Philip Gilbert Hamerton

The Sylvan Year

Leaves from the Note Book of Raoul Dubois

Philip Gilbert Hamerton

The Sylvan Year
Leaves from the Note Book of Raoul Dubois

ISBN/EAN: 9783744730136

Printed in Europe, USA, Canada, Australia, Japan

Cover: Foto ©Andreas Hilbeck / pixelio.de

More available books at **www.hansebooks.com**

LEAVES FROM THE NOTE BOOK OF RAOUL DUBOIS.

BY

PHILIP GILBERT HAMERTON,

AUTHOR OF "THE INTELLECTUAL LIFE," "ETCHING AND ETCHERS," ETC.

"Non canimus surdis: respondent omnia silvæ." — VIRG. Ecl. x.

BOSTON:
ROBERTS BROTHERS.
1882.

UNIVERSITY PRESS:
JOHN WILSON & SON, CAMBRIDGE.

PREFACE.

IN order to give more unity to these pages, it was decided, after some hesitation, to introduce one or two fictitious personages and an element of human interest. Whatever Nature may be from the strictly scientific point of view, it is interesting to the artist (whether literary or pictorial) mainly as it is related, in ways more or less mysterious, to the world of feeling which lies hidden within our own breasts. Therefore, although a man of science might have written about the forest without reference to human sorrows or satisfactions, an artist could not do so except at the risk of sacrificing his most effective forces, those which have influence by means of sympathy and association. The principal personage of the narrative was in some degree suggested by the ' Obermann ' of De Sénancour, a creation which has been, if not precisely popular, certainly very influential amongst the more sensitive and studious minds of Continental Europe during the earlier part of

the present century, and which has not even at the present day altogether lost its attraction ; for 'Obermann'
is still read by persons of culture, though the mental
condition which De Sénancour painted in that work is
much rarer in these days than it was in the days of
René and Childe Harold. The fictitious personage who
tells what there is of story in 'The Sylvan Year' is,
however, a conception quite distinct from the dissatis-
fied hero of De Sénancour, and is intended to leave a
very different impression upon the reader. The dominant note of 'Obermann' is *ennui;* the *ennui* of a character capable of long, indefinite suffering, but not capable of passing out of such suffering by the discipline of
active sight and thought. The following narrative, so
far as it paints the character of the imaginary narrator,
is intended rather to exhibit the value of external nature
as a refreshment to a spirit which, though it has suffered
greatly, has still strength enough to take a hearty and
healthy interest in everything that comes within the
circle of its observation.

THE SYLVAN YEAR.

THE SYLVAN YEAR.

I.

IN the heart of the forests between the vine-lands
of Burgundy and the course of the river Loire my
mother's family had for centuries possessed a property
which had descended to myself, but which I had visited
only on rare occasions. It required singularly little care
from its proprietor, being nearly the whole of it forest-
land, and the cuttings took place only once in twenty
years. The estate had been divided into five portions,
and the times of cutting had been so arranged that one
such period should recur every fourth year; so we came
to the place each Leap-year, like the 29th of February.
There were about four hundred acres of woodland, and
it would be difficult to find, except on the slopes of the
Alps, a similar extent of country with so little that was
level. Seven miles from the nearest public road stood
our ancestral habitation. It occupied the bottom of a
little valley, and had for its title the name of the locality,
le Val Sainte Véronique. The house was not a *château*,
nor was it (I rejoice to say) an ordinary *maison bour-
geoise*. It consisted of the remains of a monastic establish-

ment which had never been either extensive or splendid, but our religious predecessors had left upon the place that which suits my taste and temper better than either size or splendor — the impress of a quiet feeling, in harmony with the perfect seclusion that reigned there from year to year.   They had left, too, a lovely chapel of perfect fourteenth-century work, which had been used by the farmer as a barn, and so little injured (for the soft hay did no harm to the delicate sculpture), that when I restored it some years since the walls and vaults required nothing but a careful cleaning, and the only serious outlay was that for a new pavement and the repair of the external roof.   The monastic buildings pro-vided a capacious residence for one of my tenants, and a house for my own family ; but, as our visits had been so rare, we had gone to no expense in luxuries, and the furniture consisted of a few old things that had been left there by my maternal forefathers, who were people of simple tastes.   Beyond the repair of the chapel which had not been costly, I had laid out scarcely anything on these old buildings in the Val Sainte Véronique, but I thought of them always with a certain quiet affection, and sought their shelter willingly in the time of my deepest sorrow, going to that secluded place with a half-religious feeling, as if its monastic associations invited me, and made the retreat more perfect and its tranquillity more serene.

I have said that the buildings were situated in a little valley.   Three tiny meadows occupied the bottom, like a carpet of greenest velvet, and in the midst of them flowed a stream, about four yards wide, whose water was of the most lucid purity, and abundant even in the fiercest heats of summer. The hills around were so steep that they derived some sublimity from their steepness, but they were not exceedingly lofty, the highest of them not rising to more than seven hundred feet above the stream's level. Entirely clothed with wood, they offered an appearance of great richness, especially in the golden weeks of autumn, when the little valley became, for a brief season, a glorious study for a landscape-painter.

II.

Arrival at the Val Sainte Véronique — Plans for the Employment of Time — Paternal Education — Companionship between Father and Son — Sad Associations.

WHEN we came to the place — my boy and I — after the lamentable events of the war, it had not this temporary splendor, but was gray under a gray and rainy sky; and it seemed better so, more in unison with the sadness of our hearts. Our first visit was to the chapel, which, when we had last stayed here, my wife had decorated with some delicate needle-work of her own ; and here, as we knelt together, my boy and I had leisure to feel both the nearness of our lost ones and their remoteness. We chose two rooms that communicated with each other, and, before evening, had given them an appearance of tolerable comfort. This

can never be very difficult in a place where firewood is
inexhaustibly abundant. Logs were heaped on the old
rusty fire-dogs, and the most cheerful beams illuminated
the red-brick floor and the naked, inhospitable walls.
That night the good fire sufficed for us, but the next
day we busied ourselves very actively in furnishing our
little apartment with the least inconvenient of the old
things that were scattered about the mansion. This
activity was beneficial to both of us, and I was pleased
to see how Alexis suddenly regained his boyish cheerfulness in the toils of this novel occupation. Far from
endeavoring to repress this happy elasticity of youth,
I did my best to sustain and encourage it, for there is
gloom enough between infancy and age without adding
anything to it by the wilful refusal of whatever gleams
of sunshine may be permitted to us.

We passed a whole day in arranging the two rooms
that were to be, in an especial sense, our home, and
gradually they came to wear a pleasant and familiar
aspect, as we unpacked our luggage and surrounded ourselves with our little personal belongings. We set up
some book-shelves, and a rack for my pipes, and another
for our fowling-pieces ; we hung up, with a melancholy
satisfaction, the photographs of those who would come
to us no more. The juxtaposition of these details is
typical of what was going forward all the time in our
innermost thoughts, for whilst we were busy about our
things the images of the beloved ones were always near,
always ready to rise vividly in the imagination.

I had not come to the Val Sainte Véronique with-

out a definite plan for the employment of our time.
Employment is necessary to us all, and in all circumstances, but it is most especially necessary to those who
have to bear some poignant and constantly-recurring
sorrow. In the solitude that death had made for me,
I felt myself drawn nearer to my remaining son, and
resolved to have him with me for a whole year in that
lonely dwelling of the Val Sainte Véronique. If this
arrangement retarded his school-work, there might be,
it seemed, an ample compensation in the constant exercise of a beneficent paternal influence, whilst the life he
would lead with me was in the highest degree favorable to his physical growth and health. Nor was it
inevitable, either, that his studies should be neglected
during the months he passed with me. Though quite
without ambition, I had employed a life of leisure in
maintaining and extending my own culture in various
directions, and might reasonably suppose myself capable
of teaching what my boy, at his age, could have learned
in an ordinary public school. The two disabilities which
so commonly make paternal education practically an
impossibility, the want of leisure and the want of the
necessary scholarship, did not exist in my case. I particularly desired to associate in my boy's mind the love
of nature with the love of literature, and art, and science;
being firmly convinced, and knowing partly from my
own experience, that these pursuits enhance the value
of wealth to those who possess it, and are in themselves
true riches for many who have little material gold. I
determined, therefore, that we would not pass our time

in the forests like wild animals, but that some light of culture should brighten our sylvan year.

I indulged myself, furthér, in the hope—though this may have been, to some extent, a common parental illusion—that by the constant but gentle exercise of paternal influence, whatever degree of that influence I already possessed over Alexis might be increased during the year that we were to live together in such close and uninterrupted companionship. It is the misfortune of public education that our sons are separated from us in their youth and delivered into the hands of teachers, who, however conscientious they may be, cannot, in the nature of things, take that earnest and complete interest in their whole mental and physical well-being which incessantly occupies the mind of every father who is worthy of the name. Since this boy alone remained to me, I desired to establish between us relations of intimacy and friendship of a kind which cannot be incompatible with respect on one side and dignity on the other. His brothers had loved me well, and when their life-blood flowed out upon the miry ground at Gravelotte, their last thoughts, so far as they related to anything in this world, were, I doubt not, thoughts of tender affection for their mother and dutiful love for me. I know that they loved me well. There have been times and occasions in our life . . .

In vain I school myself into forgetfulness; I cannot quite forget, for all things remind me of my sons. Alexis himself reminds me of them continually, and he is constantly in my sight or in my thoughts. The place, too, recalls them to my memory, for they came here to hunt the boar in the pride of their early manhood. And why should we endeavor to forget? Do we not wrong the dead when we dismiss their memory as too disturbing and importunate? Let me rather welcome these recollections, and be thankful for that clearness of the faculties which enables me still to see their faces and hear their voices as I heard and saw them when the only war they knew was that against the wild boar and the wolf. I will build a monument to their memory near the Val Sainte Véronique. On the crest of the hill before the house two columns of spotless marble shall rise high above the summits of the trees, and as the marble mellows to the sunsets of the years that are to come, so may their sacrifice appear to me more in harmony with the great purposes of the world!

III.

The Old Building— My Herbarium — My Books — A Year of Retirement — Reading — Botany — Etching — Animal Life.

THE day after our arrival in our new home it rained incessantly, and not a ray of sunshine came to brighten the dreary November landscape. We had arrived at a time of the year that offered no prospect of cheering natural appearances. The splendor of autumn had utterly faded away; the clear brightness of the frosty winter had not yet arrived to brace us

with its healthier influences ; we had nothing around us
but the dulness of advanced decay. From sunrise to
sunset, or, more accurately in a valley shrouded by mist,
from the time when the cloud grew paler in the morning
to the time when it grew dark again in the afternoon,
we remained in the house together. Our heavy baggage
arrived from the distant railway station in the middle of
the day, and we found an occupation in unpacking the
various cases and in settling our interior arrangements.
There was plenty of space in the old building, and, with
unlimited supplies of excellent firewood, we were under
no necessity for limiting our existence to the apartments
we had especially selected as our own. We had *déjeuner*
in the dining-room, but it seemed so large and dreary,
with its broad stone floor and the black beams in the
rude old ceiling, that we determined not to eat in it any
more, and dined that evening in a circular cabinet, which
occupied the basement of one of the round towers — a
cabinet which had been used by a lady of our family
two generations before, and had still the charm of a
faded elegance that affected the mind like the faint perfume of withered flowers.

The German invaders of Lorraine had carried away
the greater part of my library and my little collection of
pictures. My herbarium, which it had taken me years
to collect and classify, had gone I knew not whither ;
possibly some scientific invader may have been tempted
by the rarer plants, and appropriated them, leaving the
rest to comrades less enlightened, who may have used
them to kindle fires. Even the cabinets that contained

them disappeared in the general ruin. All that remained
to me of my material implements of culture were a few
old books ; but these, as it fortunately happened, were
my dearest friends and favorites. Better editions may
have been printed by the enterprise of contemporary
publishers, but to my feeling no copy of a beloved
author, however fair, however faultless, can ever be
worth the copy that has long been my companion.
Books increase in value for their possessor as they
diminish in salableness at an auction of his effects.
The remnant of what had been the best private library
in the neighborhood I lived in had for me a precious-
ness far beyond that of the finest editions that were
once its glory in the eyes of others. Especially had I
loved the true immortal poets. From them, and from
them only, can we win that wondrous lore which en-
chants for us the whole material world, and admits us
into a fairy-land which is not illusory.

A year of absolute retirement would seem like an
interminable desert to any one without an occupation,
but I knew from the experience of other years that
when once we are absorbed in pursuits that are at
the same time very interesting and very laborious, the
months melt away like a treasure in the hands of a
spendthrift. It was only, indeed, by the most method-
ical arrangement of our time that we could possibly
accomplish the tasks we had voluntarily undertaken.
Besides our reading, which, for Alexis, was the most important of my plans, I proposed to collect an herbarium,
to include the entire flora of my woodland property, and

to make an album of etchings which was to illustrate everything of interest on the estate. In the selection of subjects there was but one serious difficulty — their inexhaustible and bewildering abundance. In the Val Sainte Véronique itself there were groups of magnificent chestnuts, centuries old, shadowing the woodland road that leads into the heart of the forest ; and though the dense young woods were cut regularly for their revenue, many an old giant had been spared from generation to generation, and there were hollow trunks more ancient than monarchy in France, and far more deeply rooted. I desired also to illustrate the animal life of the great woods, from the wild geese flying over their summits in the chill evenings of the dying year, to the deer in the sunny glade and the wolves in the winter snow.

IV.

An Excursion in the Forest — Dante's Suffering Trees — The Forest-road — A Hill-top — We go astray — Observation on the Adhesion of Dead Leaves — Analogy in Human Affairs — Wonderful Variety of Color — Emerson on Winter Scenery — The Forest-Fear of Dante — How I first understood it.

ON the third day after our arrival in the valley the weather, though still thickly overcast, was fair enough to encourage ideas of exploration, and we set out after *déjeuner* with the intention of making an excursion in shape something like the outline of a pear, and so getting home again about dinner-time. We began by following one of the narrow roads which from time immemorial have given access to the interior of the forest. There is evidence that some of these roads existed in the old Gaulish times, and the engineers of those days, trusting to the strength and patience of their oxen, seem to have considered mere steepness as no objection whatever. The road we followed was often closely hemmed in on both sides by impenetrable hedges of old beech, whose trunks were twisted into the most fantastic shapes long ago, when they were young, and have remained so ever since in grim deformity. Some of them were really painful to contemplate, the efforts of nature had been so thwarted. They were like powerful arms of men bound at the wrists to some immovable front of rock, with muscles swelling in vain efforts for deliverance. I thought of that dreadful fancy of Dante's, the suffering human trees, that bled dark drops of blood when a little twig was broken, and asked so pitifully, ' Why dost thou break me, why dost thou tear me, hast thou no pity ? '

> Però disse'l Maestro : ' Se tu tronchi
> Qualche fraschetta d'una d'este piante
> Li pensier ch'hai si faran tutti monchi.'
> Allor pors'io la mano un poco avanti
> E colsi un ramoscel da un gran pruno,
> E'l tronco suo gridò : ' Perchè mi schiante?'
> Da che fatto fu poi di sangue bruno.
> Ricomincio a gridar : ' Perchè mi scerpi ?
> *Non hai tu spirto di pietate alcuno ?* '

After being hedged in by these gaunt arms for the distance of nearly a mile, the road became less distinctly

separated from the surrounding forest-land ; it made
several sudden turns, and finally offered us a bifurcation.
Having nothing to guide us but a general project of wandering, we took the side which seemed most in our intended direction, and followed it where it might lead.
The wheel-ruts soon ceased altogether ; the road became
a mere footpath, and after winding in an uncertain manner
for a long distance emerged at last on the very summit
of a lofty knoll, where, in the midst of an open space of
greensward, stood four enormous chestnuts, surrounded
by tall bushes of holly with an abundance of red berries
in the midst of its varnished green.   Although we were
certainly on the top of one of the many hills which carry
this great forest upon their ample sides, it was impossible
to see anything beyond the narrow circle of the open
space around us.   We were enclosed by a sylvan wall,
penetrable indeed by a pedestrian traveller, but as impervious to his vision as if it had been built of granite
blocks.   We were certainly not on our own land ; these
giant chestnuts were not mine, for all the great old
forest-trees that belonged to me were known to me as
the richest plum-trees in his orchard are known to the
market-gardener.   It was impossible to ascertain the
points of the compass.   The whole sky was covered
with one dense low cloud, not lighter in one place than
another, so that we could not guess the sun's position ;
nor did any inclination of the trees, or any growth of
moss, give a reliable indication of the prevailing wind,
and if they had done so the indication would have been
useless to us in our ignorance of the local meteorology.

To retrace the path we came by might have been possible, though difficult; but I felt an invincible repug-
nance to a mere retreat. So partly in reliance upon
chance, and partly trusting an instinct of locality that
I cannot account for or explain (an animal instinct, like
that of the salmon or the housemarten), I determined to
push on through the dense wood till the topography of
the country became somewhat more intelligible to us.

Before quitting the great chestnuts, I made an observation which confirmed what I had observed before with
reference to the adherence of dead leaves. These trees,
as a rule, were entirely denuded of their foliage ; but
two or three branches, on the contrary, retained almost
every leaf that had adorned them in the glory of summer
—changed indeed, in color, from rich dark green to a
lovely pale gold, far more delicate than the winter coloring of beech or oak, yet scarcely altered in form, and pre-
serving great purity of curve. Now the question which
interested me was, how it happened that these branches
retained their foliage whilst all the others had lost it ?
The answer is, that a branch which retains its foliage has
always been virtually severed from the stem by fract-
ure before the fall of the leaf. Why the leaves fall from
a branch that shares the life of the tree, and adhere to
one that is separated from it, I am not scientific enough
to decide quite positively, but naturally conclude that it is
due to the continuance of circulation in the one case and
its stoppage in the other, the leaves adhering when the
sap has not been able to descend, but detaching themselves easily when the course of the descending sap has

met with no interruption. This suggested the reflection that a very close analogy may be found in human affairs. A colony severed from the mother country will often preserve words, and even habits in thought and action, which have dropped off from the parent since the separation took place, and which would also have been lost by the colony if the old closeness of connection had never been interrupted. The French Canadians are an excellent instance of this; they have preserved traditional ways of thinking, and traditional manners, which have dropped off long since from the inhabitants of France itself.

Although the season of the year was that which is generally reputed to be least interesting, and most completely denuded of the charms of color; although the sky above us was like lead, and there was not one flower on the earth beneath: still it would have been impossible for a painter, or for any one capable of seeing color in nature, not to be continually interested by the wonderful variety around us. It was not merely those pale, golden leaves of the broken chestnut branches, but the rich green of the holly with its bright red berries, and the abundant beech leaves, and the young oaks that kept their foliage as in summer, changed only in hue and in the form of the shrivelled leaves. Amidst intensities of green, of moss and holly, blood-red berries, and foliage like rusted iron or faded gilding, the grays and purples of a thousand trunks and bewildering intricate branches had a beauty that is lost in the too monotonous verdure of July. The American philosopher, Emerson, says,

'The inhabitants of cities suppose that the country landscape is pleasant only half the year. I please myself with observing the graces of the winter scenery, and believe that we are as much touched by it as by the genial influences of summer. To the attentive eye, each moment of the year has its own beauty.'

It was not without some feeling of anxiety that I quitted that open space, to enter once more the obscurity of innumerable trees. The words of Dante came to me again, this time with a deeper gravity of meaning than I had ever found in them before, —

> Mi ritrovai per una selva oscura
> Chè la diritta via era smarrita.
> Ahi quanto a dir qual' era è cosa dura
> Questa selva selvaggia ed aspra e forte
> Che nel pensier rinnuova la paura!

Gradually there came upon me a certain *feeling* that I had never yet experienced, but which Dante had known well. Hour after hour we walked through that interminable forest, and the strange new feeling became more and more oppressive, till at length I realized what the old poet meant with

> . Questa selva selvaggia ed aspra e forte.

We were so hemmed in by millions of stems, that, although free to walk everywhere, we were held in an illimitable prison. The trees began to wear a hostile and menacing aspect, as if we were wandering amongst unnumbered enemies. They had no longer for us any grace or beauty, but united together in one horrible monotony. I remembered the enormous extent of this

forest which covers a hundred square miles ; its complicated and difficult geography, not thoroughly known
to any human being ; its endless variety of hill and dale,
that it would take weeks of travel to explore in their
intricate detail.   And then I reflected on the single hour
of daylight that remained to us — one hour — and that
we were not only unprovided with food, but had no
covering besides our light pedestrian dress.   Alexis had
brought his gun.   I had my tobacco, and a good pro-
vision of matches, and a little brandy in my flask ; but
in the way of food, not even so much as a biscuit.

V.

A Shepherdess — Her Ignorance — A Shepherd Lad — I resolve to follow a Rivulet — Emerson's Feeling about the Forest — That of Dante
— How we were led by the Rivulet —Our Situation — Resolves for
the Future — The Silence of the Woods — A Wild Sow — We kill a
little Pig — Our Bonfire — Signals — Searchers — Help reaches us —
Our Geographical Situation.

THE time was past when it might have been yet
possible to retrace our steps, and the only practicable issue before us was to get out of the forest as
we might.   I knew that there were occasional openings,
little patches of tilled ground with rude habitations
for the woodmen, and in one of these openings we
should probably find a guide.   We came at last to a
clearing of about five acres on the slope of a hill-side,
and from this place were able to get a view of the
surrounding country.   All that was visible consisted

chiefly of a valley, with a stream at the bottom, in character so precisely like the Val Ste. Véronique that I concluded it to be the same rivulet, and therefore, of course, the most reliable of guides. On one side of the clearing passed a road of the kind common in these forests, so narrow in parts that an ox-cart would graze the trees on both sides, and then suddenly widening with verdant margins of pasture to the right hand or to the left. In one of these places, huddled in a coarse striped cloak and spinning from her distaff, stood the first human being we met with in these solitudes, a shepherdess with a flock of the tiny Morvan sheep, and a wolfish dog to guard them. The dog rushed at us as if we had been wild animals; the girl threw her sabots at him, and hit him rather severely, uttering violent exclamations in a language entirely unintelligible by us. I asked her whither the road led, pointing before me, and she answered '*à la fôret*' (pronounced *fôôret*) ; then I inquired whither the road led in the other direction, and she answered '*à la pâture*' (pronounced *pââture*). These two words comprised her entire conception of geography. In vain I mentioned the names of the Val Ste. Véronique, of the villages I knew, of the nearest market town, — all these were utterly unknown to her. Forest and pasture ! could we not see them with our eyes ?

We followed the road for about a mile, and met a lad of sixteen with two curs after him. Here, at last, was a reliable guide. We asked him whither the road led, and got for answer '*à la fôôret ;*' then we asked him where it came from, and he answered '*de la pââture.*'

He, too, was entirely impervious to questions about distant localities, and he did not understand French, whether from weak intellect or mere isolation I know not. He spoke the uncouth *patois* of these regions, a language more remote from French than is either Spanish or Italian. Yet even his *patois* was spoken with the greatest hesitation, as if utterance of any kind were a difficulty for him.

It being impossible to gain any information from these dwellers in the wilderness, I determined to take a resolution and follow the rivulet in the valley. If it were our own rivulet it would surely lead us homewards ; if not, we should at least escape the danger of wandering uselessly in a circle. Every stream in the forest gets out of the forest ultimately, and he who follows a rivulet, if he can only follow it long enough, will emerge at last from its labyrinthine dells.

'In the woods,' says Emerson, 'is perpetual youth. Within these plantations of God, a decorum and sanctity reign, a perennial festival is dressed, and the guest sees not how he should tire of them in a thousand years. In the woods we return to reason and faith. There I feel that nothing can befall me in life — no disgrace, no calamity (leaving me my eyes), which nature cannot repair.' How different is this from Dante's feeling about the forest! As the gloom of evening settled down upon the land the views of Dante prevailed with me more and more. I felt that our modern conception of wild nature, simply as a field for the pursuit of health and amusement, or pleasant study, is not a complete conception. The old dread of the wilderness had retained more of the early experience of man, when he found himself, in his weakness and ignorance, in the presence of natural forces that appalled but did not charm his imagination.

The rivulet led us into the densest wood once more. Our easiest path, but a wet one, lay in the very bed of the stream itself, and we floundered along, guided by twilight glimmers on the fortunately shallow water. In this way we proceeded for a long time with considerable rapidity, and might have gone on until night fell in blackness, had we not met with an insurmountable difficulty in a sudden alteration of geological character, which made the rivulet no longer a practicable path. It became closed in between precipitous rocks, and fell in a loud cascade into the depths of a ravine below. Nothing remained of daylight but a feeble grayness in the sky, every near object was invisible, and after some ineffectual attempts to get round the rocky sides of the watercourse I determined to abandon, for that night, all further effort to reach the Val Ste. Véronique. Most fortunately it did not rain, and we were in a perfectly sheltered situation. The constant exercise of our long march (we had been walking for seven hours without intermission) had kept us hitherto safe from cold, but we could not prudently rest without a fire. I had matches and a newspaper in my pocket ; we collected a heap of the driest leaves and twigs, and soon had the satisfaction of illuminating the little dell with a cheerful blaze of light, that brought the rocks and nearest trees into the most vigorous relief against the forest gloom and the starless blackness of the sky. Near to us were some resinous firs, and under them Alexis found quantities of large cones, rich in turpentine, which kept our fire up very brilliantly.

I had carefully economized my brandy, and now administered enough of it to give us a little temporary comfort; but we suffered seriously from hunger. Alexis had killed nothing with his gun, or else we might have tried our skill at such rough cookery as the circumstances permitted, but the cartridges he had with him turned out to be very useful to us ultimately. The lesson of the day's misadventure was certainly not lost upon either of us. Alexis declared that in future he would never trust himself in the forest without a mariner's compass in his pocket, and I mentally determined that on all future expeditions we would carry soldiers' rugs and a little supply of provisions. I had at least the consolation of my pipe, which aids a man wonderfully to support privation, and deadens the sense of hunger.

The hours passed one by one, and Alexis was overpowered with sleep. I cut a quantity of heather and covered him with it entirely; after which I sat watching by his bed, and supplying fuel to the fire of our bivouac. There is a death-like silence in the woods on a winter's night, but I consoled myself for the quiescence of the nightingale by the torpor of a great population of vipers which inhabit the crevices of the rocks, and are dangerous things in summer. No sound was audible but the rushing of the rapid stream and the monotonous murmur of its cascades.

About three o'clock in the morning I heard, or fancied that I heard, a movement in the brushwood, quite clearly distinguishable from the music of the rivulet. To this succeeded a crash of breaking branches, and a wild boar, or rather sow, dashed through the water a few yards above our resting-place. She was followed by a well-grown litter, which I took to be rather numerous from the noise they made. On the impulse of the moment I discharged both barrels amongst them, and killed a fine little pig, the rest of the family being immediately lost in the depths of the forest. The discharge aroused Alexis, who was delighted with this exploit, and finished the poor little brute with a hunting-knife of formidable dimensions, which he always carries about him. Here, at any rate, were the materials for a carnivorous breakfast. But this was not the only consequence of the incident. We were startled soon afterwards by the report of a gun in the distance, after too long an interval to be an echo. The inference was obvious ; we were in communication with some gun-carrying personage in the forest, either poacher or forester, or possibly a party in search of us from the Val Ste. Véronique.

Instead of attempting to set out in the direction from which the sound proceeded, which would have been useless in the dark entanglement of the forest, I determined to remain quietly where we were, and to increase our bonfire as much as possible, so that the reverberation from it on the clouds above might be strong enough to guide any seeker to our whereabouts. This may be done when the clouds are low, and it is the only advantage I have ever been able to discover in losing yourself on a cloudy night.

Alexis had a good supply of cartridges, so I told him to fire both barrels every five minutes. These signals were regularly answered, and we heard to our satisfaction, by the increasing loudness of the distant guns, that our friends were gradually approaching. It was slow and toilsome work, however, for them in the depth of the forest. We waited an hour and a half, firing regularly, before we heard a long cry from the top of the hill. This we answered, and twenty minutes later the forest was suddenly illuminated by the glare of torches, and a scene was accidentally composed which a painter could not have witnessed without finding material for his art.

The farmer who rented from me whatever little pasture and arable land there was in the Val Ste. Véronique, and my servant François, who, amongst other peculiarities, has a deep-seated unbelief in his master's capacity for taking care of himself (which the present adventure was not exactly calculated to remove), had become very anxious when we did not return at dinner-time, as we had promised. They soon arrived at the conclusion that we had lost ourselves in the forest, and organized, by the help of neighbors (who lived five miles away), a very well-arranged little expedition for our relief. François had taken care at starting to bring provisions in a heavily charged knapsack, and the first thing he did was to arrange them tidily on the ground. Alexis displayed the wonderful appetite of his age, and exhibited in triumph the ensanguined blade which had finished the little *marcassin.*

Whilst we were breaking our fast our geographical situation was made clear to us. In the first place, this was *not* the stream leading to the Val Ste. Véronique, but another rivulet leading in quite a different direction. Had we been able to follow it we should have emerged from the forest at a point about forty miles from home. We had walked thirty miles, and were fifteen from the Val Ste. Véronique in a straight line. The farmer knew of a forester's hut within a reasonable distance, and proposed that we should go there when it was daylight, as we all needed a few hours' rest to prepare us for our homeward journey.

VI.

Scenery of the interior of the Forest — The Forester's Hut — Interior of the Hut — The Forester and his Son — A little pet Wild Boar — A Boar that heard Mass — Jean Bouleau the Forester — His ostensible Trade — He is a Poacher — Poachers and Magistrates — An Indiscreet Poacher — The Temptations of Good Eating — The Protectors of Poachers — Professional *Braconniers* — Their Wonderful Skill — The Weasel — Alexis fraternizes with the Weasel — The Weasel described — His manners and habits — His affected ignorance — The Weasel's knowledge of the Forest.

WE lay round our fire in the forest during the hours that remained of the night, but at earliest dawn we started for the forester's hut. The road to it passed through a narrow gorge, so enclosed by steep hills, densely wooded with young oak, that it was impossible to see more than two or three hundred yards in any direction. After walking in single file for the distance of about a league, we came suddenly upon an abrupt turn in the little dell, and there it ended, for a barrier of hill rose directly in front of us, so steep as to be almost inaccessible. There was a little open space of natural meadow, and on one side of this stood the forester's hut, scarcely distinguishable from the dense vegetation that surrounded it, for the builder had used material ready to his hand, and simply constructed a sort of wigwam of young oak-trunks and branches, with a thatch of gorse that covered both roof and wall. A tiny rill had been artificially directed to a spout of hollow wood, and fell in a little cascade of the most perfect purity on the stony ground in front of the cabin, trickling afterwards amongst the pebbles, and finding its way to the bit of meadow below. No human dwelling could be more humble and primitive than this was. In the remotest wilds of America there may be houses equally primitive, but there can be no habitations nearer in structure and conception to man's earliest ideal of a home. The inhabitants were already awake, and we had immediate access to the interior. There were a couple of low bedsteads, made roughly from young trees and covered with sheets of canvas. There were two or three shelves, with nothing on them but a little of the commonest earthenware, and the rest of the furniture included nothing that Socrates would have rejected as unnecessary. It is just possible that Diogenes might have discovered a superfluity.

The inhabitants consisted of the forester and his son, a lad of fifteen, who seemed three years younger. They welcomed us with a surprised politeness, natural under the circumstances ; but we told our story, and this led to a more frank and intimate acquaintance. Our new host lived too far from the Val Ste. Véronique to know much about our extremity of the forest, and my name appeared to be unknown to him, but he treated us with an equal hospitality in which there was a great deal of simple dignity. The conversation turned upon our adventure, and when we told him about the little wild boar, and displayed the victim, he gave a peculiar whistle, and immediately a beast of the same species, a little older, came from a dark corner in the hut and sought his caresses like a dog. He had killed the sow in the forest, and taken this youngling home, at first with no definite intention of adopting it, but the creature had become so familiar that it now formed part of his household. The wild boar, if taken young, is very easily domesticated, and capable of strong attachment to its human friends. The men present immediately began to mention other instances of boars that had been taken and brought up in the same way, and one was mentioned which regularly followed its master to the village church, and would not be excluded, but came at last, by the toleration of the curé, to hear mass like a Christian ; till finally it grew to an alarming size, and was sold to a travelling menagerie for the sum of seventy francs. What a transition for a poor creature, that had loved its friends and enjoyed great freedom in their society, to be taken suddenly away from all affectionate intercourse and shut up in a narrow cage, and carried from fair to fair like poor Gulliver in Brobdignag, but without the tender care of Glumdalclitch! As for the future fate of this one, its owner admitted with sorrow that the time must ultimately arrive when it would be necessary to have him 'bled;' but when that day came he hoped he might be at a distance, and not be a witness of the sacrifice.

The society of people who live with Nature, though it may be wanting in the variety of thought and experience that we find only in great cities, has always some elements of interest; and this forester, Jean Bouleau, was very observant in his own way, and half a naturalist. I learned afterwards that he had the reputation of being a wonderfully skilful poacher; and indeed a man in his situation, buried in the depths of a vast forest, with no neighbors but wild animals, would naturally be tempted to lead the life of a trapper. His ostensible trade was woodcutting, and he worked at it sufficiently to give a fair color and pretext to his existence; but a hardy and adventurous spirit desires other excitements than constant physical drudgery, and this man found in poaching exactly the excitement that he needed. The reader may ask how a man so well known to be a poacher could go on year after year without exciting hostility enough to drive him out of the country; but the difficulty in this part of France is, that however strong the evidence against poachers, the magistrates will not convict. One conviction certainly did take place some

years ago, but it was owing to an extraordinary absence
of tact on the part of the poacher himself, who had not
yet learned the refinements of his trade.   The President
affected to interrogate him with great severity; on which
the prisoner was simple enough to answer, ' What ? don't
you know me ? I'm the man that supplies your own
kitchen with game.   It was I who sold that hare to
your cook only last week.'   ' Silence, prisoner!' shouted
both the President and the *Procureur Impérial*, and the
man was condemned at once ; not for poaching, but for
indiscretion.   The simple truth is, that the poachers are
the regular purveyors of all who have a taste for game ;
and as magistrates and other official persons know that
their kitchens are supplied by persons of this class, their
lenity may be counted upon if only the prisoner has the
tact to play his part in the little comedy so as not to
compromise his betters.   Even the dignitaries of the
Church are not proof against the temptations of good
eating, and sometimes consume viands which have not
been come by either legally or honestly.   There was a
certain Bishop, now dead, who took his share of responsibility in these matters with a pleasant humor.
Wishing to eat venison when not quite in season, he sent
half the body of the deer that tempted him as a present
to the Prefect, who lived in the same town, and accompanied the gift by the following little note, — ' Parta-
geons la responsabilité : chargez-vous du temporel ; je
me charge du spirituel.'

Sometimes a few sportsmen unite to prosecute poachers, but their efforts encounter the perpetual difficulty

that the lawyers and magistrates have — private feelings of the tenderest regard for the clever and adventurous men who supply the greatest delicacies of their tables. Some sportsmen heard that a great game dinner was being cooked at a certain restaurant, and they required the *Procureur Impérial* to give a warrant for seizure. Armed with this and accompanied by the police, they entered the kitchen where the preparations were busily going forward. On the spits before the fire were quails, partridges, pheasants — evidence enough against the master of the establishment; but he simply answered that, although the dinner might not be legal, for the game was not killed in season, still it would be useless to prosecute him, because the feast had been ordered by the President of the Assizes himself. The zeal of the *trouble-fête* sportsmen cooled at once on receiving this piece of information, and they desisted. The plain truth is, that conscientiousness in game-preserving is almost entirely unknown in France, and the only people who desire a different state of things are the large land-owners, who are not powerful enough to alter the habits of the whole nation. Every town of importance enough for the interchange of hospitality is sure to maintain a good many isolated *braconniers*, who supply its larders with game both in and out of what may be legally the season. They are less what an Englishman understands by the word poacher, than hunters and trappers by profession, like their brethren in the forests of America. There is still great variety of game in France, and no country could be more favorable to it if preservation of any serious kind could be resorted to ; but under present circumstances, when it is impossible to protect it efficiently, it would be impossible also to purchase game without the assistance of the *braconnier*. The land-owners do not sell, they have only enough for their own tables ; the sportsmen who live in towns, and consider themselves rewarded if, after a day's march, they return home with a single partridge, are not skilful enough to do more than procure themselves a luxury from time to time : so there is clearly a sort of need for the true professional *braconnier*, who is to ordinary sportsmen what the artist is to the amateur, and can get game in quantity enough to supply the market regularly, though often at high prices. The skill of these men is often wonderful, but no one becomes a *braconnier* who has not a strong natural aptitude for the chase, with all those animal instincts and physical powers which are necessary to an incessant warfare against the cunning and swiftness of the brute. These instincts and powers gain greatly both in delicacy and strength by incessant use, and after ten or fifteen years of a life in the woods such a man as Jean Bouleau becomes a hunting animal, the most patient and cunning of all animals, and one of the most enduring. If there is a fish in the river, or a quadruped in the woods, he will have that fish, he will have that quadruped, when the common sportsman might as hopefully propose to himself to arrest the wild swans in their longest and loftiest travelling in the upper air. I found afterwards that this man was never called by his own

name, but was known in the forest and its outskirts as
'the Weasel,' and by this *sobriquet* we will speak of him
in the present narrative.

There is an instinct in the boyish nature by which
it is strongly attracted to whatever is primitive in man,
and ·I observed without surprise that Alexis fraternized
almost immediately with the Weasel, even before he
became aware of the man's remarkable talents and ac-
complishments. It immediately occurred to me, that
if Jean Bouleau were guilty of no greater crime than
supplying the larders of rich citizens with game, which
they offered him the strongest temptations to procure
for them, merely because they had not skill and endurance enough to procure it for themselves, I need not
throw any hindrance in the way of an intimacy of this
kind, which would be an education for Alexis in habits
of self-reliance and observation, and the best possible
introduction to the study of natural history.

The Weasel was an excellent specimen of the race
of men that he belonged to, as pure a Celt as any in
all France. We, who belong to the taller races of man-
kind, are rather apt to undervalue the qualities of the
Celt. His superiorities may be summed up in rapidity
of intelligence and of action. The Weasel was in
stature even below the low standard of his race, but
he was beautifully built, with legs and arms fit for a
painter's model, and, notwithstanding his labor as a
woodcutter, the hands retained an almost feminine
delicacy. The hair on his head was richly abundant,
black, and curly ; but the beard was scanty, like that

of an adolescent. The eyes were like the eyes of a wild animal, quite clear and brilliant, but unpleasantly rapid in their movements. He spoke in the most good-humored manner, and after the first quarter of an hour became extremely polite to us. ' Would we not accept something to eat? he would do what he could for our entertainment.' Having kept a little inn some years before, he confessed to some skill in cookery, and produced as a specimen of it a large earthen pan filled with *civet de lièvre.* He had wine, too, rather rough to the palate, but sound — *vin du pays,* grown in a little experimental vineyard on the outskirts of the forest, with sufficiently good soil and a southern aspect, but much too high above the level of the sea for any delicacy of flavor. There were goats' cheeses of his own making, which were excellent ; and to conclude, he gave us coffee and a dram of *genièvre,* which consisted of brandy made from pressed grapes, in which he had steeped berries from the juniper bushes that abounded in the forest. These luxuries, and the cigarettes he smoked with us afterwards, were quite enough to prove that the Weasel did not really and truly belong to the class of woodcutters by his habits (for they live like ascetics), nor did he appear in the least anxious to go to his daily labor. His earlier life as an innkeeper, and his frequent visits to the city, where he ate in the kitchens of his patrons, had given him a taste for good living, which may have been one of the incentives to his career as a *braconnier.*

It became evident in the course of our conversation

that his ignorance of the Val Ste. Véronique had been affected, probably to shield himself from the suspicion of poaching on my estate.   The truth was that the whole of the forest was known to this man, and probably to him only.   He could find his way through its intricate hills and valleys by day or night, in fog or sunshine ; *he* needed no mariner's compass, but went about guided · by the marvellous instinct of locality. His talk about the forest interested us exceedingly, and he offered to guide us if ever we felt disposed to pursue our explorations.   It was an offer not to be rejected for the future, but for the time being we felt more disposed to return homewards with our relieving party. After a rest of three hours at the Weasel's cabin, we set off on our long march, and arrived at home before nightfall.   The principal result of our adventure was a feeling of the awfulness of the forest, which was partially diminished by subsequent familiarity, but never quite effaced. We never set out on any excursion afterwards without a mariner's compass and a small supply of provisions.

VII.

THE weather, which had been gloomy since our arrival in the Val Ste. Véronique, now became more cheerful, and as we were more settled in our new home the beauty of Nature grew more evident and more satisfying. In times of mental disturbance from whatever cause, from the pressure of affairs, or anxieties, or sorrow, we do not see Nature clearly, nor do we see it either in the dulness of *ennui*. A certain middle state is needed between anxiety and too stagnant calm, in which the mind does not either suffer from the sense of pressure on the one hand, nor yet, on the other, become dulled from the want of use. Every day my sorrow produced less of disturbing pain, and knowing the past to be wholly beyond my power, I resolved to live as much as possible in the present. This was rendered the easier by the companionship of Alexis, who, with the natural buoyancy and activity of his age, soon entered with great eagerness into the pleasures of our new existence, whilst he willingly accepted the studious discipline which I had felt to be necessary for both of us.

The month of December was passed in indoor studies, with occasional excursions in the forest, undertaken

3

rather for sport than observation.   Few incidents of
importance occurred to us during these wintry weeks.
The neighborhood of our own valley was frequently
visited by wild boars, which of late years had been
more numerous than ever, whilst the wolves were becoming rarer.   The peasants affirm that this is an
inevitable law, that the wolf and the wild boar always
increase or diminish inversely.   Why this is so I have
not yet been able to ascertain, for these animals do not
make war upon each other ; but there may be a mutual
jealousy or dislike.   However, although the wolves may
be rarer in this forest than they have been in former
years, there are still quite enough of them to occupy the
attention of the shepherds on its outskirts.   About the
middle of December I happened to witness an incident
which is not very rare.   A few sheep were grazing
quietly in a little sloping pasture along the wood's edge,
when an animal first crept out cautiously and then
rushed at the nearest sheep.   That animal was a wolf,
and his immense strength was proved by his manner
of dealing with his victim.   He got his head under the
sheep's belly and threw her weight upon his own neck,
her four feet beating the air.   Holding her quite firmly
in this position with his teeth, the wolf had strength
enough to gallop very rapidly up the steep slope back
to the impenetrable density of the copsewood, where it
was of no use trying to follow him.   Now the wolf in
this country is not a very large animal, and a feat like
this implies a degree of muscular and constitutional
power which is relatively enormous.   I could not help

admiring the courage of the little shepherdess whose flock had been thus suddenly invaded. She was very much irritated at the impudence of the wolf, but not alarmed by his ferocity ; and she threw her wooden shoe after him as an expression of most earnest though in-efficacious hostility, uttering at the same time sentiments of her own in *patois* of extraordinary volubility, which were certainly not benedictions. The girl's father told me afterwards that on one occasion she had actually beaten a wolf till he retreated, and there are so many anecdotes of a similar character that I infer a certain human influence over these animals, which as they are of canine race may have something of canine deference for humanity.

The wild boar has one indisputable advantage over the wolf — he is eatable. There is always wild boar in some form or other during the winter months in the larder at the Val Ste. Véronique. It was a fancy of mine that our guns ought to supply a great part of our food, and they did so during what remained of the season.

The month of January opened splendidly, with sunshine in the gray and gold of the forest. I think that the sadness so often attributed to winter scenery is due much more to the prevalence of cloud and fog, and to the chilly, uncomfortable temperature, than to the state of vegetation. The color of winter scenery is not without elements of variety and even brilliance. The leaves of the preceding year are important, both for the richness of the tints they give, and, when seen close at hand, for the fixed beauty of their forms. A leaf that has

passed the autumn on the tree, and dried there, is always
sure to be well worth drawing, for the force and variety
of its curvature. Even in January oak-leafage is rich
upon the trees, and though its color is often too red
and coppery to be altogether agreeable to the eye, still
it breaks the monotony of the gray stems. Saplings
retain their leaves longest, and there are varieties of
oak which have a pale yellowish-brown that a painter
might accept with pleasure. The common hornbeam
also preserves its leaves far into the following year, and
the underwood of this forest is full of it. Hardly a
single leaf of hornbeam is missing in the month of
January, but every one of them is curled up with a
graceful twist, showing the lines of ribs under it quite
distinctly, even at a distance of several yards. There is
no material better than dried oak and hornbeam for the
study of natural curvature, because you can carry a sprig
home with you, and it will retain all its forms, day after
day, as if the leaves were made of metallic gold. The
hornbeam underwood is splendid in the slanting sunshine of a January afternoon. The beech, too, is important for its winter foliage, which remains, almost all of it,
in situations sheltered from the winds. The color is a
beautiful light red brown, and the form of the leaf very
perfect indeed, with a good surface. The roads in the
forest about the Val Ste. Véronique are often bordered
on both sides with trunks of beech, and the effect in
January is rich in the extreme, on account of the splendid
freshness of the green mosses, which are in perfection
and give the best possible contrast to the beech-leaves.

No tree in January is so variously rich in color as the quince-tree. The branches (so wonderfully tortuous and interlaced) are tinted of a summer-like green — painted, I may say, by Nature with the tiniest of her green mosses ; whereas the leaves, of which very many are still remarkably perfect in form, are of a rich red brown, and the under side is of a pale golden brown, with a little down remaining. The most decayed leaves are a good deal darker. Now, although the oak, beech, or hornbeam, still retain their leaves in the following year, they offer but little variety of hue ; and though a sprig of oak might instruct and occupy a designer, the quince-tree would occupy a colorist. So, indeed, would the common bramble, with its crimson or purple stalk and leaves, often still retaining a perfectly fresh green, others being of a dark, ochrous red, but still very perfect in their form.

VIII.

Deschanel's description of an English Landscape Painter — Botany and Art — An Effect in January — The Harmony of Gray and Gold — How Diaz would have given it — Sunset-light on Dead Foliage — Use of Scientific Knowledge — The Microscope — Use of a Nomenclature — Drawing Plants — Jules Jacquemart's way of Drawing Plants — Memoranda — Colors of the Wintry Landscape — Fanaticism about Nature — Eglantine — The rich green of Broom — Woods in Mass — Edges of Woods — Birches — Lichen.

DESCHANEL, in his clever and amusing 'Essai de Critique naturelle,' gives a description of an English landscape-painter addicted to botanical study ;

a description slightly caricatured, yet probably drawn
from some living instance, and accurate in the main :
' Il s'en va herboriser par champs, s'assure que tel *vegetable* a les feuilles pointues ou découpées de telle façon,
que telle fleurette a une telle corolle et tant de pétales ;
qu'il y a d'ailleurs, dans la nature des rouges violents,
des verts crus, des jaunes impitoyables, beaucoup de
violet,' &c.   Well, this may be true with reference to
some painters of that young realist school which was
flourishing in England when M. Deschanel wrote his
book, and he may have met with some English artists
who were also botanists ; but the harm is not in the
study of plants, it is in the forgetfulness of large relations
to which this minute observation of Nature has occasionally led those who were addicted to it.   It is well to
know the plants with a loving familiarity that observes
the minutest detail, but the great harmonies of natural
effect and color concern the landscape-painter more
closely.   Here, for example, is an effect which, if painted
in a masterly manner, with sufficient taste and feeling,
would reward the labor of an artist :   One day in January I was riding in the forest, where the ground is
closely planted with young oaks, and the sun was setting
behind them.   The material was almost monotonous in
its simplicity, — one species of tree, and a sunset with
no elaboration of cloud-form, but merely a suffusion of
yellow light in a sky heavily charged with vapor.   The
trunks of the trees were all gray, the sun-gold pale
yellow ; and as the light was well concentrated, and
brilliantly scattered to right and left, but always from

one central point, it was just one of those simple and harmonious arrangements of light and color which are adapted to the purposes of art. It happened, too, that this color-harmony of gold and gray was precisely the one which an artist may attack without incurring the certainty of defeat from the unapproachableness of natural illumination; for yellow is the one color which may be made luminous in painting without much sacrifice of its chromatic quality. Had the sunset been a red one, the difficulty (as every painter knows) would have been immeasurably increased; and, indeed, would have involved the necessity of painting the whole subject in so low a key, that the beautiful grays of the forest would have been lost in dark neutral tints far below the pearly tones of Nature. This would have been seen by an artist like Diaz as a flashing of gold on gray intricacy, and he would have painted it exactly in the way best fitted to convey that impression. Another very fine effect, often visible in winter at the hour of sunset, is the illumination of the trees to the east of you. When the light of sunset catches the dead foliage of a forest of oaks their tops burst into sudden flame, so that the forest seems all on fire. The impression is greatly heightened if you are unable, from your position, to see the western sky, which is the origin of the light. Now, for the powerful rendering of such effects as these, the knowledge of plants need only be that which every artist is sure to possess who has been in the habit of sketching from Nature; but whenever a painter desires to give something of the beauty of foreground detail, and he may well desire this without abandoning his pictorial purposes and intentions, then it is most convenient for him to know the plants scientifically. I cannot think that the Englishman in M. Deschanel's book was wrong even in using a microscope, though the idea conveyed is that he did so in order to be able to delineate microscopically. There is an obvious *non-sequitur* here. It does not follow that because an artist happens to use a microscope to dissect some plant in order that he may afterwards remember it, he will necessarily draw the plant otherwise than as it simply appears to the naked eye—to the educated eye—in its subordinate place in Nature. Possibly M. Deschanel might argue that the landscape-painter need not trouble himself even about the names of plants, since he does not write their names upon his canvas, and no doubt these plants have existed for innumerable generations before any nomenclature was contrived for them ; still he may surely avail himself of what is nothing more than a convenient *memoria technica* all ready to his hand. The objection does not seem to be so much to the knowledge of a little botany, as to the habit of *drawing* plants minutely in isolation ; and this habit is not injurious for the knowledge which it conveys, but because it encourages us to neglect the more important truths of relation, and makes us think we have done something good and useful, when, in fact, we are busy in an occupation which is not fine art, and which is incomparably easier than fine art. Any young student whose eye for form has attained a tolerable degree of accuracy may soon draw studies of detached leaves very beautifully, and then he is likely to fall into a sort of mechanical routine which is the indolence of the industrious in all the handicraft trades. The only kind of study at all resembling this, which may be permitted to a real artist, is work done on the principles of Jules Jacquemart in his etchings of flowers. There you have leaf-drawing certainly, and careful copying of petals and calices, yet always subordinated to the effect of a bouquet as a mass.

Before quitting the subject of leaf-drawing let me add, that careful memoranda of leaves and other objects may often be done with great advantage by those who are not troubled with any artistic ambition. They aid the memory wonderfully, and enable it to retain truths of form and color with an accuracy that may be of the greatest advantage in many studies and occupations. Much mechanical drawing is bad, because the draughts-man has looked only to those characteristics of plants which may be technically described in scientific language : these things he sees, but he fails to see the beauty of natural curvature even in those very forms where it is most conspicuous. Now it would be perfectly possible, and a worthy object of ambition to any student who really loved Nature in a catholic and comprehensive way, to preserve the strictest botanical truth in the delineation of plants, and yet add to it the true loveliness of their forms, the exquisite changes of curve and surface which the accidents of perspective are incessantly producing. Such an enterprise might not be directly remunerative in the pecuniary sense, for scientific students appear to be satisfied with the sort of drawing which sets down what they want to know, whilst lovers of art are satisfied with nothing short of full artistic synthesis both in conception and execution, and yet the sort of work I now suggest would reward the laborer by certain delicate, intimate satisfactions of its own.

There are often very brilliant colors in the wintry landscape, but the difficulty in making artistic use of the material that it presents would be to harmonize the color-material into synthesis. You may find very fresh-looking greens, and very bright reds, but there is a want of quieter color in their neighborhood sufficiently resembling them in quality to lead up to them as a climax. The coloring of Nature is not always good or available for art, any more than all her plants for food, and it is one of the first results of culture in an artist when he is able to perceive this. It is mere fanaticism to speak of the fortuitous arrangements of color which occur in natural ·scenery as examples of divine art which it is impiety to criticise. The simple truth is, that a plant will bud or fructify at a time determined by the action of heat or moisture upon its vessels, without the least reference to its effect upon a color-composition in the landscape. For instance, you may have a bush of eglantine, which will be a perfect mass of vermilion on account of its fruit. The stalks will be a very dark purple in shade, but crimson in the evening light, and they intensify the vermilion of the berries. Ten to one, this piece of splendor will be entirely isolated, and it will kill all the delicate coloring in its neighborhood, as a scarlet coat kills a modest landscape in the Academy. Or you may have the fine rich green of broom, most valuable in itself, especially in large masses, yet by its very richness likely to make you feel more acutely the wintry poverty of the decayed vegetation around it, and the naked branches overhead. A judicious artist might avail himself of these materials, but he would never permit them to injure the unity of his work, a kind of unity necessary in human art, but outside of the aims of Nature. The seasons when Nature is most harmonious are the late summer and the earliest weeks of autumn, but in winter and spring she colors accidentally and in patches. Woods in the mass, however, are often grandly harmonious even in January, with their rich brown in nearest scenery passing through purple in the middle distance to a deep neutral tint on distant hills. On the edges of woods the white stems of the birches tell very effectually against dark purple as silvery lines, even at a considerable distance. In the immediate foreground all lichens and mosses assume an unusual importance during winter ; in the case of the mosses because they are really more brilliant, as they prosper and grow in moisture, whilst the lichens gain a more than common degree of prominence from the comparative poverty of the decayed vegetation around them. There are hedges so invaded by pale green tufted lichen that it becomes in winter the principal element of their coloring ; and not a disagreeable element, being delicate in hue notwithstanding its opacity.

IX.

THE wintry landscape is a museum of dried vegetation, bearing much the same resemblance to
the verdant wealth of summer that a mummy does to
a living human being, yet with the difference that the
vegetable mummy often retains the most graceful elegance ; and this it is to be feared, can scarcely be said
of any Egyptian princess, however distinguished in her
time.   Indeed I may go so far as to assert that some
plants are positively more elegant as mummies than
they were when the sap circulated in all their vessels.
There is the common teazle, for example, which in
winter acquires a quite remarkable perfection of curvature in all its leaves.   There is a clump of them not
far from the Val Ste. Véronique, of which the tallest is
nearly eight feet high, and so very perfect and delicate
that if some skilful goldsmith were to copy it as it stands
in pure Australian gold (silver would be too chilly in
tint) all Paris would wonder at its loveliness.   Not a leaf
of it but is fit to be the model for an archbishop's crozier,
and round the head rise the thin bracts like guards, still
perfect, every one of them, though the tall stem has

swayed in the autumn storms. As to that head itself, what a miracle of texture! Warm reddish brown in the sun, and at a short distance seeming soft as fur, but nearer a delicate net-work.

Another very fine plant in winter, happily very common in many places, is the great mullein, which, though it does not equal the teazle in elegance, far surpasses it in the expression of melancholy ruin. Still it retains some rich, thick, pale, dusty, cottony leaves, between the earth and the blackened raceme where the pale yellow flowers once clustered so gaily in the sunshine, but the large outer leaves have faded and lost form, and become mere brown rags, like the tatters of miserable poverty, drenched by the rains of winter, and draggled on the mud of the cold inhospitable earth. Of all the plants that grow, the mullein in its decay comes nearest to that most terrible form of human poverty when the victim has still, to his misfortune, vitality enough for mere existence, yet not enough to make existence either decent or endurable. Groups of them will be found together, still strong enough to bear up against the bitter wind that tears their rags into more pitiable raggedness, and flings foulness on their wet and withered leaves, to stick there, like contumely, till they die. Some freshness lingers yet within their folds, like hidden and tender recollections, some softness and a little warmth, but their misery is like that awful destitution that stands clothed in the last shreds and remnants of prosperity.

The ferns and grasses bear the season better, and

retain almost every charm but color. The forms of
fern are still complete, and the plant still bears itself
with a perfect grace, except where it has been exposed
to injury, and then it will often be broken, for it is more
fragile now than in the elasticity of summer. There
are grasses which survive with all their elegance, and
their delicate pale spears stand perfect in the air of
winter, bending at every breath, and bearing trembling
plumes, yet recovering themselves always. I value, too,
the great old dead stalks of the bramble, all quite hoary
and gray, with nothing but thorns upon them. They
are often twelve or fifteen feet long, and trail about the
hedges much more visibly at this season than when hidden under the summer leafage.

The blackthorn is valuable for the abundance of its
dark purple fruit, as big as common grapes, and covered
with a beautiful blue-gray bloom. The whole coloring
of this plant in winter is strikingly harmonious, for the
stem and twigs are of a pleasant purplish gray, which
the fruit continues in another variety. It is well worth
painting in studies of still-life for its peculiar quality of
texture. The whitethorn is less harmonious, but richer,
with the multitudes of its dark vermilion berries, in
masses quite sufficient to affect the coloring of a foreground. Whilst the blackthorn is entirely bare of leafage at this season, the whitethorn is not altogether bare,
but will often retain foliage rather abundantly in sheltered corners, and its remaining leaves are of a very
warm brown, which sustains the berries well, and is better
than the contrast of green. The way in which green will

be preserved or lost in winter is one of the most curious things about the local coloring of landscape. For example, in the case of rushes, the green remains vividly where there is water, except at the tops of the blades, which are tipped with yellow ; but in drier places the whole rush is pale yellow, often giving most brilliant and effective white lines, even when there is no sunshine to relieve them. Then you have the peculiar green of the mistletoe, often existing in such quantities as to give at a little distance quite a summer-like appearance to the tree it has chosen to establish itself upon. Seen nearer, the green is made perceptibly less powerful by the wax-like berries, which, being of a very pale greenish white, neither intensify the green by contrast, as scarlet would have done, nor yet sustain it by a continuation of its own color. The mistletoe is, to my taste, one of the most beautiful plants we have ; and I like its coloring exceedingly, both because the hue of the leaves is not a vulgar green, and also because the fruit has the most exquisite delicacy of hue, in such perfect harmony with the leafage, that it seems tinted by·a faint reflection.

There is a great deal of pleasant green in winter, due to the delicate minute mosses that often cover the bark of certain trees ; as for instance, the quince-tree and the acacia. In some such cases the bark seems positively painted, and is quite bright in the wintry sunshine. Such moss-painted trunks and branches are a great resource when there happens to be holly in the foreground, which is dangerous from its isolation and the intensity of its green, derived from contrast with the scarlet berries. One of the best things about the holly is the variety given by the lighter color of the under-side of the leaf, but it is not a very safe plant for the painter, as it offers a peculiar temptation to obtrusiveness both of crude color and of what may be called irritating detail, neither has it any softness of mass or grace of contour. For any one who enjoys the sight of red berries in the most jewel-like splendor there is nothing in winter like the viburnum, the species we call *viorne obier* (a relative of the guelder-rose of gardens) ; and if you meet with a fine specimen just when it is caught by the level rays of a crimson sunset, you will behold a shrub that seems to have come from that garden of Aladdin where the fruits of the trees were jewels. The birds love these splendid berries, and it is said that in Norway they are served at table for dessert. I have not forgotten the mountain-ash, but in January, although it still has berries, the most of them are withered and have lost their beautiful color ; however, they still keep a rich crimson vermilion tint. Nothing in the beginning of the year can be prettier than the hazel, with its thousands of pendulous catkins, all of a very pale and tender and lovely green in the sunlight ; they remind one of filigree, or the work in the fringe of epaulettes.

It is a great advantage of the winter season for the study of sylvan nature that it enables us to see the structure of trunks and branches so much better than we ever can do when they are laden with summer foliage. Of all trees at this season of the year my favorite is decidedly the walnut. Its bark is magnificent in the strength of the deeply-furrowed lines which mark it (tempting beyond measure to an etcher), and its fine pale grays exhibit to perfection that wealth of dark mosses which the landscape-painter knows and values. Besides this, there is so much grandeur in its far-spreading, powerful arms, that it is well for us to see them during part of the year without their voluminous green sleeves. Happily for the beauty of many a village the walnut is productive during life, so that it is allowed to come to full maturity. The oak is inferior both in form and color, and expresses only a sturdy strength. The ash shows her grace of structure, her tall and elegant limbs, whilst her bunches of 'keys' hang like ornaments on the lofty branches ; and there will be a little rich green moss, perhaps, about her foot, and on her trunk one or two different kinds of lichen, either gray or golden. As for the towering poplar, there will be nothing whatever on all his height but here and there a remnant of last year's leaves, withered and curled, whilst the branches whiten towards the summit. The alder would be almost as naked were it not for the quantities of brown catkins, which give a deep and rather rich color at a distance. All the branches of the horse-chestnut are tipped with brown buds, whose abundant adhesive varnish protects the tiny leaf rudiments, all snugly wrapped in cotton. The ground beneath is strewn with the sere leaves of the preceding year, and the smooth-rinded old mahogany-colored fruit.

4

X.

Improvements — Wood-cutting — Importance of fine Trees in Scenery — Giant Brethren — Spenser's Conception of the Forest.

MY presence in the Val Ste. Véronique had the good effect of saving some trees from the woodman's axe, and by way of compensation I gave myself the pleasure of making an opening here and there to obtain glimpses of scenery, where the brushwood was as impenetrable as a jungle. Of all country occupations I think this is the most interesting, whilst planting is perhaps the most satisfactory. It is flattering to the vanity of a creature so ephemeral as man to feel that he is settling the fate of oaks that might live for a thousand years. No sentiment can be more foolishly thrown away than that which would preserve all trees until they were rotten : it is best to cut them in their fullest maturity before decay begins. Still there are exceptions to this rule, and the chief of these are the cases where a tree is valuable in life, either from its position as an ornament of scenery or else from association with past generations of men. How much of the beauty of the scenery we love best may be dependent upon the magnificence of a few trees which, once gone, a hundred years would not replace, we do not adequately realize until accident or avarice has removed them. All scenery that is not positively mountainous owes to sylvan beauty nearly all its charm and attraction, and even where trees abound the whole dignity and character of some house or village may be dependent upon the immediate neighborhood of two or three venerable oaks or walnuts. And in the heart of the forest, remote from any human habitation, there may be scenes of the most striking grandeur, which would be utterly ravaged by the destruction of some venerable company of giants who have lived there side by side for full five hundred years. There is one such solitude in a narrow dell about a league from the Val Ste. Véronique. It is just at the end of a little valley, where a streamlet glides down a grassy slope rounded into the smoothest curves. On this slope stand twelve gigantic brethren, chestnuts, which by a happy fatality have escaped the axes of many successive generations. They have no definite association with human history ; they have dwelt together in this solitude undisturbed by the fall of dynasties or the noise of distant battle-fields. No king has ever sought refuge in their foliage, no general has encamped or held council beneath their shade. Only the birds have made nests in their world of leaves, and the wild deer found repose in the coolness of their shadowy seclusion. No poet has ever sung them, no lover ever carved linked initials on their bark. And yet the man would be dead to all sylvan feeling, who could go into that valley, axe in hand, and look at these ancient brethren with a base calculation of their price. Can we not spare a narrow spot of ground, where ground is worth so little, in order that one group of trees may

reach the limit of their age, in order that we may see
both what they are and what they may become? Every
sapling in the forest gains dignity from their imposing
presence, and he who has once beheld them in their
place may read with better understanding the verse of
those great old poets who wrote when such princes of
the forest might be met with more frequently in the
land. Think what was Spenser's conception of the
forest, and what in our own time is too often the uninteresting reality! He thought of it as a country
shaded by a great roof of green foliage, which was carried on massive stems always so far apart that one or
several knights could ride everywhere without inconvenience; but we find the reality to be for the most
part an impenetrable jungle of young trees, that will be
cut down in a year or two for firewood. Ah, let us still
preserve some dwelling of sylvan majesty, where the
poet may dream and the artist may study, and both may
forget the cares and interests of the present! Are there
not still left to us, here and there in the deep woods, such
vales of ancient peace that wandering Una may haply
meet us there; or some splendid knight of fairy-land,
like him whose glittering crest danced joyously as the
rustling foliage of an almond-tree,

'On top of greene Selinis all alone?'

XI.

Mild Winters — Arctic Sleep of Nature — Beauty of Hoar-Fiost —
Fairy Work of the Hoar-Frost — One Day — Snow — Wild Boars
— The Weasel — He becomes my Gamekeeper — A Snow-storm —
Winter Reading — Cowper's Description of the Ice-Palace — Thom-
son — His Ficelles — The Man Lost in the Snow.

OUR winter in the Val Ste. Véronique had been
hitherto one of those mild southern winters
which deceive us with promises of a calm transition
from the glow of autumn to the green of spring, as if
there were nothing between the two seasons but an
interval of grayer sky and briefer daylight, without
any severity of temperature, or any white enshrouding
of the departed year. Rarely, however, does the course
of Nature in these latitudes entirely avoid the season of
arctic sleep, and if it is delayed till the spring flowers
are ready to blossom, it is almost sure to come down
suddenly upon the earth, like a fit of somnolence on a
weary human frame. So it happened that one day near
the end of February the thermometer went down very
rapidly, and every creature that was susceptible of cold
began to feel the bracing of a keener air. It was evident that we were to have real winter after all, though
probably a very brief one.

It came upon us in a single night ; and as men have
gone to rest with hair all black or brown, and the next
morning looked in the glass and seen a head white like

the foam of the sea, so did our forest darken in the twilight and whiten in next day's dawn.

It is certainly not my intention to trouble the reader
much with mere changes of the weather, but I mention
this because it produced one of those enchantments
which belong to sylvan scenery, and to sylvan scenery
alone. The beauty of hoar-frost is nothing by itself,
nothing on naked rock or mountain, nothing in the
streets of the city, and out at sea it is visible only on
the ship's cordage, if by accident it may whiten it for
awhile. But on sylvan landscape it settles like a fairy
decoration. No human work is delicate enough to be
compared with such delicacy as this, no human artificer
in silver or in ivory ever wrought such visible magic as
these millions of tiny spears that thrust out points of
unimaginable fineness from the lightest spray's utmost
extremity. The perfect beauty of this adornment is
visible only on tree-branches, and most visible on the
thinnest and lightest; on the dark thin twigs of the
birch, that bend under the weight of a robin, or on
the slender long sprays of the bird-cherry tree, that the
little birds love so well. And it is not every lover of
Nature, however keen his perception, however inveterate
his habit of observation, who has had the good fortune,
even once in his whole existence, to see the hoar-frost
in perfection. It needs a calm so perfect that a ship
with all her sails would sleep motionless upon the sea;
it needs also a low cloud upon the earth, whose watery
particles, or hollow spheres, or whatever in their infinite
littleness they may be, may fall and settle slowly in the

stillness of the night, and freeze and fasten on the tiniest point they touch. Not once in a dozen winters does this fairy building prosper to its completion ; but when the time is come, and the fairies are permitted to do their work without any disturbance from the great, strong gods of the tempest; or the rays of far-darting Apollo, then a strange enchantment descends upon the forest, and a fragile beauty clothes it ; so fragile that the alighting of a bird will shatter it, or the wind from his rapid wings.

The hoar-frost lasted for one day in this perfect beauty, as abundant as ˙a considerable snowfall, but incomparably more exquisite, being indeed to the opacity of common snow what the lace of a princess is to the linen of ordinary life. During this one day of strange tranquillity I walked mile after mile in the narrow woodland roads, deeply enjoying the solemnity of their silence, and watching without sorrow the beautiful death of Nature. The next night came a storm of wind and rain that washed out all fairy-land ruthlessly, and after the rain came snow, and when the snow was deep in the meadows down in the valley the sky cleared and the stars shone as night deepened with that peculiar scintillating splendor which belongs to a frosty night, and a young bright moon cast a broad shadow from the wood's edge down a slope of snow untrodden by man or beast.

Alexis and I were watching this scene from a terrace in the garden, when he seized my arm suddenly, and pointed in silence to the broad shadow above mentioned, in which we discovered with some difficulty several slowly-moving objects, that seemed to be emerging from the blackness of the wood. They came out into the moonlight, half-a-dozen of them, all fine wild boars, and Alexis was just going to fetch his rifle when a shot was fired from the wood on the opposite side of the valley, and the largest boar rolled over on the snow. The others were lost immediately in the recesses of the forest.

Soon a dark human figure became visible as it crossed the narrow open space before us. We quitted our post of observation, and went towards the boar as quickly as the depth of the snow would let us. It was a noble beast, weighing more than three hundred pounds; and the successful *chasseur*, perceiving that his exploit had not been without witnesses, made no attempt to avoid us, but came up with perfect assurance. It was our new acquaintance, the Weasel, and he saluted us with an ease of manner like that of some considerable landowner, who finds himself by accident a trespasser on his neighbor's domain. He begged pardon for having yielded to an irresistible temptation, and said that he would ask of my generosity a pound or two of boar's flesh for himself. I had resolved before to keep on good terms with this active and enterprising neighbor, whose depredations it was impossible to prevent; so, instead of wasting words in ineffectual anger, I simply observed that he would have done better to ask my permission, which would have been freely given, and added that he might remove the beast whenever he chose to fetch it.

He stayed at the farm that night, and the boar was carried on a rough litter to the house, where the Weasel performed the office of butcher with a degree of skill which gave clear evidence that the task was not new to his experience. The next day I came to a decision, and offered to take him into my employment as a gamekeeper ; which he agreed to more readily than I had expected, for his independent existence must have been in many respects more agreeable to his tastes and habits, and probably more lucrative also, though it was likely enough that he would never entirely abandon his private business as a *braconnier*, even after his engagement in my service. I did not regret this decision afterwards, for the Weasel was of the greatest use to us in subsequent sylvan labors and explorations. He occupied a vacant cottage in the Val Ste. Véronique, and attached himself more particularly to the service of my son. I was glad that Alexis, who wandered a great deal in the forest from the beginning, should have such a competent servant and guide.

Although winter had come upon us late, the severity of it was enough to make amends for its want of punctuality. A tremendous snow-storm confined us to the Val Ste. Véronique ; all the roads were impassable, and the house was isolated from the world. But what do we know of winter, what can any one know of it, in the latitudes of the chestnut and the vine ? Even where the oak will not grow freely the winters are still supportable, and wherever the yet hardier pine-tree can bear the rigors of the long dark nights man lives through the months of gloom, in crowded Lapland huts. The perfect winter, more horrible than any dream of poetry except Dante's frozen hell, is the winter of Spitzbergen, where indeed some timber may be found, but only driftwood, washed by the surf of the Atlantic on that treeless northern shore, or fragments of hapless vessels crushed long ago like nutshells in the ice.

I suppose that every European who has written any thing about winter has certainly alluded to the one indisputable benefit which that season brings to us, in inclining us to be more studious of books. We never read so profitably, I think, as we do by the fireside on a winter's evening ; and if in a future state of existence there should be any hours that we have passed in this world to which we may look back with feelings of tenderness and regret, it would be those fire-side hours in which our minds have sought a light that is not the sun's light, and which comes to us through literature.

Amongst other readings that seemed more particularly adapted to the season, I had selected passages of English poets who had described winter with great earnestness of manner, though not always with equal felicity of style. It is not easy, in the blank verse of Cowper, to find a passage that may be quoted without the wish to pass over some line that is either halting or prosaic, or else that slips away too suddenly from under you ; but there is one — the description of that famous freak of the Empress Catherine, the ice-palace on the shore of the Neva — which is firm and sound throughout, and very grand. The subject is introduced by a few weak and prosaic verses, which injure the effect in the original, but when the nobler lines are detached from these the ore is pure indeed :—

'No forest fell
  When thou wouldst build ; no quarry sent its stores
To enrich thy walls : but thou didst hew the floods,
And make thy marble of the glassy wave.
In such a palace Aristæus found
Cyrene, when he bore the plaintive tale
Of his lost bees to her maternal ear :
In such a palace Poetry might place
The armory of Winter ; where his troops,
The gloomy clouds, find weapons, arrowy sleet,
Skin-piercing volley, blossom-bruising hail,
And snow, that often blinds the traveller's course,
And wraps him in an unexpected tomb.
Silently as a dream the fabric rose ;
No sound of hammer or of saw was there.
Ice upon ice, the well-adjusted parts
Were soon conjoined : nor other cement asked
Than water interfused to make them one.
Lamps gracefully disposed, and of all hues,
Illumined every side ; a watery light
Gleamed through the clear transparency, that seemed
Another moon new risen, or meteor fallen
From heaven to earth, of lambent flame serene.'

Surely these lines have qualities which will survive the vicissitudes of taste ; but we are so impeded in our judgment of the poets by the fashions of two epochs, by their fashions and our fashions, that it is almost impossible for us to arrive at an unprejudiced appreciation

of their work. And I think that no poets are farther
removed from ourselves than those of the eighteenth
century. There is Thomson, for instance; how difficult
it is to read him without being arrested at every page
by a too clear perception of the minor tricks or *ficelles*
of his craft! At the time he wrote, these were the
accepted and customary *ficelles*, and probably attracted
so little attention in themselves that the mind of the
reader was left perfectly free to enjoy the thoughts
and imagery of the poet; but to us the work is old-
fashioned, and strikes us as we are struck by whatever
is just old-fashioned enough to be *passé de mode*. And
yet, although his descriptions are not treated on the
same principles as ours, although he has not learned
the more temperate and perfect art which has resulted
from a completer culture than the culture of his time,
and has not been aided (as contemporary work is aided)
by the development of the modern school in painting,
there is still great force in his most finished passages.
The episode of the man lost in the snow is one of the
best of these:—

> ' As thus the snows arise ; and foul and fierce
>   All Winter drives along the darkened air ;
>   In his own loose-revolving fields, the swain
>   Disastered stands: sees other hills ascend,
>   Of unknown, joyless brow ; and other scenes,
>   Of horrid prospect, shag the trackless plain ;
>   Nor finds the river, nor the forest, hid
>   Beneath the formless wild ; but wanders on
>   From hill to dale, still more and more astray ;
>   Impatient flouncing through the drifted heaps,

Stung with the thoughts of home ; the thoughts of home
Rush on his nerves, and call their vigor forth
In many a vain attempt.

      *   *   *   *   *   *

In vain for him the officious wife prepares
The fire fair-blazing, and the vestment warm ;
In vain his little children, peeping out
Into the mingling storm, demand their sire
With tears of artless innocence. Alas !
Nor wife nor children, more shall he behold ;
Nor friends, nor sacred home. On every nerve
The deadly Winter seizes ; shuts up sense ;
And, o'er his inmost vitals creeping cold,
Lays him along the snows, a stiffened corse !
Stretched out and bleaching in the northern blast.'

XII.

Sudden Change from Winter to Spring — Floods — Spring is come —
The Sweet Time — Thomson — Nash — Daubigny — The Spring
Feeling — Constable — His Love of Spring — Harmony of good Art-
Work — Nature not harmonious in the Spring — Charms peculiar to
Spring — The Regrets which the Spring suggests.

WHEN the winter comes very late in our latitude,
as it does from time to time, we pass to spring
quite suddenly. The temperature rises in the course of
a single night as if we had travelled far southwards, and
felt the breezes from the African shore of the Mediterranean. The snow and ice thaw rapidly ; the little
streams become impassable torrents ; the rivulets be-

come rivers; the rivers spread themselves over the plain, and carry ruin to a thousand homesteads. There was something ominous in the excessive mildness of the temperature when we awoke one morning in March. The snow lay deep upon the earth, but the air was warm and enervating. Already the tiny stream in the Val Ste. Véronique had increased in volume, and before nightfall it roared angrily, its turbid waters confined between steep banks, carrying logs of wood that had been purposely laid along its sides, and other burdens that had not been so intentionally confided to its care. Most of the little wooden bridges are removed in a flood of this kind, the earth is washed away from the roots of the trees, and many an alder falls.

With the thaw came a deluge of rain, and the torrents roared in all the glens. We who were at the head of the waters began to expect evil tidings from the plains. Every drop that now fell on the soaked earth of the forest must find its way ultimately to the Loire. Fortunately the hills were richly clothed with wood, which retards the departure of the rainfall, and converts what would be a sudden crisis of devastation into the endurable floods of twelve or twenty days. And still the waters descended rapidly enough to give ample reason for anxiety. We in our hills were safe, and the buildings in our valley had been so arranged by the foresight of the monks who first erected them as to be clear from any possible inundation; but already the torrent was washing the stone-faced embankment of the garden-terrace, and if the monks had not built their stone bridge lower down, which to strangers always seemed so uselessly wide in summer, our road communication would have been entirely interrupted. I felt curious to see the effects of the flood, and, notwithstanding the incessant rain, we quitted the Val Ste. Véronique and drove in the direction of the Loire.

The morning after our return to the valley we rose early, and breathed an air at once so mild and pure that we knew the spring had come.

Spring is much rather the season of poets than of painters. What delights us in the spring is more a sensation than an appearance, more a hope than any visible reality. There is something in the softness of the air, in the lengthening of the days, in the very sounds and odors of the sweet time, that caresses and consoles us after the rigorous weeks of winter. It is natural that poets should love the spring, which comes to them with a thousand flowers, with songs of birds, with purer, brighter light, and such refreshment that it is like a fountain of *jouvence*. So they hail the season with their most melodious invocations, sometimes in grave earnestness, as if its benefits were too great to be treated lightly, and sometimes in frolic merriment like the dancing of kids or lambs. Thomson is grave and stately : —

> ‘Come, gentle Spring, ethereal mildness, come,
> And from the bosom of yon dropping cloud,
> While music wakes around, veiled in a shower
> Of shadowing roses, on our plains descend.’

Nash greets the spring in another tone and measure : —

> 'Spring, the sweet spring, is the year's pleasant king ;
> Then blooms each thing, then maids dance in a ring.
> Cold doth not sting, the pretty birds do sing
> Cuckoo, jug-jug, pu-we, to-witta-woo ! '

These extracts are as dissimilar as can be, and yet in both of them we may observe a characteristic they have in common. It is much more the sounds and sensations of the pleasant time than any thing that is to be seen which awaken the enthusiasm of the poet. The 'ethereal mildness' of Thomson, with the shower of shadowing roses and the awakening music, strike his imagination before any landscape distinctly rises before it. Nash says that 'cold doth not sting,' and he imitates the songs of the birds, which serve him for a refrain. On the other hand, I well remember a large picture of Spring by Daubigny, which was very disappointing both to myself and others ; and the disappointment was most probably due to the inevitable absence of those very delights of sound and sense which refresh us so much in Nature, and of which the poets are so careful to remind us. What would spring be without the *spring feeling* — that quite peculiar exhilaration that comes to us, we know not how, like far-off reminiscences of youth ?

The only landscape-painter who ever dedicated his powers to this season of the year with a devotion all but exclusive of every other was Constable. He liked the freshness of the season as a pleasure for the eye, and his own eye longed for it and loved it, because he was in a state of intense antagonism to the brown doctrine in landscape-painting, and the spring greens were all on his own side of the controversy. In estimating the value of Constable's opinion on this matter we ought therefore to remember that it was not quite an unbiassed opinion, that his mind was not at all in a neutral or judicial state, but that he was like a Protestant theologian seeking texts against tradition; and that his texts were the young verdure, the shade and shower, the cool and pearly light, and soft blue shadow beside it, the sparkle and glitter of daisy-pied pastures in the moisture of an English April. Now whatever a good artist paints is sure to be harmonious, for the simple reason that he makes it so; and there is no doubt that any first-rate landscape-painter who chooses to paint a spring scene will get a harmony out of it (as he will out of any thing in the world), which may be used afterwards as a critical argument in favor of the 'year's pleasant king.' But the plain truth is that *Nature* is not harmonious at this season, she is only in the way of becoming so. The colors that she gives are delicious separately, as we happen to come upon them, and they do our eyes good after the chills of winter; the green especially is good for us, and we welcome it with an uncritical gladness: but when we think of painting, it may be doubted whether any season of the year is less propitious than this to the broad and noble harmonies which are the secret of all grand effects in art. A patch of green in this place and that, quite crude as yet and utterly isolated; a constant contradiction between the sunshine and the wintry-looking woods; a few plants

5

precociously early, and nobler ones lagging behind, — the season resembles nothing so much as that uncomfortable hour in the daily life of a household when some of its members, the early-risers, are already walking about as if they did not quite know what to do with themselves, and others have not yet come down to breakfast.   No, summer and not spring is the landscape-painter's time of harmony, — late .summer, when the peasants go to the harvest-fields, and come home with songs in the warm-toned, mellow moonlight, and all the trees have had time to assume the fulness of their foliage.

Yet spring has its own charms, especially for young people, who have it within their breasts. I think perhaps, as we get older, and are saddened by the gloomier experiences of life, that the recurrence of the earliest leaves and flowers does not always increase our cheerfulness very much* We know too well the limits of a year, how short a space it is, how little that will be satisfactory afterwards can be done in it whilst it lasts. We think of the other springs that now lie far behind us, and how we lost them in vain pleasures, or profitless labor that seems to us still more vain. Will this year be better used? Already it is slipping away from under us, and pray what have we done? Made plans, perhaps, to be afterwards modified, and, it may be, finally abandoned, to join all those other ghostly schemes and projects so various in conception, so monotonous in the negative result. It is only, I imagine, the simply and intensely practical who are never assailed by any such regrets as these ; to them the business of living seems a very plain, straightforward business, and they follow their own lines, as loco-motives do, with the least possible friction or loss.

XIII.

IN the life of men who work in great centres of popu-lation, and see nothing of the sylvan world except what may happen to have been planted in a plot of ground which they dignify with the name of a garden — a few gardeners' plants so altered from the Divine ideal as to be unrecognizable, and so arranged as to be entirely without that charm of unexpected surprises which is the great source of interest in Nature — there will often occur a sudden awakening, about the begin-ning of June, to the fact that the world has somehow painted itself green again, with touches of white, and crimson, and blue. In such lives as these the spring is often simply omitted, unless from time to time some breath of vernal mildness may reach them across the barrenness of the brick wilderness they live in. It hap-pened to me once to be confined by urgent business during the spring season in the heart of a great English city, in which there were no green boulevards or avenues, and whose only refreshment in that kind was a park that had been recently purchased by the common council, far outside in the suburbs. After many delays my business came to an end, and I fled at once to a little corner in the country that was frequented only by artists and anglers — a clean little inn by a river well shaded by ancient trees. We had got to the middle of June and I had not seen a leaf or a flower; or if my eyes had seen one, the mind had not perceived it in the midst of wearing anxieties. When, therefore, this sudden leisure came upon me, in the glorious birth of summer, I felt the transition like the change from Purgatory to Paradise. No summer ever seemed to me so wonderful as that did. Every leaf was a marvel, every flower was a delight; I lay down in depths of dewy grass, and watched the pure sunshine streaming through the perfect young leaves till they softened it to a quiet green light all around me, that seemed at once to strengthen my jaded eyes and soothe them. Three days afterwards the marvel had passed away, but the recollection of it has ever since remained with me, and explains for me the delight of the citizen in green leaves, and the intensity of sensation about Nature which we find in poets who were bred in towns; whilst those who have lived much in the country, though they know and observe more, seem to feel more equably, and to go to Nature with less of sensuous thirst and excitement. Exactly the same difference may be observed between horses which have daily access to the pasture, and those which, after being kept in stables during a prolonged town season, are sent to grass in summer. The former will conduct themselves reasonably when the released prisoners of the town-stable will indulge in the most extravagant demonstrations. There is in men and animals a natural thirst for summer that begins to agitate them about the month of March, and if they live in rural freedom the advance of spring very gradually satisfies this craving, like slow-dropping rain on a parched land ; but if they pass into summer suddenly, and omit the spring from their experience, then the change is like the arrival of thirsty camels on the bank of the abounding Nile. Yet, although there is a deep delight in thus bathing ourselves in the full rich green of summer, when we have longed for it many a day, I like better the slow increase of satisfaction that the spring-time hourly brings to us, however parsimoniously, and I would not in exchange for months of what is commonly reputed to be pleasure, miss the sight of the first leaves on the willow and the scent of the violets where they grow.

I remember a boy who for many months, even for years, suffered agonies from a disease which was perhaps even the more terrible that there was no hope of release by death ; and one day, after he had been in bed so long and had suffered so much that he had lost his reckoning of time, his mother brought him a great full-blown rose that filled all the chamber with its fragrance. The lad took the flower very eagerly, and, after almost burying his face in the soft and perfumed petals, turned wonderingly to the giver and said, 'Is it summer now, dear mother?' He, poor fellow, had missed his spring altogether, and missed it doubly; for the spring of his life was passed on a couch of suffering, amidst odors of medicines, visits of grave-faced doctors, and a weariness almost without hope.

Happier in this, at least, at the Val Ste. Véronique we were out every day from the very beginning of the new season, and watched the slow brightening of it like a dawn. Where, in early March, will you find a plant already in the fullest pride of all its greenery, not yet in flower it is true, but in leaf abundantly? The water precedes the land in the contest for spring primers, and our finest streams are full of the water-ranunculus, waving in the shallows like long green hair, — the richest of all greens, certainly, though it might be treason to some paler and fairer land plants to affirm that it is also the loveliest. The water at this time is quite clear and abundant, and very swift in those depths of two or three feet where the ranunculus is happiest; so that all the fine linear segments of its subaqueous leaves, the only ones yet developed, are washed by millions of gallons of pure water every day of their lives, and kept so exquisitely clean that no fragment of earth can ever adhere to them for an instant. It is very different later in the year, as we shall see when the time comes, but the plant is never so lovely as it is now, even when its flowers are all out in the sunshine and it has two sorts of leaves to boast of. I thought sometimes as I watched it waving so unweariedly with the motion that the current gave it, and flashing dark emerald from one end to the other like the scales of some swiftly-gliding serpent, that it seemed to have more than simply vegetable life, and to be a water-spirit tied fast in the stream's path and seeking relief in ineffectual struggles. Strangely enough, one of my horses came exactly to the same conclusion ; for as I was riding him across the river at a ford down in the plain, where the stream had a certain width and a depth of two feet or thereabouts, he saw the green ranunculus waving in the clear current, and, being at once persuaded that it was some living creature likely to do him bodily harm, became frantic with fright, and bolted with me down the stream's bed till he got into a deep pool, where the necessity for swimming brought him to his senses again. I do not know whether artists have ever cared much for this plant, but it adds infinitely to the beauty of some rivers at this early time of the year, the effect of the waving various green through the lightly-rippling transparent water being a beautiful variety in the otherwise rather monotonous topaz of river-sands.

Alexis and I quitted our retreat amongst the hills for an excursion in the low country to see the opening of the spring season, which occurs about a fortnight earlier there. The plain was rich in trees and foreground plants that were not so common in our forests, and the most conspicuous of these, at this time of the year, were the willows. During a walk of a few miles we found half-a-dozen varieties, the most frequent and most effective near the rivers being the purple willow, whose thin red stems, all speckled with young shoots of pale green, were brilliant in the first spring sunshine. Then there was the sallow-willow, with its soft white downy blossoms, and the brilliant silver of the osier changing so beautifully, according to the direction in which you look at it ; for if you look in the direction of the down it is silvery, but if against it, then you see a delicate gray purple. This purple reddens later as the anthers become visible, and finally turns to a golden yellow with pollen, but the yellow is beautifully moderated by being always on a gray ground. Hardly any thing in Nature is more lovely than the round-eared willow in full blossom, especially the glory of the male tree, with the mingled greenish gold on its flowers, where the anthers make a sort of light golden filigree on a ground of tender green. The female tree is much less splendid, but her pale flowers are pleasant as young foliage is, with their soft grayish verdure on which lies no dust of gold. A little later in the season the common white willow is sufficiently leaved to show a delicate green bloom in the distance when caught by the sun, but when the sun is clouded the bloom seems to disappear, and in certain positions relatively to the light the green will be scarcely, if at all, visible. This adds much to the liveliness and variety of the spring landscape, as the color comes and goes under the sunshine and cloud, adding greatly to our sense of motion and change in Nature, — a sense that some artists have had in great strength, and even expressed verbally, which is rare with them. There is nothing prettier in the natural landscape than the appearance, and vanishing, and

sudden reappearance of the fresh young green on willows, at a distance, as the light touches or abandons
them. We have something of the same kind, but more
sublime, in the evanescence and reappearance of crags
or knolls on the sides of all noble mountains, whose
structure can never be quite accurately ascertained
unless you can make models of them by tedious sur-
veys, and which cheat us and amuse us by endless alterations and disguises.

XIV.

The Willow — Associated with Unhappiness — Desdemona — Barbara's
Song — Ophelia — The Willow cheerful in Itself — Cheerful use of
Willow — In Tennyson — In Virgil — Melody of the English Name
— The Latin Name — The Italian Name — The French Name — In
Lamartine.

I WONDER how it is that so cheerful-looking a tree
as the willow should ever have become associated
with ideas of sadness. Yet the association was established by the great poets long ago, and must have been
found by them already in the popular mind. It is especially connected with unhappiness in love, and unhappiness on the side of the woman when neglected and
forsaken. So Desdemona says, —

> ' My mother had a maid called Barbara :
> She was in love ; and he she loved proved mad,
> And did forsake her : she had a song of " willow ; "
> An old thing 'twas, *but it expressed her fortune*,
> And she died singing it.'

Then Desdemona sings Barbara's song, with the refrain,—

> ' Sing willow, willow, willow ;
>   *Sing all a green willow must be my garland.'*

And in ' Hamlet,' when Shakspeare wishes to give a poetical melancholy to the brook where Ophelia was drowned, he introduces a willow in the very beginning of the Queen's description, so that the word occurs in the first verse, and is the first substantive in the verse : —

> ' *There is a willow grows aslant a brook,*
> *That shows his hoar leaves in the glassy stream ;*
> There with fantastic garlands did she come
> Of crow-flowers, nettles, daisies, and long purples,
> That liberal shepherds give a grosser name,
> But our cold maids do dead men's fingers call them :
> There, on the pendant boughs her coronet weeds
> Clambering to hang, an envious sliver broke ;
> When down her weedy trophies, and herself,
> Fell in the weeping brook.'

This association seems the more curious that the willow is one of the lightest, liveliest, and most cheerful-looking of all the trees that grow. There is nothing funereal about its leaves either in form or color, and they play in the wind like butterflies. See how well the tree comes in when Tennyson uses it in the pleasant allegro overture to the ' Lady of Shalott ' : —

> ' Willows whiten, aspens quiver,
> Little breezes dusk and shiver,
> Through the wave that runs for ever
> By the island in the river   .
>   Flowing down to Camelot.'

And how sweetly and cheerfully the willow occurs to

Virgil's mind in connection with a passage of pure congratulation, as a tree whose flowers would be haunted by the bees of Hybla:—

> 'Fortunate senex! hîc, inter flumina nota
> Et fontes sacros, frigus captabis opacum!
> Hinc, tibi, quæ semper vicino ab limite sepes
> Hyblæis apibus florem depasta salicti
> Sæpe levi somnum suadebit inire susurro.'

But what an advantage the English poets have over all others in the melody of that sweet word 'willow'! How beautifully it takes its place in verse, — so beautifully that the mere repetition of it is music in itself.

> 'Sing willow, willow, willow.'

Virgil was not nearly so fortunate as Shakspeare in this respect, for *salictum* is a word which can never have any beauty of sound, though it may be made, of course, to fit neatly into a Latin hexameter; neither is *salix* any better for euphony. And even the great softening process which Latin underwent before it was moulded into other languages has not very much improved the word for poetry. *Salce* and *salcio* are both harsh; and *saule*, though softer, is far inferior to willow for syllabic melody. Here it is, for example: the word occurs in some fine lines of Lamartine, but the adjective which follows it is immeasurably more important in the structure of the verse:—

> 'Là, contre la fureur de l'aquilon rapide
> Le saule caverneux nous prêtait son tronc vide,
> Et j'écoutais siffler dans son feuillage mort
> Des brises dont mon âme a retenu l'accord.'

XV.

Perceptible Changes in Foregrounds — Honeysuckle — Yellow Iris —
Furze — Soapwort — Arum — The Names of the Periwinkle in dif-
ferent Languages — The unfortunate English name, Periwinkle —
Brilliant Contrasts in early Spring — Viburnum — Spindle-tree —
Precedence of Leaf or Flower — Hawthorn and Blackthorn — Oak.

ALTHOUGH there is nothing at this early season
which shows from a distance like the willow,
whose silvery catkins and tiny nascent leafage have
really an importance even in the general landscape,
still the foreground is beginning to decorate itself with
leaves that count for something, even before they are
fully grown or accompanied by their sweet sisters, —
the flowers.   The very tardiness of some plants gives
greater consequence to those which precede them by a
few weeks ; for instance, the honeysuckle is a more important hedgeplant in March than it is two months later ;
for when the hedges are bare of every thing but a few
incipient buds of thorn, or wide-apart scattered little
leaves of eglantine, it is a great thing to find the soft,
rather dark-green leaves of honeysuckle quite rich and
abundant, so much more abundant as it seems to us
than even in the height of summer, when they are lost
in the general profusion, and only the flowers attract
us by their color or their perfume.   So by the edges
of streams, although the yellow iris is a fine attractive
plant at all times when it is visible, and most especi-

ally so when it displays its regal flowers, still one
welcomes it in March with a new sense of its value
when the young pale-green blades stand straight out
of the water, their points about six inches above the
surface. There is, in truth, plenty to be seen in the
young vegetation of the foreground, and there are more
leaves everywhere than we think; but most of them
are so small yet that they escape attention individually,
and only please the eye in the mass by a general sense
of reviving greenness. So it is with the tiny green leaves
of furze, an innumerable multitude, which as yet, however, seem less numerous than its thorns. And there
are plants which will be of great size and splendor in
their maturity, and which have already quite a mature
look on a much smaller scale, so that any one who did
not know them would think they were satisfactory
enough already. The young soapwort is an example
of this; few young plants are better worth drawing,
for the leaves take curves almost as good as those of
fine naturally-dried leafage, and there is an interesting
transition of color from the fresh green of the well-
formed leaves down to purple near the root. Other
plants, which will never reach any great height or size,
are of consequence, because their leaves, though few in
number, and close to the ground, happen to be relatively of rather large dimensions; such a plant is the
arum, which is often visible now in damp nooks with
more than a mere promise of verdure yet to come.

I have said something about the beauty of the
English word *Willow.* Other plants are less happy in

their English names, and more fortunate in the names that have been given them by other nations. For example, there is that charming little spring flower which is called in Latin the *Vinca*, or *Pervinca*, because it is supposed to conquer (vincere, pervincere) either the frosts of winter or some malady, whichever it may be, for etymologists suggest both explanations. And now for the changes that we have made in the Latin name. The Italians, to begin with, have been in this instance singularly conservative, and they call the flower *pervinca* still; but the French have softened the word, and made it more beautiful by changing it into *pervenche.* How sweetly it occurs in the following verses, addressed by a poet to a young lady who had captivated his admiration! —

> 'Je voudrais être la pervenche,
> Qui joue avec tes noirs cheveux,
> Ou ton beau miroir qui se penche,
> Quand sur lui tu mires tes yeux.'

The English, on their part, have also deviated from the Latin, but not, I think, with so happy a result. They have changed *pervinca* into *periwinkle*, and I submit that it is simply impossible to write about this flower in sentences worthy of its charm and beauty when you have to introduce such a barbarous word as that.* A poetical lover might wish to be a violet or a rose, but he would never, in written verse, have the temerity to wish he was a periwinkle.

---

* I suppose the change must have come gradually, and through the form *pervinke*, which Chaucer uses.

Early spring is not the season of the most brilliant contrasts ; but they occur occasionally, and may be briefly alluded to in passing. You have the viburnum, for instance, which in the late winter is so splendid in its innumerable berries, with their jewel-like transparent red. In early spring a good many of these berries remain, and though their splendor is rather dimmed and faded by this time in reality, it seems to be revived by the effect of contrast, for the fresh green leaves have sprouted amongst them. Another little tree, whose foliage sprouts about the same time, is the spindle-tree, or *fusain*, which one can never see without thinking of its two very opposite uses. The charcoal from it is, it appears, especially approved for the manufacture of the powder used in cannons, whilst at the same time artists prefer it for charcoal-drawing. Both these two things — cannon powder and charcoal-drawing — have been immensely improved of late years ; so war and art, barbarism and civilization, go on together yet as they did in old Greece, in old Rome, in the Europe of the Middle Ages, and in the time of the great Renaissance.

The mere precedence of flower before leaf, or leaf before flower, is in itself quite sufficient to insure variety in the early aspects of vegetation. It is illustrated by many plants which might be paired together in this connection as examples ; but it is enough to mention two of the commonest and best known, the hawthorn and the blackthorn. The leaves of the hawthorn will be all sprouting over it abundantly and rapidly covering the hedge with their fresh light-green, probably rather in-

tensified by the contrast of a few old haws that may
linger yet from winter ; whilst, at the same time, the
blackthorn will just begin to be abundantly dotted with
little white buds which, here and there, are bursting into
flower, the leaf-buds meanwhile, though contemporane-
ous, being of no visible importance, mere points compared
with the flower-buds. If the blackthorn were often an
isolated plant it would scarcely, in early spring, be a
cheerful-looking one, notwithstanding its abundant efflorescence, for the eye desires a little green amidst so much
white and black ; but, as it very frequently happens that
the hawthorn is not far off, this defect is fully compen-
sated by the green and leafy neighbor. Besides this,
in our scenery at least, you are never very far from an
oak, and last year's leaves still remain very abundantly,
offering another contrast which is not, I think, always
quite harmonious or agreeable, but which, at any rate,
is a variety.

XVI.

A Larch-Wood — Rosy Plumelets — Horse-Chestnut — Quince Tree —
Ash — Walnut — Oak — Keys of Ash — Acacia — Elder — Privet —
Bird-cherry — Wild Gooseberry — Daffodil — Wordsworth's Poem on
the Daffodil — Herrick's Poems on Daffodils — The Poet's Narcissus
— The Legend of Narcissus — καλὰ νάρκισσος — Keats — His Poem on
Narcissus.

BY far the most charming sight in the early spring
is however, to my taste, a larch-wood. There is
such a delightful mystery in it, just when the leaves begin
to sprout — a pervading green-gray bloom, from the gray

of the branches and trunks, and the delicate green of the
young leaves. Still more beautiful is it rather later,
when the rosy catkins come into being, as Tennyson
says, —

> 'When rosy plumelets tuft the larch,
> And rarely pipes the mounted thrush ;
> Or underneath the barren bush
> Flits by the sea-blue bird of March.'

About this time, too, the leaves of the horse-chestnut
have pushed vigorously through their varnished scales,
and are now visible all wrapped together in a great
ogive bud, in softest cotton down. The quince-trees,
always interesting in one way or another, are especially
pretty at this time, for downy little pale leaves are coming all over the tree in little clusters, each cluster almost
like a flower, the effect at a short distance being that
of a scattering of light-green points, as if a swarm of
small green butterflies had alighted on the tree. The
ash and walnut, like the oak, show no change as yet
at a distance, although the work of a new creation is
elaborating itself within their closed buds ; but the
'keys' of the ash catch the sunshine strongly, and are
important and elegant from their vertical hanging —
a quality which never fails to add a certain grace to
trees whenever it occurs ; as, for example, in the flowers
of the acacia and many others not so beautiful or conspicuous. The elder, privet, and bird-cherry tree all
advance simultaneously, and amongst the shrubs the
wild gooseberry is in great haste to clothe itself with
fresh green. This unpretending little shrub has been

6

strangely unfortunate in being scientifically misnamed *ribes* — a name which the Arabs gave to an acid rhubarb, and a Frenchman by mistake applied to the wild gooseberry.*

But of all the plants that flourish at this season of the year not one is equal to the daffodil in its splendor of golden yellow on pale dusty basis of long green leaves. The causes of the singular and almost blinding intensity of the color are a gradation from semi-transparent outward petals, which are positively greenish in themselves, and still more so by transparence owing to green leaves around, to the depth of yellow in the womb of the flowers, where green influences are excluded, but yellow ones multiplied by the number of the petals. So in the heart the color is an intense orange cadmium, not dark, but most intense — a color that we remember all the year round. Wordsworth found that this floral splendor haunted him, —

> ' I gazed — and gazed — but little thought
> What wealth the show to me had brought.
> For oft when on my couch I lie
> In vacant or in pensive mood,
> *They flash upon that inward eye*
> *Which is the bliss of solitude.*'

It is well for our northern yellow daffodils that they should be thus associated with one of the most beautiful passages in which any poet has ever revealed to us something of the working of his own memory and

---

* I allude to the *Ribes Grossularia*, sometimes called *Ribes Uva-crispa*, the Gooseberry Ribes ; not to the *Ribes Rubrum*, *Ribes petræum*, or *Ribes nigrum*, various species of currant Ribes.

imagination. And then we have a very exquisite little poem by Herrick, in which he laments their too early disappearance; a regret which has been felt by many others who have loved the flower, yet never, it is probable, expressed with such exquisite conciseness, —

> ' Fair daffodils, we weep to see
> You haste away so soon.
> As yet the early-rising sun
> Has not attained its noon :
>   Stay, stay
> Until the hasting day
>   Has run
> But to the even-song,
> And having prayed together we
> Will go with you along.'

But of all the associations which are attached to our golden narcissus, the most ennobling is its near relationship to the ' poet's narcissus' of the Mediterranean, which bears a solitary flower of pure white, with a yellow crown often edged with orange or crimson ; and this is believed to be the flower to which the beautiful Greek legend has given the charm and interest which belong to imaginative tradition, and to that alone. The different stories of Narcissus agree in these particulars, that he contemplated the reflection of himself in the river Cephisus or in a fountain, and afterwards became a flower, either because his blood was changed into one after suicide, or because a flower grew beside his grave after he died of sorrow for his twin sister, unheeding the charms of Echo. The stories differ as to his reason for gazing upon his own image ; some say that he became enamoured of it fancying it to be a water-nymph, and others that he could not help looking at it because it reminded him of the sister that he had loved too much and lost. The popular impression seems to be that Narcissus was 'a beautiful youth who simply admired his own beauty, and gazed upon his form as it was reflected in the smooth water, afterwards becoming a flower on the river's brim, and continuing, as a flower, the habit of self-admiration which he had contracted in his human adolescence. This last interpretation, or simplification, of the old legends, whose details it drops altogether, is still very happily in accordance with the genuine old Greek spirit, the spirit of a time when no possessor of eminent physical beauty could remain unaware of a gift so much appreciated, but would see it reflected, not only in the waters of the Cephisus or other rivers, but in the admiring eyes of all Greek men and women whenever he appeared in public. In any shape it is peculiarly an artist's legend, having so direct a reference to beauty, so that it has often been illustrated by modern painters and sculptors. We do not feel very grateful to those later classical writers who have been at the pains to inform us that our καλὰ νάρκισσος (as Theocritus called it) has no especial association with beauty, and is not called so after the beautiful youth who was beloved by Echo, but takes its name simply from νάρκη, or, ναρκάω, with reference to its narcotic properties. Was the flower called νάρκισσος before the legend existed, and is the legend itself, as Keats imagined, simply the beautiful fancy of some early poet who, 'in some deli-

cious ramble,' found the flower looking at itself in the
water, and imagined for it the story that we know?

> ' And on the bank a lonely flower he spied,
> A meek and forlorn flower, with nought of pride,
> Drooping its beauty o'er the watery clearness,
> To woo its own sad image into nearness :
> Deaf to light Zephyrus it would not move ;
> But still would seem to droop, to pine, to love.
> So while the poet stood in this sweet spot,
> Some fainter gleamings o'er his fancy shot,
> Nor was it long ere he had told the tale
> Of young Narcissus, and sad Echo's bale.'

XVII.

Young Hemlock — Socrates — Authorized Suicides — The Death of
Socrates — Peach-bloom — Apricot Blossoms — Value of Old Walls.

THERE is a corner of a neglected old garden at the
Val Ste. Véronique in which grows a certain plant
very abundantly, that inevitably reminds us of an ancient
philosopher. Towards the end of March it is all carpeted
with young hemlock, which at this stage of its existence
lies almost perfectly flat upon the ground, and covers it
with one of the most minutely beautiful designs that can
possibly be imagined ; the delicate division and sub-
division of the fresh green leaves making a pattern that
would be fit for some small room, if a skilful manu-
facturer copied it. Our own hemlock is believed to be
identical with that which caused the death of Socrates,

but its action in northern countries is much feebler than in the warmer climate of the Mediterranean. The Athenians added poppy-juice to the infusion of hemlock, that the approach of death might be painless ; and it is said by Valerius Maximus that the civil authorities of Marseilles kept a supply of this drink always ready for weary ones who had obtained the permission of the Senate to lay down the burden of existence. Those indeed were waters of oblivion ; and it is astonishing how easily, in certain conditions of society, men have come to look on death as a deliverer, to be invoked whenever life is felt to be unpleasantly painful, or even simply *ennuyeuse.* But the death of Socrates, half voluntary, was grander than their death which was wholly voluntary. His dignity seemed to him incompatible with flight, and he awaited the fatal cup with that perfect mental clearness which is so well known to us. He died for having preached the philosophy of the conscience, which the Athenians instinctively felt to be opposed to the antique religion of the State, however careful he might be in external conformity to its rites.*

In the same old abandoned garden where the hemlock grows on the walls there remain a few fruit-trees,

---

* 'En vain prenait-il soin d'assister à toutes les fêtes et de prendre part aux sacrifices; ses croyances et ses paroles démentaient sa conduite. Il fondait une religion nouvelle, qui était le contraire de la religion de la cité. On l'accusa avec vérité "de ne pas adorer les dieux que l'état adorait." On le fit périr pour avoir attaqué les coutumes et les croyances des ancêtres, ou, comme on disait, pour avoir corrompu la génération présente.' — *La Cité antique,* by M. FUSTEL DE COULANGES.

and amongst these some peaches and apricots. They
are in full bloom towards the end of March, and of all
the beautiful sights to be seen at this time of the year
I know of none to be compared to these old peach-trees
with their wealth of rosy bloom, which would be beautiful in any situation, but is so especially in this because
there happen to be some mellow-tinted walls behind
them, the very background that a painter would delight
in. There is some pretty coloring in the apricot blossoms, on account of the pink calyx and the pinkish brown
of the young twigs, which has an influence on the effect,
but the peach is incomparably richer; and after the
grays of wintry trees and wintry skies the sight is gladdened beyond measure by the flush of peach-blossom
and the blue of the clear spring heaven. But to enjoy
these two fresh and pure colors to the utmost we need
some quiet coloring in the picture, and nothing supplies
this better than such old walls as those of the monastic
buildings at the Val Ste. Véronique; walls that Nature
has been painting in her own way for full four hundred
years, with the most delicate changes of gray and brown
and dark gleamings of bronze and gold. There is something, too, which gratifies other feelings than those of
simple vision in the renewal of the youth of Nature,
contrasting with the steady decay of any ancient human
work; and in the contrast, between her exquisiteness,
her delicacy, her freshness, as exhibited in a thing so
perfect as a fresh peach-blossom, with its rosy color, its
almond-perfume, its promise of luscious fruit, — and the
roughness of all that man can do, even at his best.

XVIII.

IT is one of the most striking peculiarities of the scenery around the Val Ste. Véronique, that although the country is almost entirely covered with dense forest, and although the land is a sea of hills with narrow valleys between them, there are here and there little patches of it in full tillage, and these are often placed in the most unlikely situations. You will occasionally come upon a little field, islanded in the forest, and occupying very likely just the most awkward bit of steeply-sloping hillside that is to be found there, and yet this little field will be ploughed and sown with the utmost diligence and affection. I know two or three such places, which not only are on a most inconvenient slope to begin with, but have also on their own surface a variety of minor inconveniences, in the shape of miniature hills and valleys, or lumps and holes, which seem as if they would baffle the most ingenious ploughman who ever stood behind a team of oxen. With horses, it is unnecessary to observe, such work as this would be simply an impossibility. The heaviest and most sluggish breed of horses in the world would still

be far too impatient for a kind of labor which is as trying to the patience of animals as if it were expressly
contrived to irritate and torment them. The oxen go
through it in their own inimitably firm and patient way,
often dragging the plough against a slope so steep that
merely to climb it, without dragging any thing at all,
would be in itself an exhausting kind of labor, yet keeping up to their work always steadily and well, as if they
were inwardly sustained by the firmest sense of duty.
Such is the difficulty of the ground that a light plough
requires six oxen to work it, and often eight. There
is a certain field on a hillside visible from the Val Ste.
Véronique which especially interests me when the farmer
is ploughing it, which he does so conscientiously that his
example would be excellent if transferred to the intellectual sphere ; and many a student, who finds the
ground before him irregular and arduous, would do well
to imitate that thoroughness which will leave no corner
of it untilled. There is one place which interested me
most especially, a sort of cup or hollow just on the edge
of the field, so that the forest advanced into the very
middle of it, and you could not go down one slope and
up the other, which would have been comparatively convenient, but must necessarily, if you would plough the
place at all, take your team of oxen straight into the hollow, then turn them, and bring them out again up a slope
as steep as a house-roof. Would the peasant attempt
this ? I watched him the first day to see what he would
do, but the question was very soon decided. He took
his eight oxen straight over the edge of the hole, down

into the bottom of it, where they were huddled in temporary confusion, then calling them by their names got
them into order and bravely ploughed his way out again.
This he repeated till the sides of the hole were as well
ploughed as any other part of his little field, and the
groupings of his eight oxen when they got into it, with
their grandly strenuous labor as they were getting out
of it, were well worth the study of an animal-painter.
The clear early sunshine cast them into strong light and
shadow, and the creamy white of the oxen was splendid
against the dark reds and yellows of the earth.

That word 'splendid' which I have used just now,
without especially thinking about it, reminds me of the
right and accurate employment of the same word by
Virgil with reference to a ploughshare. His '*sulco at-
tritus (incipiat) splendescere vomer*' is just one of those
touches which show an artist's sense of what has been
called the poetry of common things. Anybody can see
that the Shah's diamonds are splendid, and perhaps the
most essentially vulgar minds are the most likely to be
strongly impressed by a splendor so much associated
with great pecuniary value; but only an artist or poet
would notice the shining of a common agricultural implement. And yet few things in the world are more
resplendent than a well-used ploughshare as it catches
the glory of the sunshine; and it may be doubted whether
even the glitter of martial steel can awaken more poetical
associations. It is a fine sight to see a flash of sunshine
run along a restless line of bayonets, or on the burnished
helmets of some emperor's regiment of guards; but a

true poet would be set dreaming just as surely by the
polish of the ploughshare — a polish not due to any intentional scheming about effect, but simply a proof of
labor, like that noble polish which comes of itself upon
the laborious human mind when it has toiled in the intellectual fields. The mere fact that Virgil noticed the
shining of a ploughshare nineteen hundred years ago is
of itself a poetical association, as Thomson felt when he
wrote : —

> ' Such themes as these the rural Maro sang
> To wide imperial Rome, in the full height
> Of elegance and taste, by Greece refined.
> In ancient times, the sacred plough employ'd
> The kings and awful fathers of mankind.
> And some, with whom compared, your insect tribes
> Are but the beings of a summer's day,
> Have held the scale of empire, ruled the storm
> Of mighty war ; then, with victorious hand
> Disdaining little delicacies, seized
> The plough, and greatly independent lived.'

' I was bred to the plough,' wrote Burns, 'and am independent ; ' the two ideas of ploughing and independence connecting themselves together very easily, in
part perhaps because the ploughman whilst he works
is not commanded by another, but is lord of his own
team, and guides his own implement as it makes the
long furrow in the earth. There is certainly a great
dignity in the grand old agricultural operations ; so
much dignity, indeed, that they are compatible with the
grandest traditions of religious or political history. One
is tempted to avoid the allusion to Cincinnatus because

it is so familiar to every one, but I may observe that the very familiarity of it, the universality of its reception and preservation in the memory of the cultivated world, is the proof that we have an ideal sense of a certain harmony and compatibility between the dignity of ploughing and the dignity of government which finds its satisfaction in the story of that worthy Roman. And I think the true dignity and grandeur of this labor is never so conspicuous as it is under circumstances such as those which I have just now attempted to describe, when the earth·to be subdued is so difficult and rebellious, and it is necessary to have a strong team of six or eight well-trained oxen thoroughly under command. Think of the long hours from early dawn to sunset, with the incessant exercise of resolute will and strong, controlling arm on the plough-handle; a guidance needing far more strength than that of the seaman's tiller, whilst the team of animals is not so mechanically obedient as the unresisting ship! Steadily they all go forward together, team and plough and ploughman, through wind and calm, through shine or shower, and still the iron coulter turns up the heavy soil, resisting always, and always resisting vainly!

XIX.

OF at least equal dignity is the great religious act of sowing, with its sublime well-grounded confidence in the natural repayment of what we wisely trust to Nature. We are so familiar with this act of confidence that the meaning of it is almost lost to our apprehension, yet man's trust in the order of the universe is never more grandly proved than when he goes forth from some poor house where the children have scanty bread, and carries the precious grain and scatters it on the ground. There is another kind of sowing on which it is not always possible to have such secure reliance, because it is so difficult to know accurately the condition of the soil. He who sows corn sows it in earth that can be analyzed, and agricultural chemistry can tell him with great certainty what may be his chances of success; but who knows the minds of nations and *their* chemistry? who can tell whether the most precious seed-thoughts of philosophy will lie utterly unproductive or yield illimitable harvests? The condition of *that* soil varies from year to year; one year you might as well sow corn on icebergs as trust any living thought to the deadly coldness of the world, and yet a few years later this same world will be no longer an iceberg but good earth waiting for the seed. We all of us know the parable of the sower, how 'the sower soweth the word' by the wayside, and on stony ground, and amongst thorns, and finally on good ground also. That is the way the preacher sows his doctrine, and in every age from the day when that parable was first spoken the preacher has had exactly those chances of success. But it is not quite the same in the intellectual sphere, for here the soil itself all changes together, and in one age it will be all stones or thorns, whilst in another it will be good ground ready for the reception of great thoughts or astonishing discoveries. And whatever may be the faults of the age in which we live, whatever may be the crudeness, rawness, uncouthness, of our half-developed industrial system with the unpleasant forms of human life which it has made discouragingly conspicuous, one thing at least may be boldly advanced in defence of it ; namely, that it is incomparably more favorable than any age that has preceded it to the sowing of the seeds of knowledge.

There is an old peasant near the Val Ste. Véronique whom I like to see especially at this time of the year. He is very tall and thin, with large bones, and a white head carried high with natural dignity. When he walks steadily along the furrow, casting the seed with that regular motion of the hand and arm which comes from years of practice, I look at him and think that, of all the great works that ancient tradition has handed down to us, there is none more full of majesty than this. The old man has sown crops that were harvested long ago, and his fathers before him have done this also for unnumbered generations. When the legions of Cæsar swept through the country in pursuit of the Helvetii, there were great granaries in the hill-fortresses that the Gauls had filled from their well-cultivated cornfields. In what far Eastern land, I wonder, did the sower first go forth to sow? And what keen-minded, far-seeing, early discoverer, aided by no hint from Science, first conceived the notion of cultivating those utterly unpromising gramina which were shortly to become corn, and wheat, and barley? Nobody knows how long the human race used the cereal grasses before the clever bakers found out at last the art of making what we call a loaf of bread. It was nearly six hundred years after the foundation of Rome when the Roman bakers developed their art to a degree before undreamed of, and produced what at that time was a novelty and a luxury, but is to us a matter of primary necessity. Before that they made bread indeed, but of the sort that was eaten by the besieged Parisians, with bits of straw and awns in it; and soldiers on the march carried a sack of ill-ground flour, that they mixed with water when they came to a spring or stream. We know nothing of the first discoverers, humanity's earliest benefactors, but not the least among them were the discoverers of the cereals. The author of ' Lothair ' did well to remind us of what we forget so easily — the merits of discoverers whose discoveries have been long familiar.

We think that nothing can be more natural than the growth of the cereals, but it is not so : the wild grasses with tiny uneatable seeds, these are natural, and not the nourishing cereals.

XX.

The Common Reed — Music of Reeds — Pan and a Reedy Stream — Sadness of the Willow and of Reeds — Tennyson's use of them — Song of the Dying Swan — 'The Morte d'Arthur ' — Association of Reeds with a dreary Scene — Mrs. Browning's Association of Reeds with the Sacrifice of the Poet to his Art — Associations of noble Utility — Various practical uses of Reeds — The Reed's Motto — The lesson of the Reed not very noble — Pascal's comparison of man to a Reed.

AMONGST the good gifts of Nature which have needed absolutely no amelioration by human care or culture, one of the best and handsomest is the common reed, and March is its harvest-time. There is hardly any thing in Nature more delicately beautiful than some damp corner where the reeds have grown undisturbed, and turned finally to that pale reed-yellow, a tint far exceeding in refinement the golden hues of straw. The long lanceolate leaves seem like fairy papyrus, on which some elfin bard might indite his exquisite inventions, and the tall stalks rustle together as the cool March wind blows through them, and the sound is very sad and melancholy ; because although the glorious spring is coming, when the earth will be covered with flowers,

these last year's reeds will never be green again, and
they watch the spring as old people watch sadly some
festival of youth. Their music is not unknown to thee,
great Pan !

> ' Who lovest to see the hamadryads dress
>   Their ruffled locks where meeting hazels darken,
>   And through whole solemn hours dost sit and hearken
>   *The dreary melody of bedded reeds*
>   In desolate places, where dark moisture breeds
>   The pipy hemlock to strange overgrowth,
>   Bethinking thee how melancholy loth
>   Thou wast to lose fair Syrinx.'

And in another poem by Keats, where Pan and a
reedy stream both recur to his fancy, we have in the
space of four lines a strong expression of pity, with
weeping, sighing, and desolation : —

> ' Poor Nymph — poor Pan — how did we weep to find
>   Nought but a lovely *sighing of the wind*
>   *Along the reedy stream ! a half-heard strain,*
>   *Full of sweet desolation, balmy pain.'*

As the willow is associated with the sadness of disappointed lovers —

> ' The willow, worne of fornlorne paramours ' —

so whenever the poets speak of reeds, it is in connection
with dreariness or weariness of some kind, and always
to give sadness to the landscape. This may be because
no plant answers so exactly to our idea of ghosts as
reeds do when they stand still in their places, so changed
and pale, when the sap no longer flows, and a phantom

7

of their former self remains, all ghastly in the twilight
So Tennyson says : —

> ‘ Ever the *weary* wind went on,
> And took the reed-tops as it went.’

And farther on in the same poem the song of the
dying swan is associated with

> ‘ The wavy swell of the soughing reeds.’

And in the ‘ Morte d’Arthur,’ where the poet has
sought every circumstance which could heighten the effect of melancholy sublimity, — the ‘ dark strait of barren
land,’ the sea-wind singing ‘ shrill, chill, with flakes of
foam;’ ‘ the winter moon,’ — he has not failed to remember the poetical use of reeds : —

> ‘ Better to leave Excalibur conceal’d
> *There in the many-knotted waterflags*
> *That whistled stiff and dry about the marge.’*

And a few lines farther on, —

> ‘ “ I heard *the ripple washing in the reeds*,
> And the wild water lapping on the crag.”
>   To whom replied King Arthur, faint and pale,
> “ Thou hast betrayed thy nature and thy name.” ’

This reference to the reeds occurs a second time with
the effect of a mournful refrain : —

> ‘ Then spoke King Arthur, breathing heavily,
> “ What is it thou hast seen, or what hast heard ? ”
>   And answer made the bold Sir Bedivere,
> “ I heard the water lapping on the crag,
> *And the long ripple washing in the reeds.”* ’

Even in Mrs. Browning’s fine little poem, ‘ A Musical

Instrument,' there is an undertone of regretful melancholy. The 'great god Pan' goes 'down in the reeds
by the river,' and hacks and hews at them till he has
got the material for his instrument ; but then comes the
deeper meaning of the poem — the regret that poetical
culture and discipline should so isolate us from the
common world ; and pray just observe how sadly sweet
are the final cadences of the verse, and how much the
sadness is aided by our old association of melancholy
with reeds : —

> 'Yet half a beast is the great god Pan
> To laugh, as he sits by the river,
> Making a poet out of a man.
> *The true gods sigh for the cost and pain, —*
> *For the reed that grows nevermore again*
> *As a reed with the reeds in the river.'*

Reeds have many associations of utility as well as
poetry. The reed-pen, still used by a few artists and
greatly valued by them on account of its qualities as an
instrument for powerful and picturesque design, was in
the early centuries of our era universally employed by
authors and transcribers, so that the plant has been a
servant both to literature and art, and has the dignity
which belongs to every instrument of culture.* Besides
these delicate uses, the reed has aided the early steps
of civilization by providing its first requisite, — a roof ;
and a requisite only secondary to that, φράγμα, a fence,

---

* To this might be added some reference to the papyrus of antiquity, which was the leaf of the Nile reed, so that this plant has supplied
both pens and paper.

so that botanists have called it *Arundo Phragmites.*
The moralists, on their part, have found the reed
extremely useful as an illustration of weakness and in-
stability, which may however save itself by a timely
yielding to forces that cannot be resisted. The reed's
motto is given with the neatest brevity by Lafontaine : —

'Je plie, et ne romps pas.'

But although the reed in the fable had practically the
advantage over the oak that the wind uprooted, and although worldly prudence always counsels us to do as
the reed did, and bend, — still it may be observed that
the reed's lesson is not a very noble one, and that humanity scarcely requires it, being only too ready to bow
before every breath that assumes the tone of authority.
And it may be observed, farther, that whatever political
liberty, and whatever intellectual light, may be at present enjoyed by the most advanced nations of the world,
are due to exceptional men, who had much more of
the oak in them than the reed ; men who often paid
their resistance with their life, but who were not failures, since their example has bequeathed fortitude to
their successors. Pascal said, '*L'homme n'est qu'un
roseau, le plus faible de la nature, mais c'est un rcseau
pensant.*' Surely, however, the thinkers are of robuster
quality than that.

XXI.

April — Play of Light and Shadow — Genuine April Weather — Hills in April Weather — The Willow in April — Streams in April — Constable — His observation about Clouds — His Affection for the Spring-time — Chaucer — His wonderful Passion for Landscape — His description of Spring — The Draba Verna — Figwort Ranunculus — Wordsworth's Poem on the Little Celandine — Buttercups — The Lesser Celandine in Decay — Unresisting nature of Decay in Plants — Resistance to Decay in Men — Beautiful Association of the name Celandine.

IT happened that the month of April opened with April's own characteristic weather. March had ended with a gray sky through which sunshine filtered, as it were, in a way much more trying to the strongest eyesight than the intensest glare of summer. All Nature was a picture of the most various and delicate grays, with fresh green sparingly scattered ; a sort of coloring quite peculiar to the season and full of a quiet charm, when we are in a mood quiet enough to enjoy it. But the first of April brought with it a perfect revolution. Instead of the almost uniform gray sky, broken only by gleams of semi-transparence in the universal cloud-canopy, we had now separate clouds, having a magnificent individuality, and sunshine in perfect though temporary splendor. No weather is, to my feeling, so delightful as this genuine April weather. The play of light and shadow, so rapid in its transitions, so powerful in the suddenness of its unexpected yet most effective contrasts, would of itself be a subject of inexhaustible interest in any country where the landscape is not too irremediably dull for any thing to make it lively; but this is not all. In genuine April weather you have not only the play of light and shadow, but that of mystery and definition, caused by the frequent showers, which pass before the hills at one time with the half-transparence of a veil, at another with the opacity of a curtain ; so that it is hardly possible to find any considerable extent of hill-scenery of which one part will not be in' the clearest definition that brilliant sunshine and a pure atmosphere can give to it, whilst another will be ·in purple shadow, and a third paled by a light-gray shower. It is a season, too, which will give to ordinary hill-scenery much of the life and glory of the true mountains. A forest-covered *colline*, which in summer is simply a rising land of rather sombre green, with a monotonous outline on a blue sky, becomes, under the lively effects of April, as rich in purple and blue, and silvery grays of distance, as a mountain-range in the north of Scotland. Nothing can exceed the vivacity and brilliance of these effects in April, and their brilliance is heightened to the utmost by the freshness of the unsullied greens in the foreground, which are made splendid by the glittering varnish of the rain. This is the time of the willow's pride and glory. He is as yet almost alone amongst the trees, and begins the concert of the year with a delicate and tender solo, to which we are all sure to listen ; and he is sustained by an accompaniment of

purple background, with such variations of sunshine that
his singing, not naturally of the strongest, is made to
seem quite powerful for the time. All the streams, too,
are in a season of prosperity; for although they are
rather swollen by frequent showers, they run plentifully
but not foully as they did in winter, and all their little
islets are like emeralds with the new grass that the clear
water refreshes as it flows past them.

It is impossible to watch the effects of April without
thinking of a painter who loved and understood them
better than any other, and who painted them in all
their freshness at a time when the connoisseurship of
all Europe was in the brown stage of art-criticism, and
liked nothing so much as thickly-varnished old canvases,
so obscure that it was not always easy to distinguish
what the artist had intended to represent. Constable
said that he preferred spring to autumn, in which I find
it difficult to agree with him; but as he loved the spring
pre-eminently he studied it earnestly, which landscape-
painters who pass the season in great cities have few
opportunities for doing. There is a description of an
engraving from one of Constable's pictures of Spring,
written by the artist himself, which is well worth quoting
for its truth of observation about clouds. 'It may perhaps,' he says, 'give some idea of one of those bright
and silvery days in the spring, when at noon large
garish clouds, surcharged with hail or sleet, sweep with
their broad shadows the fields, woods, and hills; and
by their depths enhance the value of the vivid greens
and yellows so peculiar to the season. The *natural*

history, if the expression may be used, of the skies, which are so particularly marked in the hail-squalls at this time of the year, is this : the clouds accumulate in very large masses, and from their loftiness seem to move but slowly ; immediately upon these large clouds appear numerous opaque patches, which are only small clouds passing rapidly before them, and consisting of isolated portions detached probably from the larger cloud. These, floating much nearer the earth, may perhaps fall in with a stronger current of wind, which, as well as their com- parative lightness, causes them to move with greater rapidity; hence they are called by wind-millers and sailors *messengers*, and always portend bad weather. They float midway in what may be termed the lanes of the clouds ; and from being so situated are almost uniformly in shadow, receiving a reflected light only from the clear blue sky immediately above them. In passing over the bright parts of the large clouds they appear as dark ; but in passing the shadowed parts they assume a gray, a pale, or a lurid hue.'

Notwithstanding Constable's passionate affection for the spring-time, and the advantage of possessing an eye that had been educated by the constant practice of art, it may be doubted whether he felt its influences more keenly than did a great early English poet, who had been influenced by no such general appreciation of the beautiful in Nature as that which exists (or seems to exist) in modern society, and is so continually stimulated by modern writers and artists. It is truly amazing that a poet situated as Chaucer was situated, who had seen

no landscape art but such as existed in the backgrounds
of illuminated manuscripts or the sylvan scenery of
hunting-pieces in mediæval tapestry, who had read no
literature in which the landscape sentiment was more
developed than it is in the Eclogues of Virgil, should
have felt as Chaucer felt, and seen what he perceived.
I do not mean that he wrote from the landscape-painter's
point of view, for that has only been done by quite
recent poets, and the attempt has in most instances been
injurious to their compositions as literature, which is not
painting, and ought not to imitate painting ; but I mean,
that to any one who thoroughly realizes what Chaucer's
situation was, it must be matter of astonishment that he
loved Nature with such intensity.   There is a sort of
quiet enjoyment of Nature in the classical pastorals.
Theocritus and Virgil evidently liked a country life, and·
they mention different kinds of trees and shrubs, and a
few flowers, with a tranquil contentment that occasionally becomes almost affectionate ; but they have nothing
like Chaucer's passion.   The note of the following extract from 'The Flower and the Leaf' may, it is true,
seem delicate and tender rather than passionate, yet its
tenderness is passion in repose : —

> 'When shoures sweet of raine descended soft,
>   Causing the grounde fele times and oft
>   Up for to give many an wholesome aire,
>   And every plaine was clothed faire
>
> 'With new grene, and maketh small floures
>   To springen here and there in field and mede,
>   So very good and wholesome be the shoures

That it renueth what was old and dede
In winter time ; and out of every sede
Springeth the hearbe, so that every wight
Of this season waxeth glad and light.'

If from the 'small floures' of Chaucer we descend to particulars, and ask of what 'small floures' the verse at once reminds us, I think we can hardly fail to remember the common Draba, or *Draba verna*, which is both small and early, and as pretty in its elegant humility as many little plants that happen to be more popularly known.   Tiny as it is, with stalks just strong enough to carry its little pods and flowers, and not burdened by any leaves, for they lie on the ground about its root, it still has an appreciable effect on the color of an April foreground, which it powders with white like a hail-shower, and even at a distance it will make the green of a pasture grayer.   The power of small plants in the coloring of landscape is often forced upon the attention of artists, and there are many remarkable examples of it in different parts of the world.   The Draba does not strike the eye as it would if the flower were scarlet or bright blue, but it has its influence nevertheless as a moderator of crude greens.

A much more important spring flower in size and splendor is the Figwort Ranunculus, which, happily for its reputation, possessed a much prettier and more musical name ; probably the great motive that induced Wordsworth to write about it.   The rose might smell as sweetly by another name, and yet not occur so favorably to the euphony of verse.   Wordsworth, in a footnote, called the Figwort Ranunculus 'common pilewort,' but he was extremely careful not to call it so in the stanzas of the poem itself. Hear how prettily the poetical name ends the first stanza : —

> ' Pansies, lilies, kingcups, daisies,
> Let them live upon their praises ;
> Long as there's a sun that sets
> Primroses will have their glory ;
> Long as there are violets,
> They will have a place in story :
> There's a flower that shall be mine,
> 'Tis the little Celandine.'

And again, the last stanza but one : —

> ' Ill befall the yellow flowers,
> Children of the flaring hours !
> Buttercups that will be seen
> Whether we will see or no ;
> Others, too, of lofty mien ;
> They have done as worldlings do,
> Taken praise that should be thine,
> Little, humble Celandine ! '

It is curious what a hold this flower seems to have taken on Wordsworth's affections. He wrote three poems about it, two in the rather jingling measure of the stanzas just quoted, and a third, of far more serious tone and deeper meaning, in a measure adapted to the expression of earnest thought ; and so closely does the noble sadness of these stanzas associate itself with the flower by which they were suggested, that it is impossible for any one who has read Wordsworth as poetry ought to be read,

not to remember them when he sees the Lesser Celandine
in her decay.

> ' But lately, one rough day this Flower I passed,
> And recognized it, though an altered form,
> Now standing forth an offering to the blast
> And buffeted at will by rain and storm.
> I stopped, and said with inly-muttered voice,
> *" It doth not love the shower, nor seek the cold,*
> *This neither is its courage nor its choice,*
> *But its necessity in being old.*
> *The sunshine may not cheer it, nor the dew ;*
> *It cannot help itself in its decay." '*

Surely in all the range of poetry there is no finer and
truer description of the real nature of decay — that there
is no courage in it, nor choice, but only necessity and
helplessness — yet in the association with old age in man,
which occupies the concluding stanza of this poem, one
cheering consideration is omitted, that the note of melancholy might be wholly unrelieved. It is certain that by
courage and strength of will men really can resist, for
long years, some of the worst evils of old age, and at
least one happy consequence of the modern feeling *de
senectute* (so different from Cicero's) is that men not only
try to keep themselves young, but actually succeed for a
very long time in doing so. In the vegetable world there
is neither courage, nor choice, nor effort, but only sub-
mission. The plant is rooted in its place, and can seek
no shelter against the weather, nor any protection against
its enemies, neither can it strengthen by voluntarily directed nervous force the resisting power of stalk or
branch. We are so much accustomed to that old artifice

of the poets, so suitable to the childish condition of the intellect, by which they attribute human feelings to the oak and reed, to rose and lily, that we have a difficulty in realizing the true nature of a plant's existence. And yet there is poetry in the truth also, as my last quotation proves.

The Lesser Celandine attracts us by scattering a little bright gold on the earth so early in the season, but its yellow is neither more modest nor more beautiful than that of the later flowers that Wordsworth playfully sacrificed at the shrine of his early favorite. It is evident, however, that in addition to its sweetly-sounding name, the poet found another attraction in the Lesser Celandine — the idea of connecting his own fame with that of the flower permanently, and of conferring fame upon what had been hitherto unnoticed ; an idea that has always been pleasing to poets, from Horace downwards. Wordsworth does not appear to have remembered that the name which pleased him by its music is associated with, and even derived from, the name of one of the most beautiful and poetical of the birds. Celandine is a corruption of the French *chélidoine*, which in Italian is *chelidonia* or *celidonia*, in Latin *chelidonium*, in Greek χελιδόνιον, from χελιδών a swallow.* Opinions differ as to the reason

---

* The classical reader may remember the beautiful passage in the thirteenth idyl of Theocritus, where Hylas goes down to the fountain to fetch water for the heroes who are eating. Several plants are mentioned by name : —

Περὶ δὲ θρύα πολλὰ πεφύκει
Κυάνεόν τε χελιδόνιον, χλοερόν τ' ἀδίαντον,
Καὶ θάλλοντα σέλινα, καὶ εἱλιτενὴς ἄγρωστις.

Liddell and . Scott suggest that κυάνεόν (which presents a little

why the Greeks associated the celandine with the swallow; some say that it is because the celandine* (not the lesser) comes when the swallows come, and stays as long as they remain with us; but others affirm that it is because the swallow used the plant (in which a caustic juice circulates like blood) to give sight to her little ones. Be this as it may, the plant takes her name from the bird.

XXII.

The Common Primrose — Nooks where the Primrose grows — Etymology — Beauty of Primrose Yellow — Cowslip and Oxslip — Influence of Agriculture upon Landscape — French Dislike to Solitude — Nature and the Farmers — Wheat-fields in April — A flowering Rape-field — Gentians and Heather — The Blackthorn — Its Chilling Effect — Leafless Oaks.

A MUCH more delicately beautiful flower is the common primrose, but her praises have been sung so often that it is difficult in this century to say any thing of her that can be either new or interesting. Still, if we can say nothing that is new, there is always a delightful novelty, not unpleasantly mingled with half-melancholy

difficulty, as there is no positive blue about the plant) may have stood for γλαυκόν; and this is the more probable that the underside of the leaves might be accurately described by the latter adjective.

* The Figwort Ranunculus, which Wordsworth wrote about, has scarcely any thing in common with the true Celandine but the color and the name. The two plants do not even belong to the same family botanically. The figwort belongs to the *Ranunculaceæ*, and the true celandine to the *Papaveraceæ*.

reminiscences of by-gone years, in the sensation of meeting with primroses for the first time in the spring, especially if they happen to be in great rich clusters, in some corner where we come upon them unexpectedly. There are several nooks in the Val Ste. Véronique which the primroses have elected for their homes, particularly one place between the rivulet and a great wild cherry-tree, where there must be two or three thousand of these flowers. *Prima veris*, first of the spring, *primevère*, and first not only in the sense that it is earliest, but first also in the perfection of its loveliness, if you think only of the delicate corolla, and not of the great coarse leaves, which seem as if they had been put there for nothing but to make us feel the exquisiteness of the pale corolla more completely. That corolla is the perfection of Nature's yellow, for it shows all the delicacy the color is capable of; and if you seek that coloring elsewhere, you need not look for it on the earth, but may haply find it once in a twelvemonth in the purity of the clear heaven after sunset. The bees are glad when the primroses bloom in the grassy hollows, and they come to them from far, well knowing that there is honey down in the tube of the one soft beautiful petal. And whilst the primroses live in great companies in the shady places that suit them best, the cowslip and oxslip, their very near relations, live out in the meadows and pastures, over which also the bees range at this time very busily.

The influence of agriculture upon landscape is one of those questions which force themselves irresistibly upon our attention when we think about art and Nature.

There are two quite opposite schools amongst artists and poets in reference to this rather difficult and complicated subject. Constable was entirely on the side of agriculture, and plainly said that he liked the fields the farmers worked in, and the work they did in them ; in short, the Nature that Constable loved best was Nature modified by man, and so he painted a well-cultivated country with villages, and mills, and village-steeples seen over the hedges and between the permitted trees. This feeling about Nature is a very common one in France, where people will often tell you that such a place 'is delightful for its scenery — you can count the steeples of eight villages, and you cannot drive two miles in any direction without passing either a village or a country-house.' The essence of .this feeling is the dislike to solitude, and a sense of oppression when not relieved either by the companionship of man or by visible evidence of his presence. On the other hand there have been several modern landscape-painters, and a few writers, who believe in wild Nature as an article of faith, being persuaded that nothing that occurs in ' unspoiled Nature ' can by any possibility be defective from the artistic point of view — a dogma of natural religion which is seductive by reason of its simplicity, and because it offers what man so much desires, an infallible authority and guide. But supposing that a thinker were to approach this subject armed with a good deal of artistic taste and experience, yet not in the least inclined to pin his faith to any absolute dogma on one side or the other, what would he be likely to decide ? He would say most probably that both Nature and the farmers often made arrangements which might be good and reasonable on the solid earth that we inhabit, but which, for the clearest artistic reasons, would be perfectly intolerable in a picture ; and such an opinion would be compatible with the profoundest reverence for the Divine arrangements, and a sincere respect for the useful work of agriculture. The material world was not made exclusively for the purpose of being painted ; it has other uses, and there may be some incompatibility between those other uses and the exigencies of artistic color or composition. Who would venture to paint a wheat-field at the beginning of April ? Its intense crude green may be in itself agreeable as a refreshing change after the grays and browns of winter, but it harmonizes with nothing else in the landscape, and the quantity of it is unmanageably great for a color of such intensity. And if a wheat-field is too dangerous to be thought of, what shall we say to such a blinding phenomenon as a flowering field of rape ? The difference between color and colors could not be more vividly illustrated. In the artistic sense the rape is devoid of color, though it is of the most glaring yellow, and a patch of it on a hillside flares over leagues of landscape. Not only ought artists to avoid painting crudities of this kind, but they ought even to avoid looking at them. It is enough to paralyze any delicate color-faculty to live near a flowering rape-field, at least so long as the abomination lasts. The balance of color in the entire landscape is destroyed by it, and the eye is rendered insensible to modulation. There are times when even wild plants may be a danger to the general harmony, but a belt of azure from the gentians on an Alp, or a large patch of rather crudely purple heather on the flank of a Scottish mountain, has always the great advantage of irregularity about its edges, which also lose themselves with more or less of gradation in the vegetation round about. The rape-field, on the other hand, is as obtrusive from the mathematical definition of its outline as from its insupportable intensity of hue.

The spring of the year, like the adolescence of the mind, is especially the time of crudities. May I venture to observe that even the blackthorn, which the poets have sung with affection, is at this time rather a crudity also, and not very much better, from the colorist's point of view, than snow on the hedges in winter? Of course, if you go close up to the flowers, and look at them as a lady does at her bouquet, you will perceive the yellow of anthers and green of calyx, but these have little effect at a distance, and we feel the need of leaves. It is curious how far a flowering shrub can make us feel its importance, for good or evil, in the landscape. A single blackthorn can chill the edge of a forest, and this is the easier that the forest, being as yet leafless, has a wintry look in contradiction to the genial weather. A forest of oak is even *more* leafless now than in the month of January. The smaller oaks will retain the mass of their dead leaves, but the larger ones, being more exposed to the wind, will have lost the greater part of theirs, leaving a few only in the light sprays, which catch the sunshine as specks of ruddy gold.

XXIII.

Cherry-tree — Aspen Poplar — Stem of the Birch — Birch trunks in Sunshine — Young Beech — Birch against the heavenly Azure — Young leaves of Horse-chestnut — Their apparent newness — Dried old Leaves — Old Scales — Their ornamental Utility — Dry Oak Foliage — Last Year's Leaves of Bramble — Their rich Coloring — Principle of Coloring in good Glass and Oil Painting — Deathly Opacity — Vigorous advance of many Plants — Nettles — Great Mullein — Arum — Meadow Bittercress — Its Constellations — Marsh Marigold — Creeping Bugle — Small-flowered Calamint — Broom in Flower — Broom Yellow — Prudence in Art — Criticism of Nature — Fanatical Opposition to it — Artistic and Natural Color — The Materials of Art in Nature.

AMONGST the wild forest-trees in the Val Ste. Véronique one of the finest is the cherry-tree, which is believed to be indigenous here, and as the soil and climate are most favorable to it, grows to such a size that it may almost, in that respect, claim equality with the oak and the beech. At the end of the first week in April the wild cherry-trees are all in full bloom. At a distance of fifty yards the flowers so entirely eclipse the leaves that the latter are invisible, but the young leaves take their place beautifully when you are close at hand, not only for their form (the cherry-leaf is one of the most beautiful of all leaves for a good designer), but for their color also, which is not crude, as young leafage generally is, but enriched with a reddish brown. There is one huge old cherry-tree just outside the wood, with plenty of space for growth, and a quite congenial situation. It is a great world of flowers, and the bees are constantly going and coming between it and their hives. Not only what are popularly called flowers may produce an effect, but even the less generally admired catkins may under certain circumstances acquire pictorial importance. One of the finest sights at the beginning of April is a tall aspen poplar in full morning sunshine, with its thousands of pendent catkins, which at a little distance take a rich dark crimson tint, and strikingly contrast with the light gray stem and branches. But the stem of the aspen is not to be compared with that of the silvery birch, which is one of the master-pieces of Nature. Every thing has been done to heighten its unrivalled brilliance. The horizontal peeling of the bark, making dark rings at irregular distances, the brown spots, the dark color of the small twigs, the rough text-ure near the ground, and the exquisite silky smoothness of the tight white bands above, offer exactly that variety of contrast which makes us feel a rare quality like that smooth whiteness as strongly as we are capable of feeling it. And amongst the common effects to be seen in all northern countries, one of the most brilliant is the oppo-sition of birch trunks in sunshine against the deep blue or purple of a mountain distance in shadow. At all seasons of the year the beauty of the birch is attractive, and peculiarly its own. The young beech may remind you of it occasionally under strong effects of light, and is also very graceful, but we have no tree that rivals the birch in its own qualities of color and form, still less in that air and bearing which are so much more difficult to describe. In winter you see the full delicacy of the sprays that the lightest foliage hides, and in early spring this tree clothes itself, next after the willow, with tiny triangular leaves, inexpressibly light in the mass, so that from a distance they have the effect of a green mist rather than any thing more material. When the tree is isolated sufficiently to come against the sky, you may see one of the prettiest sights in Nature, the pure deep azure of heaven with the silvery white and fresh green of the birch in opposition. And yet it is not a crude green, for there is a great deal of warm red in it, which gives one of those precious tertiaries that all true colorists value.

No young leaves are more interesting than those of the horse-chestnut, which every lover of Nature who passes the spring in the country must have watched daily in April, if the tree happened to grow within a little distance of his residence. When they get fairly out of the cotton, in which they have been so snugly protected against the severities of the early season, they first hang straight down in the most languid manner, and it is only after many days that they begin to spread themselves in the air like the fingers of an extended hand. No leaf but that of the beech looks *newer* than the young horse-chestnut. There is a great difference amongst trees in this respect, for some young leaves have a very old look indeed, and might be taken by a half-observant person for remnants of the later year; but when the horse-chestnut leaf is young, it has that air of newness which is seen in human work that has

just left the hands of the workman. The impression is
much increased by the quantities of leaves from the preceding year, which will generally be found on the earth
beneath, for the horse-chestnut leaf is very durable, and
retains its shape and substance long after it is dead and
sapless. Painters are not generally very partial to this
tree, because the size of the leaf and the definition of
its forms require more accurate drawing than can be
easily made compatible with the mystery that landscape-
painters desire ; but from the opening of the leaf-bud
to the ripening of the fruit the end of a horse-chestnut
twig presents a constant succession of interesting models
for a designer of ornaments. Even such a detail as the
position of the old scales, which remain after the accomplishment of their especial protective function, is of importance from the ornamental point of view, as one
soon discovers after carefully drawing the extremity of
a twig in full detail, when the leaflets are still hanging
together vertically, or just gaining strength enough to
begin to spread themselves, and the scales decorate the
point from which all this new vegetation has issued,
making the separation between the old woody twig and
the fresh green leaf-stalks of the present year.

How long the coloring of foregrounds is affected by
the remains of the previous season ! and what astonishing contrasts are produced by this juxtaposition of
death and birth ! All along the sides of the April
woods you may see the red of the dry oak foliage
close to the fresh green of the willow and the white of
the blackthorn, three colors as distinct as possible ;

whilst in the nearest foregrounds the last year's leaves of the bramble are still visibly an element in the landscape, with their stains of red and passages of russet and dark green. Sometimes you may get a few such leaves between you and the morning sunshine, and then, if the coloring of them happen to be favorable, you will see that which in all wild Nature comes nearest to the effect of a painted window. The middle of the leaflet will probably still retain some of the original green coloring matter (being nearest to the midrib from which the sap was supplied), and its edges will be quite brown and dead ; but between these there will be gradations from light crimson to deep purple, precisely of that quality which Jean Cousin and his school successfully tried for in their glass-painting — that is, color intensified to the utmost by light unequally transmitted. The same principle is well known also to oil-painters, and can be (by means of glazing) to a great extent acted upon in their art, though not so strikingly as in glass-painting. When this principle is absolutely neglected or ignored, as it is in vulgar stained glass, in which a flat pane of blue is put by the side of other flat little panes of yellow or red, the color is never really luminous, nor can it be.*

Besides the jewels of transparence, last year has bequeathed to us much deathly opacity, which lingers

---

* It does not follow, however, that to obtain luminous quality in color each piece of glass should necessarily have a gradation *painted upon it.* Luminous quality may also be obtained by the graduated arrangement of small fragments, which, taken separately, had no gradation ; in a word, by glass arranged on the principle of mosaic.

only too long in the spring landscape. There are great quantities of dead light-brown rushes, which for my part I am weary of, and should like to see hidden away under fresher and greener growths. It is consoling that so many plants come vigorously forward at this season. The enormous roots of the bryony, hidden away in so many places where no one suspects their existence begin to prove their vigor by sending forth a few green leaves, which give promise of graceful festoons. Nettles are growing in great abundance under the hedges, which they border with a fresh and beautiful green ; and many wild places are adorned with the richer and better coloring of the ground ivy, which the peasants in France, I know not wherefore, have chosen to dedicate to St. John. The great mullein sprouts handsomely in April, with his fine large cottony leaves, and it is a pleasure to meet with him again when we remember his summer grandeur. Contemporary with the great mullein, the barbed leaves of the arum, smooth and glistening, with their irregular spots of dark, grow quickly in their shady retreats. By the streams no April-flowering plant is prettier than the meadow bitter-cress, and I know some places where it clusters in splendid constellations that bend over the water, and are reflected on it

'Like stars on the sea
When the blue wave rolls nightly on deep Galilee.'

The flowers being of the purest possible white, or else just delicately tinted with pinkish purple, show strongly in the evening when the first approaches of twilight have darkened the damp recesses behind them. You will find, too, in similar situations, the marsh marigold, often in the most splendid abundance, making a rich yellow foreground color, and those more modest little plants, the creeping bugle and the small-flowered calamint, both which are good and agreeable in hue, and some places are known to me where the small purple flowers of the calamint are sufficiently powerful from their quantity to deserve the attention of a painter.

I suppose that no prudent artist would undertake to paint a field of broom in full flower, as we see them towards the end of April. The broom is certainly less objectionable than a field of flowering rape, for the yellow is more supportable and not so unmixed with green ; besides, the green is much richer and darker than that of the rape plant, even if the latter were visible ; but the broom yellow is too powerful to be acceptable in landscape-painting unless in very moderate quantity. It is conceivable that an artist might admit a broom amongst other plants in his foreground, but only with the greatest care and moderation as to the painting of its flowers ; and in saying this I do not wish to main-tain the authority of the brown masters, but that of sober and right judgment, which in art, as in other matters, must always predominate in the end. When-ever an artist admits any glaring and positive color in quantity relatively great, he incurs the risk of not being able to harmonize it with the quieter hues of which the rest of his picture is composed ; and I may add that Nature herself, from the artistic point of view, does not always succeed in doing so. I have met with people who consider any criticism of Nature as a sort of heresy, who, having adopted the theory that Nature is infallible, will not listen to any reasoning on the subject, and tell you that a field of cabbages is a finer sight than a gallery of masterpieces in painting ; but if such persons could understand what art is they would abandon this fanaticism. All who have practised art are well aware that natural composition, though a suggestion of artistic composition, is never quite good of itself, and has always to be altered by the artist ; and why should Nature be more artistic in her color? I believe the truth to be, that artistic color is as far removed from natural color as artistic composition is from natural composition, and that it will be found on investigation impossible to produce what artists call fine color by the simple copyism of Nature. It has been a vulgar error of the uneducated, whether practically painters or not, to imagine that things in Nature were suitable for painting which in fact were altogether outside its province, to believe that they had only to paint whatever struck their fancy out-of-doors, and that *toute verité* was *bonne à dire.* There could not be a greater mistake. It is true that Art finds her materials in nature, but she chooses them as we choose mushrooms for the table, and if she were not careful in her selection it would be at her own great peril. And even when the material has been judiciously chosen it is only raw material still, but the finished work of art is material that has been both modified and reorganized by human taste, intelligence, and invention.

XXIV.

Early Rising — Not a virtue, but a Compensation — Chaucer's Early Rising — His passionate Love of Daisies — Chaucer's way of observing Nature — How Etymology may be Poetical.

I F early rising were so much of a virtue as its practitioners generally assume, then indeed, in this respect at least, should we be eminently virtuous in the Val Ste. Véronique. We are all of us up and stirring before the dawn, not for any particularly laudable passion for an ideally perfect life, but in the case of the poor peasants and servants who surround us from immemorial tradition simply, and the daily necessities of existence; and in my own case from taste and choice, and the love of a kind of pleasure which is blameless, and no more. Indeed, I think that early rising is not so much a virtue in people who live in the country as one of the many pleasant compensations of their existence. They cannot go to the opera in the evening, and they miss a hundred delights and advantages of great cities; but they have certain pleasures of their own which it is wise to enjoy to the utmost, and early rising is one of them. We had kept late hours at Paris, as every one must who lives with and in the life of a great capital; but here in the Val Ste. Véronique we followed the life of Nature.

Of all early risers that ever witnessed the beautiful Aurora, surely old Chaucer was the happiest, and the most keenly conscious of his happiness. What seemed to him sweetest and purest of pleasant hours was that cool, calm hour of the early morning, at the beginning of the dawn, when having put on his 'gear and his array' he walked forth into the fields and woods with the serenest cheerfulness in all his well-tuned feelings. If it is true that Nature with all her beauty is mere desolation until reflected in the eyes and soul of man, then there must be gradations in the beauty of the image according to the brightness or imperfection of the living mirror; and if so, how fortunate were those dawns, and those dewy fields and flowers, that were in the deep, clear, happy, poet-soul of Chaucer! If it were possible to go back into the past, and enjoy the companionship of the illustrious dead, I should like two things most of all — a drinking-bout with Socrates (not for the wine's sake) and a very early walk in the morning with Dan Chaucer, yet not perhaps on the morning immediately following the before-mentioned Athenian symposium : —

> 'Wherefore I mervaile greatly of my selfe
> That I so long withouten sleepe lay,
> And up I rose three houres after twelfe,
> About the springen of the day ;
> And on I put my gear and mine array,
> And to a pleasant grove I gan passe
> Long er the bright Sonne up risen was.'

Such was Chaucer's way in the pleasant spring-time,

especially when he could count upon seeing plenty of
daisies, the flower he loved before all others.

> ' Of all the floures in the mede
> Than love I most these floures white and rede,
> Soch that men callen daisies in our town ;
> To hem I have so great affection,
> As I said erst, whan comen is the May,
> *That in my bed there daweth me no day*
> *That I nam up and walking in the mede,*
> To see this floure ayenst the Sunne sprede,
> Whan it upriseth early by the morow
> That blissful sight softeneth all my sorow.'

In some verses that follow soon after these we have
an account of the poet's own way of observing Nature ;
and notwithstanding the intensity of the modern passion
for natural beauty, it may be doubted whether there
exists in any writer of the eighteenth and nineteenth
centuries any passage so full of the true feeling as
this is : —

> ' My busie gost, that thirsteth alway newe
> To seen this flower so yong, so fresh of hewe,
> Constrained me, with so greedy desire,
> That in my herte I fele yet the fire
> That made me rise ere it were day,
> And this was now the first morow of May,
> With dreadfull herte, and glad devotion
> For to been at the resurrection
> Of this floure, whan that it should unclose
> Again the Sunne that rose as redd as rose,
> *And downe on knees anon right I me sette ;*
> *And as I could this fresh floure I grette,*
> *Kneeling alway, till it unclosed was*

> Upon the small, soft, swete gras,
> That was with floures swete embroidered all.
>
> * * * * *
>
> In which methought I might day by day
> Dwellen alway, the joly month of May,
> Withouten sleepe, withouten meat or drinke.
> *Adown full softly I gan to sinke,*
> *And leaning on my elbow and my side,*
> *The long day I shope me for to abide*
> *For nothing els, and I shall not lie*
> *But for to look upon the daisie,*
> That well by reason men it call may
> The daisie, or els the eye of the day.'

Who shall say, after this, that etymology may not be poetical, since Chaucer teaches it us in his own sweet, unpedantic way? If he loved the daisy for itself, he loved it also for its association with the day, and liked to see in it the opening of the dawn. So, too, the French *marguerite* has its own beautiful origin. In the Latin Bible *margarita* is the word for pearl, from the Greek μαργαρίτης; and Littré thinks that the Greek word in its turn comes from the Persian word *mervarid*, which means pearl also. So here we are again *en pleine poésie*, and just as Chaucer's English derivation may be explained in verse without lowering its tone, the origin of the French word might be prettily dwelt upon by any French poet who chose to write about the flower. Shelley, indeed, though an Englishman, having in his mind very probably the beautiful Greek association, uses it as an epithet, —

 ' Daisies, those *pearled* Arcturi of the earth.'

XXV.

SHELLEY'S allusion to constellations reminds one of a flower, or family of flowers, to be seen in the very greatest profusion in the beginning of May, and which have certainly much more the effect of stars upon the earth than daisies ever have. Everybody seems to have been struck by this, as the name implies, *stellaria*, *starwort*, *stellaire*. It seems almost a crime to compare any thing with the daisy to its disadvantage, and yet so far as mere appearance goes the starworts are greatly superior. In quantity they may often be found, like the stars in a clear sky, by myriads, their brilliant whiteness illuminating the shadiest places; and if you come near enough to see the individual plants, if you lean on your elbow and your side, as Chaucer did when he studied daisies, then are you rewarded by the beauty of one of the most graceful amongst the lighter vegetable forms. The light green stems are elegant beyond the common grace of Nature, and there is much delicate curving in the slender pedicels. The whole stalk is but

just barely strong enough to support the narrow lanceolate leaves, and the thin, all but imponderable petals.
I confess, too, that I feel a certain reasonable preference
for plants that carry well-cut leaves in the air to those
other plants which, like the daisy, have what botanists
call radical leaves, that never get much above the root,
and lie for the most part helplessly, making only a
sort of leaf-pattern on the green carpet of the earth.
Finally, notwithstanding my love and reverence for
Chaucer, and all the dear associations that we have
with the unpretending daisy, it seems to me that, when
we know enough of botany for ideas of *structure* to be
inextricably bound up with our conceptions, a composed
flower, or congeries of flowers like the daisy, must always
seem to have much less individuality than a simple
flower like the starwort; and it seems easier to me to
fall in love with an object that is clearly individual than
with a collection of objects such as the florets of the
compositæ.   This may be fanciful, but there is always a
great element of the fanciful in these things; and it is
highly probable that Chaucer loved his favorite all the
better for not being aware that what he thought of as
a flower was, in reality, a sort of floral village, perched
on the top of a stalk.

If the starwort looks like constellations on the land,
the water ranunculus covers at the same season the
shallow streams and ponds where it has fixed itself with
other constellations of its own.   Early in the year its
wavy hair of green is wonderfully lustrous in the rapid,
limpid water: but that green, the most beautiful of all

greens in the world, has now become very dull ; yet out of its dulness springs a novel life and beauty, as the plant no longer limits itself to its old subaqueous filaments, but sends forth leaves to float on the surface in the sunshine, and covers the water with white blossom. I find that people who see Nature from the gardener's point of view have a hatred and horror of this plant, because it is very prolific and persistent, and invades little streams and ponds very rapidly when once it has got a footing there ; but for my part I feel very grateful to it for two quite distinct kinds of beauty : first and above all, for the lovely, intense green of the moving filaments in February and March, and afterwards for the gayety of its prodigally abundant afflorescence.

There is a common belief amongst landscape-painters that the minute study of vegetation is a waste of time, and even a snare for them, impeding their broader and more comprehensive observation of natural appearances. It is certainly true that any artist who studied too much from the botanical point of view would be likely to lose himself in unnecessary detail, but it may be shown very easily that a very minute detail may become of immense importance when multiplied, as Nature often multiplies it, by millions. One of the best instances of this amongst very familiar plants is that humble little member of the Polygonum family, the sheep-sorrel dock. Its flowers are so small, that one of them, taken separately, is a mere unintelligible speck, until you apply the microscope to it ; and yet with these little specks will Nature stipple and color vast spaces of landscape. The flower is red-

dish or greenish, and it often turns so red that whole
fields and hill-sides are painted with it early in May, —
painted a deep, rich, hot color, of the sort which people who do not observe accurately are accustomed to
associate exclusively with autumn.   Now I cannot but
think that it is an advantage to an artist to have such a
resource as this rich color affords him, and to know
the cause of it ; and I think also that it would perhaps
be well if critics knew enough of Nature not to be taken
by surprise when a landscape-painter happened to avail
himself of this coloring.   There are tints in spring, of
which this is an example, that everybody would call
autumnal in a picture, and yet in Nature they often com-
pensate for the crudeness of the early greens by mingling with them in large masses.   Amongst the numerous
varieties of oak that are indigenous in western Europe
there are species whose young leaves, freshly sprouting
in the month of May, give the richest golden color,
deepening into red, especially glorious when the sunshine filters *through* them ; and so, in a minor degree,
do the leaves of the aspen poplar in their season.

Although the May landscape is richer in floral
splendor than that of any other time, and splendor
of that kind is difficult to harmonize, it is still much
nearer to artistic harmony than the hues of April.   The
hawthorn, having abundant leafage intermingled with
its flowers, escapes the extreme chilliness of the snow-
like blossoming of the blackthorn, and the plentifully
sprinkled starworts carry the white down into the
hedge bottoms.   Hardly any color at this season is un-

pleasantly isolated. The note that is pitched amongst the branches of some tree or shrub is pretty sure to be repeated on the ground by some humble wild-flower. Notwithstanding the variety of flaming gold and blue that may be found wherever the brooms and bugles are abundant, the chief colors of May are the white and green of Chaucer, as he describes them on one of his customary early walks : —

> ' Anone as I the day espide
> No longer would I in my bed abide,
> But unto a wood that was fast by
> I went forth alone boldly,
> And held the way down by a brooke side
> *Till I came to a laund of white and grene.*
> So faire one had I never in been ;
> The ground was grene, y-poudred with daisie,
> The floures and the greves on hie,
> *All grene and white, was nothing els seene.'*

And now, if I were asked to name one plant as typical of the color and fragrance of this sweet season, what other could it be than that modest and singularly beloved one, the lily of the valley ? I know not whether it is from some dear early association, from having seen one who is gone to her rest long ago arranging these flowers that were her favorites, and setting them in clear water on her work-table to be companions for her in bygone months of May, but it is certain that of all the flowers that grow this little one most surely touches the tenderest place in my heart. And every year when the time comes for its blossoming, and when first I find it in the cool and shady spots that suit it best, there comes a film of moisture across my eyes, not quite consistent perhaps with the hardness of perfect manhood. But let each of us live after his own nature; for of the two figures that we remember as most characteristic of the middle ages, — the poet lying on the earth all through the sunny day dreaming and doting on the flowers, and the knight sheathed in complete steel crushing them under the hoofs of his war-horse and sullying them with the blood of his enemy, — it is the first who has my sympathy. Where in the world can there be any thing more perfect than these lilies of the valley? Look at their twin-leaves, outlined so delicately, just two of them, perfect as the wings of a bird, and the few white bells that tremble on the slender stalk, shedding the sweetest perfume! Be sure that here we have one of Nature's most complete conceptions. You may look upon a mountain and wish that it were loftier or more precipitous, upon a river and wish that it were clearer, upon a tree and desire for it some farther spreading of its boughs, some richer filling of its foliage, — but you cannot look upon a lily of the valley and wish it to be other than it is. Only one addition is possible, and that is given in the cool of the early morning, when there hangs upon each of those fairy bells one pure, bright drop of dew.

It is curious that a plant so humble and sweet as this should have had a great reputation for giving strength to the weary and the weak; but with that strangely groundless faith that characterized the pre-scientific ages, our forefathers were quite strongly convinced upon this point, and distilled from it a miraculous water, — the 'Golden Water,' as they called it ; and whoso drank thereof was believed to be sure of regaining the strength that had left his limbs. Is it not sad that we may no longer put trust in all those wonderful remedies — there are a hundred of them — which in old times gave hope at least, if they could not restore to health ? There is another humble little plant that flowers in May (and also in October) in pastures and waste places, and was called Potentilla, because it was believed to be so potent as a remedy. In these days we see its pretty yellow flowers without reverence for its potency. Just in the same temper of ready credulity on the most fanciful grounds our forefathers used to believe that the plant they called Lung-wort (*Pulmonaria*) must be good for the cure of lung disease, because its leaves were blotched like the lungs of a consumptive person ! What a wonderful piece of reasoning that was ! How remote from the scientific spirit ! We may laugh, and yet that is exactly the sort of reasoning which finds ready acceptance with the untrained minds of the vulgar, and a hundred things are still believed by uneducated persons of all ranks on grounds at least equally absurd.

XXVI.

White of Selborne — The Songs of Birds — Canaries — Birds in Liberty — Our Love for the Songs of Birds Poetical and not Musical — The Warbling of Birds really Discordant — Disillusion — Reason and Sentiment — Condescension of the Divine Mind — Poets and Birds — Mingled Warbling — The Dominant Songster — Chaucer's Fancy of the Religious Singing-birds — The Throstle — The Peacock — The Owl — The 'Romaunt of the Rose.'

IT is just a hundred years since Gilbert White of Selborne lamented the 'frequent return of deafness' that incommoded him, and deprived him of much enjoyment and many opportunities of observation. Especially did he lament that when this deafness was upon him he 'lost all the pleasing notice and little intimations arising from rural sounds,' so that May was 'as silent and mute with respect to the notes of birds as August.' Here, indeed, was a sad loss to one who so deeply appreciated the pleasures of a country life, and who used his senses so well for the work of a naturalist while he possessed them. All true rural poets and observers have loved the songs of birds. There are occasionally to be found beings unfortunate enough not to enjoy these melodies, and I know one wretch who says he does not much care for his country-house at a certain season of the year 'on account of that bothersome noise of nightingales.' Certainly this bird-music may sometimes become importunate. There is a land-scape-painter in Paris who is a great canary-fancier, and has a very large cage full of these birds in the studio where he paints. So long as he is alone it may be very delightful, for perhaps his little yellow friends sing to him with moderation ; but no sooner does a visitor enter the room and try to begin a conversation than all the canaries set up such a clatter that no human voice is audible.

The birds in the free woods fill the air incessantly in spring with their merry noises, but their garrulity never tries our patience like that of the poor prisoners in cages. Is it really music that they make, and do they charm the ear as music does, or move some fibre of poetic sentiment in our hearts ? I believe that the feeling they reach within us is a poetical and not a musical feeling. The notes of birds may be imitated with deceptive accuracy, and yet a concert of such imitations would not attract an audience. The wild bird utters its notes and we are delighted ; the human imitator accurately reproduces the same notes with in-geniously contrived whistles, and we remain indifferent. Here, too, is another consideration which may be worth notice. So long as one bird performs a solo it may be a melody, but when half-a-dozen are singing at the same time is it concerted music that they sing ? Does each of them take his part in a general harmony, like a chorus-singer at the opera ? No, their science is not equal to any thing requiring subordination of parts. And the plain truth is, that the warbling of a multitude of birds must necessarily be full of discords ; yet people of musical taste endure it, and even delight in it.   For the birds are pets of ours, they have especially been pets of the poets, and we regard their performances with the most tender and affectionate indulgence.   It has occurred to me more than once to hear what I took for birds' notes, and to think 'what delicious purity of tone, what softness, what ravishing quality !' and immediately afterwards to discover that these wondrous notes had been simply whistled by some boy behind a hedge, after which discovery all their fine qualities vanished.

So much for the criticism of reason ; but when we let sentiment have her way, as in this matter we may and ought to do, then we fall at once under the old charm and can listen enraptured, as Chaucer did.   For the songs of birds convey to us far more than the mere sound ; they are voices of Nature speaking to us joyously, tenderly, caressing the childish part of our being with simple lullabies, and thus gently effacing the too sad or awful impression which many other sounds of wild things make upon us ; such as the screeching of churchyard owls, the croak of the raven, the wild cry of plovers toppling over in the wind on the ridges of desolate moors.   We love the little singing-birds because they so prettily tell us that, notwithstanding the hard regularity of the laws that govern the world, the Divine Mind condescended to take pleasure in cheerful little beings that sing of gladness only, and know no other theme. Who can tell what man himself may have gained from the singing of the birds, how much his heart may have been cheered by it, and his labor lightened? All the poets, without exception, who have written of what is charming and beautiful in Nature, have spoken lovingly of singing-birds; and therefore it may be presumed that the great multitude of 'poets who have never penned their inspiration,' and the still greater multitude who, without being mute poets, have nevertheless some share of poetic faculty or feeling, do all take pleasure in this simple sylvan music. In aviaries it easily becomes over-powering, but in the open woods it is mellowed by many various distances; and as there is a perspective in what we see there, as the trees at a distance mingle a thousand various tints into a quiet harmony of color, so do the songs of a thousand birds mix together into a delicious indistinguishable warbling, of which the most perfect ear could never analyze the elements. And just as some one branch or leaf will detach itself brilliantly in the sunshine from the rich mystery that lies behind it, so will the voice of one songster pipe clearly over all the rest till it is lost again in the pervading atmosphere of sound.

Every one who cares for old poetry will remember the stanzas in Chaucer's 'Court of Love,' where he makes all the birds sing religiously in May, — one of the quaintest and prettiest of his fancies, but worked out too fully in detail to admit of any complete quotation. Here are just a couple of stanzas as specimens of the whole : —

    ' " *Te deum amoris*," sang the throstel cocke;
      Tuball himself, the first musician,

With key of armony could not unlocke
So swete tune as that the throstel can :
" The lorde of love we praisen " (quod he then,
And so done all the foules great and lite),
Honour we May, in false lover's despite.
" *Dominus regnavit,*" said the pecocke there,
" The lord of love, that mighty prince ywis,
He is received here and everywhere.
Now *Jubilate* sing." — " What meaneth this ? "
Said then the linnet : " Welcome, lord of blisse."
Out sterte the owl with " *Benedicite,*
What meaneth all this merry fare ? " (quod he.)'

There is no end to the allusions to singing-birds in
Chaucer, but one of the most delicately charming of
these consists of three couplets in the ' Romaunt of the
Rose,' which always come back to my memory when I
hear the birds in May. ' Harde is his heart,' says the
poet : —

   ' Harde is his heart that loveth nought
   In May, when all this mirth is wrought,
   When he may on these branches here
   The smalle birdes singen clere
   Hir blissful sweet song piteous,
   And in this season delitious.'

XXVII.

Hymn of the Birds to the Sun, by Gawin Douglas — The Birds hail the Sun with Welcomes — How the Poets love the Birds — How the Bird-catchers love them —The Mistletoe — St. Lambert's Poem of the Four Seasons — Gentle Heartlessness — The Bird-catcher in Buffon — The Work of Nest-building — Are Birds Architects or Masons ? — Magpies — The Labor given to a Magpie's Nest — Thrush, Tom-tit, Linnet — Greenfinch and Goldfinch —Wren — Excellent Arrangement of Wren's Nest — Building a House — Building for Oneself — Varieties of Nest-building — Raising and Fixing of Material — Adhesion of Martin's Nests — Birds that like to be rocked in their Nests — The Cuckoo — Poet-cuckoos — Birds and Plants — The Cuckoo-pint —Value of the Common Arum for Artists.

OF all the fine passages in old poetry concerning the life of birds in Nature, the most magnificent is the hymn of the birds to the Sun in Gawin Douglas's prologue to the twelfth book of the 'Eneid.' I should have been glad to abridge the quotation had it been possible without spoiling it, but I find, as the reader will also, that the series of verses beginning with the word 'Welcome' could not have their due effect if given by themselves ; the mind needs to be led up to them and tuned to the proper poetical pitch before it can fully enter into the fine spirit of the hymn itself. As for the little difficulty with the old Scottish words it vanishes on the second or third reading, and such poetry as this is worth reading a hundred times : —

> ' The cushat crouds and pykkis on the rise,*
> The sterling changes divers steunnys nise,†
> The sparrow chirpis in the walles cleft,
> Gold spink and linnet fordynnand the lyft.‡
> The cuckoo galis,§ and so twitteris the quail
> While rivers reirdit ;∥ schaws and every dale,
> And tender twistis tremble on the trees,
> For birdes song and bemyng of the bees,
> And all small fowlis singin on the spray, —
> " Welcome thou lord of light and lampe of day,
> Welcome thou fosterer of herbis grene,
> Welcome quickener of freshest flouris shene,
> Welcome support of every root and vein,
> Welcome comfort of al kind frute and grein,
> Welcome depainter of the blooming meads,
> Welcome the life of every thing that spreads,
> Welcome restorer of all kind bestial,
> Welcome be thy bright bemes gladding all." '

What is pleasant in these passages of the quaint old poets is their hearty love for the birds themselves and full participation in their gladness. The sylvan feeling of the bird-catcher is of a very different character; he, too, rejoices in the woods ; he, too, likes to hear the birds sing, for if they sing they exist, and if they exist they may be ensnared, and afterwards sold or roasted as poverty or gluttony may suggest. The mistletoe is in full berry in the month of May, and its berries, which

---

* The dove crows and picks on the bush.
† Tuneful voices.   ‡ Heaven.   § Cries.   ∥ Sounded.

seem like waxen pearls at a little distance, suggest some
rather painful reflections.   The birds plant the mistletoe
on the branches of trees by depositing its seeds there,
undigested ; man comes and makes bird-lime from this
very mistletoe, which by a strange fatality causes the
destruction of the very creatures to whom its own propa-
gation is due.   Could any poet rejoice over their miserable fate, and think those moments sweet when his
victims are hopelessly struggling?   Yes, M. Saint-Lam-
bert, whose poem of 'The Seasons' is, to say the least,
a piece of beautiful versification, sometimes rising into
more elevated regions, expresses the keenest delight in
that exquisitely cruel business of bird-catching, and avows
his crimes in verses of the most finished harmony : —

'Cent fois, dans ma jeunesse, aux rives des ruisseaux
 J'ai semé les buissons d'innombrables réseaux :
 Avec quel mouvement d'espérance et de joie
 Vers la fin d'un beau jour, j'allais chercher ma proie !
 A présent même encor, sous les rameaux naissans ;
 De l'oiseau de la nuit imitant les accents,
 Des habitans des bois j'entends la troupe ailée
 S'avancer, voltiger autour de ma feuillée.
 J'écoute, en palpitant, leur vol précipité ;
 D'un transport vif et doux mon cœur est agité
 Quand je les vois tomber sur ces verges perfides
 Qu'infectade ses sucs l'arbrisseau des druides,
 O doux emploi des jours ! agréables momens ! '

It would be difficult to find any thing more gently
heartless and amiably selfish than these last well-polished
verses   It is like the gentleness of the mild-minded
angler enjoying the pleasant sunshine and the purling

stream, whilst the living bait writhes in torture on his hook. *Agréables momens!* Not for the birds, surely! not for the birds! And before quitting this subject let me just observe how painfully the bird-catcher is continually reappearing in so great a writer as Buffon. He never fails to give his readers instructions, in this line of business, and generally tells them whether every little bird is good to eat or not. Fancy eating a brace of wrens, or of tom-tits! It is true that we eat smaller creatures still, — shrimps, for example; and the Burgundy vine-snail is both good and nourishing: but our sentiments are not enlisted in their behalf. To my feeling the most agreeable bit of information about bird-catching that I ever gleaned from the great naturalist of Montbard is, that the wren, from its extreme smallness, gets through the meshes of the finest nets and so happily escapes. I wish all the other birds could do likewise.

The wonderful work of nest-building goes on with immense activity in the spring. What a difference there is in relation to this business between a human couple and the wedded birds! The human couple either inherit a nest already made, generally without the most remote conception of the labor it cost to make it, or else they hire another nest without much serious interest or affection; but the bird and his wife are their own masons, and also their own architects, being usually more successful in this latter capacity than the unprofessional human designer of habitations. Or is it not more accurate to say of them that, strictly speaking, they are masons only, working after the plans of a greater Architect than those who devise big palaces in stone and mortar? If masons only, at least they are most industrious masons. The Marquis de Cherville, who is an accurate observer of what passes too often unobserved in the quiet routine of Nature, says that he watched a pair of magpies from the beginning of their nest-building to the end. They had fixed themselves in a large poplar, just before M. de Cherville's window, and he watched them both from his desk and from his bed, missing hardly any thing that they did. The work lasted for forty-seven days, during which, especially in the morning and evening, the two birds carried materials with a feverish activity. In a single day he counted two hundred and eight journeys in quest of material, and this was not the whole. But the nest of a magpie is a very rude affair, indeed, when compared with the highly finished and delicate workmanship of many other birds. The thrush, the tom-tit, and some kinds of lin-net, are master-builders in different ways. The thrush makes the outside of his nest with almost any thing that comes to hand, — with moss, with straw, or dried leaves; but his great skill is displayed in the fabrica-tion of the stout mill-board that constitutes its inner wall or shell, made of wet mud well beaten, strength-ened with bits of straw and roots. The thrush likes this hard and smooth interior, not caring for the lux-ury of soft feather-beds, but some other birds are more luxurious. The greenfinch and goldfinch are amongst the cleverest of bird upholsterers. They know how to feather their nests well, and have an English taste for carpets and interior comfort, well knowing the value of bits of wool, and hair, and feathers. The wren has another English taste also, for he likes his house to be not only comfortable, but big; and, small as he is, he has large ideas in the way of architecture. I like his plan of a little doorway in the side, just big enough for his small person to pass through; it is infinitely more snug than the commoner system of sitting in a sort of enlarged egg-cup: and, besides these advantages, the wren's house is not easily discovered, being apparently a shapeless lump of moss, though so artfully shaped within. How interesting it would be if some observer, like the Marquis de Cherville, could watch a couple of wrens at work from the very beginning to the moment of their happy house-warming, when the soft clear down was all arranged snugly as a lining to the wee dwelling, and just ready to receive the wonderfully tiny white eggs! Is not this much more interesting, as well as more admirably laborious, than the furnishing of some house in a row run up by some speculator, with balconies that you dare not step out upon for fear that they should fall with you down upon the dangerous-looking railings? I think there must be an infinite pleasure in building one's own house, — not as rich people use the words, when they say ‘I am going to build,’ but in doing it with one's own hands — a pleasure founded upon the primitive depths of our original wild nature. It has sometimes occurred to me to talk with very poor men who really had done this with their own hands, and the satisfaction their rough work gave them was evidently of a kind that no wealth could ever purchase. Observe the zest with which travellers in wild countries, who have been compelled to erect dwellings for themselves, describe the interesting process, and gravely give directions to others, a spirit of the keenest enjoyment being visible throughout the prudence of their precepts!

I have noticed the wide difference of refinement and skill in nest-building between such different birds as the magpie and the thrush, linnets, &c., but Gilbert White remarked that there was a great disparity in this respect between 'birds of the same genus, and nearly correspondent in their general mode of life; for while the swallow and the house-martin discover the greatest address in raising and securely fixing crusts, or shells, of loam, as *cunabula* for their young, the bank-martin terebrates a round and regular hole in the sand or earth, which is serpentine, horizontal, and about two feet deep. At the inner end of this burrow does this bird deposit, in a good degree of safety, her rude nest, consisting of fine grasses and feathers, usually goose-feathers, very inartificially laid together.' Here, in a very few words, he perfectly describes what is most wonderful in the skilful toil of the swallows and house-martins, their address in raising and *securely fixing* the crusts they build so cleverly. The *raising*, however, is comparatively mechanical; it is the *fixing* that always surprises one. Some windows in the old house at the Val Ste. Véronique had been left unopened for years, and the *hirondelles des fenêtres* had fixed their nests in the corners, partly on the woodwork and the stone sides, but partly also upon the very glass itself. It seemed necessary to air these chambers and to open the windows, which I did with the greatest regret, but it afforded a singularly good opportunity for ascertaining the actual strength of adhesion in the nests, which was truly surprising. Not only are the birds themselves perfectly safe in them, for they weigh scarcely any thing to speak of, but it would require a considerable weight to detach the little structure from its place ; and even after the nests had been torn away from the windows, large fragments of them still adhered obstinately to the stonework. I imagine that these birds, which are almost always in movement, have a particular satisfaction in feeling that their nest is firm and substantial ; so they fix it to the strong work of human masons that is not shaken by the wind. In this preference for what is fixed and substantial they differ notably from some other birds that like their nests to be rocked like a sailor's hammock, which one would imagine must be fatiguing in windy weather ; however, it is their taste, and there is no disputing about tastes. Buffon remarks that goldfinches like to build upon thin and weak branches, especially of plum-trees and walnuts, that are rocked by the wind. It is to be supposed that these little creatures are independent of the sensation of sea-sickness.

One has a particular respect for the industrious nest-builders that have houses of their own and establish

themselves respectably in life ; but it is difficult to feel
any such sentiment towards the cuckoo when we hear
the two notes of his monotonous ditty, and see him
pass from grove to grove with his silently gliding flight.
But if the cuckoo is not a respectable personage, since
he will neither build his own house nor bring up his
own offspring, he has an advantage in common with certain celebrities in literature and art; which is, that everybody knows his voice. It requires considerable sylvan
experience to distinguish some birds by their voices,
and it is only the most observant naturalists who can
recognize each of them with certainty ; but the citizen,
who rarely visits the country, knows the cuckoo when
he hears him. The reader at once perceives the moral
which is impending. The cuckoo is like a poet who
says but little, and always repeats that little without
variety, yet who enjoys a great reputation because his
one song is at the same time agreeable, perfectly
original, and perfectly inimitable. There have been .
such poet-cuckoos.

Nothing is more curious in popular botany and
ornithology than the way in which popular beliefs
associate together certain birds and plants. Why, for
example, is the cuckoo particularly associated with the
common arum, which is called the cuckoo-pint ? Is
the bird supposed to drink the dew or the rain-water
from the spatha ? The explanation of the popular
fancy about cuckoo-spit, which is the frothy exudation
of a certain larva, was suggested with great probability
by Buffon. He thought it possible that a cuckoo might

have been observed in the act of seeking the larva in
the froth, and that the rustic observer had concluded
the froth to be the cuckoo's own saliva; after which
it might have been noticed that an insect came out of
such froth, whence the conclusion that vermin was
engendered from the saliva of the bird. And what a
strange old notion it was that the cuckoo travelled
on the back of a kite, which was thought to be amiable enough to submit to the inconvenience of such a
burden! It is almost impossible to imagine any observed fact which may have given rise to such an
improbable myth as this.

Whether or not the cuckoo takes any particular
interest in the common arum, it is a valuable foreground plant for artists, being one of the earliest in
the season of those whose leaves are large enough to
be of some consequence in a picture. The only misfortune about it is a love of shelter, which makes it grow
almost always in situations where it is half concealed,
such as nooks and thickets, and shady places under
hedges. One of the earliest of our botanical experiences is a feeling of astonishment about its peculiar
way of flowering, and the incipient botanist is sure to
feel at the same time interested and puzzled by the long
spike and the leafy spatha, which he always remembers
afterwards.

XXVIII.

Water Iris — The Royal Flower — Lychnis — Origin of the Name — The Spurge Family — Bitter Reverie — A Poet's Botany — Use of Poets' Fancies.

OF other plants that show themselves in May it would be easy to make a considerable catalogue. There is the water iris, for example, which in this part of the world has tall blades early in the month and flowers towards the end of it, giving considerable magnificence of color to the banks of streams. It is remarkable amongst flowers as having been chosen by the kings of France to decorate their shields and banners, for in the middle ages it was called the *lis.* This, at least, is the more probable view, considering the form and color of the flower, though the popular belief is that the large white lily is the royal flower of the Bourbons. But the white lily bears no resemblance to the fleur-de-lis, whereas the water iris curves out its petals in such a way as to produce a very striking likeness to the heraldic flower. Besides this, the *fleur-de-lis* is *or* in heraldry, and, without attaching too much importance to the choice of the metal, one cannot but think it likely that a sovereign who had felt pleased with the white lily would have preserved the record of its whiteness by blazoning it *argent.* For my part I feel no doubt about the matter, and the golden flowers of the water iris have, for me, associations with history as well as landscape.

From the beginning of May there are also immense quantities of flowering lychnis, whose bright red is like gems scattered prodigally by field and river. The plant was used in Greece for garlands, and it seems possible that in this way it may have been associated with the idea of a light-giving gem that was called λυχνίς also. I am aware that another interpretation has been suggested. It is said that the Greeks used a plant of this kind for lamp-wicks, and as they called a portable lamp λύχνος the flower got its name from this more utilitarian origin I cling by preference to the association with the gem rather than the lamp, and I should like very much to know what was the color of the gem λυχνίς. If it were red, that would almost settle the question. But whatever may have been the origin of its name, the lychnis is one of the brightest and most abundant of wild flowers, giving a wonderful gayety to foregrounds wherever it occurs.

A perfect contrast in this respect are the members of the humble spurge family, with their flowers, green-like leaves, and their cold, white, milky blood, caustic and pungent. With a poet's felicity of choice Rossetti selected this unattractive plant as the object of contemplation in an hour of bitter reverie:—

> ' Between my knees my forehead was, —
> My lips, drawn in, said not Alas !
> My hair was over in the grass,
> My naked ears heard the day pass.

My eyes, wide open, had the run
Of some ten weeds to fix upon ;
Among those few, out of the sun,
The woodspurge flowered, three cups in one.

From perfect grief there need not be
Wisdom or even memory :
One thing then learnt remains to me, —
The woodspurge has a cup of three.' *

This, of course, is a poet's botany, and one does not expect it to be very accurately scientific. Rossetti means, by his 'cup of three,' the pair of flowers at the end of each ray of the umbel, and the floral leaves beneath the pair which are connected into one large orbicular leaf. The two flowers and the orbicular leaf below make up the number three, and this is the only explanation I can venture to suggest. Is it worth while to dwell in this way upon poets' fancies in connection with the subjects of our study? Yes, I think it is ; for experience proves that nothing impresses natural objects upon the memory so much as association with human thought and fancy, even when, as in the case of many popular superstitions, it has no foundation in fact.

* D. G. Rossetti's Poems, Roberts Brothers' Ed. p. 249.

XXIX.

ONE of the most striking examples of the difference
between artistic ideas of beauty and those ideas
of beauty which we derive directly from Nature without
the intervention of painting is supplied by the horse-
chestnut.   In Nature it is one of the most noble of all
trees, yet it has rarely been celebrated by landscape-
painters, who, when you talk to them about it, almost
invariably express a dislike for the peculiar quality of
its foliage; nor have they been more attracted by its
magnificent efflorescence, although in our northern
countries no other tree of equal dimensions bears such
splendid flowers, or any thing comparable to them.   The
reason is easily discovered.   In the art of painting there
is always a peculiar embarrassment in dealing with
things that are countable and yet exceedingly numerous.
Such things require great labor for their individualiza-
tion, because the eye so easily detects a failure or in-
sufficiency in design ; whilst, on the other hand, there is
a difficulty in passing from this complete individuality
of the things seen near at hand to the mystery of the
things that are utterly past counting.   When things are

large enough, and shapely enough, to require careful drawing, an artist does not wish them to be too numerous ; thus, there is no work that can be offered to a figure-painter more distasteful to his artistic feeling than a crowd of a hundred faces, of which every one must be a portrait, since the mere attention to individuality imperils the unity of the whole work. On the other hand, if the numbers are *very* great the painter likes them to be far past any possibility of counting, so that his only duty may be to represent the mystery and infinity of the innumerable. Thus, in leaf-drawing, the greatest figure-painters have always designed a *few* leaves of the kinds whose forms are beautiful, both pleasurably and successfully, and such a thing as a wreath of laurel is perfectly agreeable to their taste ; whilst, on the other hand, the great landscape-painters have delighted in the immensity of *foliage*, where the leaf is nothing individually and only the mass is seen. The objection to the horse-chestnut is, that to render it perfectly we should need the skill of the figure-painter drawing a wreath of laurel, and the skill of the landscape-painter sketching the masses of a forest. The leaves are so large, and so peculiar in their form, that they *cannot* be treated negligently, for the negligent hand would commit errors in shape and scale that the first comer would at once detect ; yet, at the same time, they are so numerous, that any attempt to draw them individually, as you would the twin-leaves of the lily of the valley, must inevitably spoil the unity of the tree, not to speak of the still vaster unity of a picture. The consequence of this is, that the horse-chestnut is hardly ever painted, and never painted quite sufficiently and successfully. But now, having stated the artistic difficulty, let us turn our backs for the moment upon all picture exhibitions, and, forgetting art altogether, go straight to the world of Nature. The horse-chestnut, in the earlier weeks of May, is a sight for gods and men. If you are well outside its branches, you see the richly-painted flowers rising tier above tier on all its glorious slope up to the odorous heights that belong to the birds and the bees; if you are under its shadow, you walk in a soft green light that comes through the broad-spreading leaflets. No transparencies are finer than this sun-illumined canopy of green, and whilst the leaves are quite young and perfect, they are cut out so clearly as to have a grandly decorative effect. Next, as to direction of line and surface, this tree is very remarkable for its bold and decided contrasts. You have the curve of the twig, first downwards and then upwards, where it carries the flowers at its extremity. The tendency of the flowery spike itself is to be vertical, and the large leaves spread themselves out horizontally and as flatly as possible to right and left. The flowers themselves are amongst the very richest of spring blossoms. The coloring of the petals is made lively by the presence of white, but admirably preserved from crudity by dashes of red and yellow. When the spikes or cones of flowers are in their full splendor, the horse-chestnut reminds one of a magnificent Christmas-tree, carrying a thousand lighted tapers upon its branches,

but with the difference that the flowers promise life,
and the renewal of, life; whereas when the pretty
Christmas tapers are lighted upon a tree they are a
sign that its end is near, according to Andersen's melancholy story. The horse-chestnut has only been an
European tree for the last three centuries, and is one of
the happiest importations from Asia. There is an octa-
gon of them at the Val Ste. Véronique, and the eight
brothers are all equally well grown, — tradition says, that
eight boar-hounds are buried under them, a hound under
each tree. In the heat of summer they offer a delightful shade, for their broad leafage makes an impenetrable
dome of verdure.

XXX.

Willow — Spanish Chestnut — Walnut — Ash and Walnut — Beech —
   Young Beech-leaves — Light through them — Birch — Character of
   Birch — It bears extremes of Heat and Cold — Birch-bark — Sap of
   Birch — Prejudices against Trees — Abuse of Painters who study
   certain Trees — Trees and Politics — The Birch always Beautiful —
   Willow — Spanish Chestnut — Its Strength and Longevity — Beauty
   of Foliage of Chestnut — Oak and Chestnut — Bird-cherry Prunus.

THE horse-chestnuts are amongst the earliest of
the trees in leaf and flower. The willow, as
we know, is earlier still, and its leaves are now fully
developed, glittering a great deal in the sunshine, when
the pleasant May breezes move them. The young green
leaves of the Spanish chestnut are rapidly making foli-

age now, and hide already the heavy, magnificent stems, at least in places. The young leaves of the walnut are pleasant upon the cool gray of the stems, being of an exceedingly warm green, that differs greatly from the crude color of most of the other vegetation. The reader may have observed how peculiarly rich are the dark mosses upon walnuts, but the glory of mosses is not in the time of leaves. The French word *noyer* comes in a very roundabout way from the Latin *nux*, a nut, so that *noyer* means the nut-tree *par excellence;* and the Latin name *Juglans* comes from *Jovis glans*, Jupiter's nut, as the fruit of this tree was thought good enough for the father of the gods. The ash and the walnut come on very nearly together in the spring, and are not much advanced in the middle of May; the beech at this season is more attractive, from the particularly lovely and fresh green of the leaves, which have all the exquisiteness of Nature's softest and prettiest *new* things. Their green is delicately pale without being crude, and they have downy edges, and are so soft that it is a luxury to touch them ; then, on the upper side, they are protected by a gloss of varnish. I spoke of the transparence of the horse-chestnut leaves ; that of beech-leaves, when they are young and fresh, is still more delicate and beautiful, and the light under them is like what one fancies the pale sea-green light where the mermaids live in submarine grottos and gardens.

As for the birches, they are in full leaf in May, as if it were the height of summer, and their shining silvery

stems, so brilliant in wintry sunshine, are now greatly
overshadowed by their foliage. Nothing can be more
decided than the *character* of the birch, and the leaves
add to its expression. In winter it is simply the most
graceful of trees, but in summer it seems nervously
sensitive and easily disquieted. The slightest breath
of air sets it all in a flutter, and it has the appearance
of the extremest delicacy of temperament. However,
in this case, as in some human constitutions, the appearance of delicacy is in the highest degree deceptive,
for the birch is gifted with singular powers of resistance. I do not believe that a tree can be mentioned
which bears so well the extremes of heat and cold. It
lives high on the sides of the Alps and thrives in the
terrible Lapland winter. The last trees near the polar
ice are birches, and yet at the same time the birch lives
uninjured through the burning summers of Burgundy,
and does not apparently suffer from a temperature that
ripens the grape, the peach, and the apricot. The bark,
too, that looks so fragile on account of its thin white
epiderm, so easily torn and never without a rent, is
really of considerable thickness, and quite remarkable
amongst vegetable substances for its all but unlimited
durability. The tree is respectable for its uses, especially for the uses of the bark, out of which the ingenious northern races have contrived to make many
different things, including canoes, ropes, roofs, drinking-
vessels; shoes, and even food, whilst that product of
high civilization called Russia leather is tanned with it.
The abundant sap is good to drink, and an alcoholic

beverage is prepared from it.   Haller says that the catkins' yield wax.   Therefore, although the birch does not
give fine timber like the oak, nor abundant edible fruit
like the walnut and what are commonly called the fruit-
trees, it is still óne of man's best friends, and a friend
to him in climates of such rigorous severity that the
rich southern fruit-bearers cannot live there.   The
Southerner may know the birch by sight, for its slender
stem gleams here and there in his forests ; but he does
not know the tree as the Laplander knows it, in the
hardship and adversity of a life so little cheered by the
genial gifts of Nature.   What the reindeer is to him
amongst animals, the birch is amongst trees.

I spoke about the suitableness of the horse-chestnut
for the purposes of the landscape-painter, and I showed
a reason why artists have so generally abstained from
any attempt to represent the horse-chestnut in their
works.   But if there are reasonable objections to trees
that may be beautiful in Nature, there are also unreason-
able ones, that are due to the most absurd prejudices, —
prejudices so absurd that the existence of them would
be absolutely incredible if we did not meet them from
time to time in reading and in conversation.   One of
the clearest and most outspoken expressions of such
prejudices that it was ever my lot to meet with occurred
in an ultra-conservative French newspaper, which is
taken in by my neighbor the *curé*, and I made an extract from it as a curiosity.   It is certain that many
trees — and the graceful birch is one of them — were
systematically neglected by the landscape-painter of

former centuries, and have only of late years had their
beauties reflected in the mimic world of painting. It
is not probable that, in illustrating these neglected yet
not less noble species, the artists of this generation have
had any feeling of hostility to the trees which their predecessors studied, not too affectionately, but too exclusively; they have simply acted with that independence
of tradition and that large desire to study the whole of
Nature which are distinguishing characteristics of our
age in art, as in science and in literature. But now see
how they get abused and ill-spoken of for their largeness : —

' It looks like a conspiracy.   The painters of the old *régime,*
the artists who were faithful to tradition, sought for and honored certain beautiful and aristocratic trees, and considered
them alone worthy of the selection and the efforts of art ; the
majestic oak, the elegant poplar, the pompous pine, and the
funereal cypress.

' "Let us upset tradition !" say the realists.   "Down with
the trees that are symbols of superannuated and odious distinctions !   Let us lift up the humble and insignificant ; let us
open a broad way to the new '*couches sociales*' of the forests ;
there is the truth, the strength, and the honor of the societies
of the future !"   And with these fine reasonings we see the
rustic apple-tree, the shivering birch, the amphibious willow,
the crude and hard Spanish chestnut, come out of their enclo-
sures, or their rocks, to display themselves outrageously in gilt
frames on the walls of palaces and galleries that were never
built for them !   It is a new form of the democracy which is
about to overwhelm us.   The populace of the woods puts
itself on the level of the populace of the *faubourgs.*   It was
not enough to have beheld the noisy and unsavory crowds cast

themselves upon the Louvre and come to Versailles and the Trianon : we must, in addition, endure the contact of the inferior species in our woods, justly rejected to the second rank, and condemned to inferior functions.' *

Now, on behalf of the birch especially, I protest energetically against this comparison with the lowest Parisian democracy.   So far from being coarse and offensive, it is the most delicately elegant of all the trees that prosper in our climate.   It is *always* beautiful : in winter for the exquisite refinement of its ramification, only to be followed by the most finished and accomplished drawing ; in spring and summer for the beauty of its cloud of light foliage ; in autumn for its color. The writer just quoted mentions also, and with equal disdain, the willow and Spanish chestnut.   The beauty of the natural willow is very little known, because the farmers almost invariably make a pollard of it, which is the artificial production of a painful and horrible deformity.   Very possibly the critic may have supposed, as many people do, that willows are born so ; but the truth is, that if you only have the kindness to let the willow alone he becomes a very good landscape tree, and there are species which cast their arms out with a noble freedom and grace, having also a fair stature.   Of the Spanish chestnut one can scarcely exaggerate the merits.   His expression is that of sturdy strength : his trunk and limbs are built, not like those of Apollo, but

* This passage is quoted from 'L.'Union,' Sept. 2, 1873. It is a very curious example of a political spirit invading the domain of art.

like the trunk and limbs of Hercules; and though for
his inflexibility he loses an arm now and then in the
hurricane, he lives to be a Methuselah amongst trees,
and dynasties rise and fall, empires are built and de-
molished, literatures flourish and decay, whilst he is still
green in his old place, unheeding the lapse of time.
His foliage is magnificent in mass and beautiful in the
individual leaf; it is always worth drawing and painting,
both for its lines and shadows: it *cannot* be mean or insignificant.   Whether he is an aristocratic tree, or a tree
tainted with democracy, I am not subtle enough in social
distinctions to determine, but tradition informs us that
the chestnut of Mount Etna once sheltered a queen and
her hundred nobles, and is called for this reason the
' Chestnut of the Hundred Horses.'   In the comparison
of the chestnut with the oak, it is fair, too, that we
should remember what animals are fed by each.   The
oak feeds herds of swine, but the chestnut supplies to
great multitudes of human beings a food as agreeable
as it is nutritious.   There are countries where it is the
staff of life, and its alimentary importance is greater
than that of any other tree that grows, with the single
exception of the date.

Amongst the shrubs which are almost trees, and
sometimes fully deserve to be called so, let me not
forget, in connection with the month of May, to mention
the *bird-cherry prunus*, of which we have some exceptional specimens in the Val Ste. Véronique, where they
grow to a height of sixteen or twenty feet, and have the
most perfectly graceful proportions.   I have often much

regretted that this tree was not more common in this fully developed form ; ordinarily it is a mere shrub six or eight feet high, to be found in luxuriant hedges. As a tree it shows splendidly in blossom, and the drooping racemes of flowers are not only very graceful, but fill the air with a delicious odor.

XXXI.

Broom — Flaming Flowers of Broom — Fortissimo in Color — Pansies — Their Variety — Heartsease — Poetry in the Language of Science — Daisy — Buttercup — Disagreeable Scientific Name — Ranunculus Aquatilis — Lousewort — The Rose fortunate in her Name — Name of the Horse-chestnut — Cuckoo-flower — Marsh Caltha — Names of the Marsh Caltha.

IT is rarely that I feel myself capable of any thing like hostility towards any plant that grows wild in our country, but there is one of them — the broom — which tires my patience a little in its flowering season by the very loudness of its self-assertion. At all other times of the year it is welcome enough, and its pleasant green is often most agreeable to the eye when very little green of a cheerful kind is to be found upon any thing else ; but really, when the yellow flowers are all ablaze, I feel that we have too much of a good thing, and are positively incapacitated for the enjoyment of delicate color by this all but intolerable glare. A strong pure color of this kind ought not to be sur-

rounded by delicate tertiary colors, because it kills
them at once. What it requires is the neighborhood
of other colors pure enough to hold their own against
it. This theory is fully borne out by the coloring of
two places which I will now describe. The first is a
beautiful bit of river-shore, very delicately tinted and
covered with pansies and violets, with a mountainous
distance usually in tender gray. All this is lovely indeed
till the broom explodes into flames of chrome-yellow,
but after that what becomes of such a thing as a pansy?
You may take it up, of course, and satisfy yourself by
minute inspection that it is a beautiful flower of pale
parchment-yellow, with a bold touch of cadmium on the
lower lip of the corolla, and seven effective little black
streaks; but the moment you look at it on the ground
you can see nothing but gray. The other place is the
edge of an abandoned quarry, where the red earth is as
hot in the sunshine as it can be; and as you look up
at it from below, the edge is brought against the intensest azure of the sky. Just along this edge grow twenty
or thirty magnificent plants of broom, and between the
azure of the sky and the fiery red of the sun-lighted
earth below they hold their own effectively enough with
their blaze of yellow, but are unable to extinguish either
the azure or the red. It is just one of those tournaments
of natural colors that the English painters seem born
to enjoy, and the French to run away from, — a spectacle
to delight the strong natural sense in its *naïveté,* but not
either the tender or the educated sense. It answers in
music, to a brass band playing *fortissimo* with blare of

trumpet and clash of cymbals ; it answers, also, in gastronomy, to the hottest of London pickles, of which one knows not which element is most fierce.

I mentioned pansies just now, but did not stop to dwell upon them.   They have several notable merits and pleasant associations.   One of their merits is that of variety.   Hardly any plant in a wild state is so various as the pansy ; other plants become various in the hands of the horticulturist, who obtains curious novelties by selection and culture, but Nature herself does this with the pansy, and you have it purple, or yellow, or whitish, or mixed in ways that it would be an endless business to describe.   Another merit is that it flowers for many months ; unlike the broom, which blazes only for a week or two, and is then completely extinguished, like a fire that has burned itself out. Then one likes the pansy for its pretty association with kindly and affectionate thought, with the memory of those we love who are separated from us by distance. Pansy is the French word *pensée*, scarcely even corrupted, but rather written phonetically in a rude, approximative way ; and in France the flower *pensée* is connected only with thoughts of a tender and kindly nature.   Many such a flower, that bloomed in a bygone summer, is still religiously preserved in an old letter or book, and never looked upon without a moistening of the eyes.   So Ophelia said, ' There's rosemary, that's for remembrance : pray you, love, remember ; and there is pansies, that's for thoughts.'   In English the pansy violet is called heartsease also, showing in another form the close connection between tender human feeling and this flower, which has somehow mysteriously established itself. Science, of course, ignores all such associations, but it would be a pity, surely, to lose and forget them altogether. The writer of a lively and fanciful little volume, called 'La Vie des Fleurs,' is indignant against men of science for their barbarity; yet even the men of science, hard as their hearts may be, do sometimes wrap up a little kernel of poetry in the rough and repulsive covering of their Greek erudition. They will not call a pansy a pansy, but they call it *viola tricolor;* and some of them have fancied that *viola* came from ἴον, and ἴον from the heifer Io, which fed on flowers of this kind. So difficult is it to shut out poetry altogether from language, even from the language of stern Science herself!

There are some exceptions, but the rule is that the popular names for plants are either charming for some sweet rustic association, or else from a direct reference to the deep feelings of the human heart. I showed how prettily Chaucer introduced etymology into his verse with reference to 'the daisie, or els the eye of the day;' and the rustic name 'buttercup,' which explains itself without analysis, is redolent of the dairy and the farm. The common French name, *bouton d'or,* has reference to the flower in the bud; the English one, to the flower full-blown. And now think of the learned name, *Ranunculus acris;* how disagreeably it grates upon the ear! The popular name hits at once upon what is agreeable in the plant, — its pretty yellow color; the scientific one refers to what would be disagreeable if we went out of our way to try it, namely, its acrid taste ; but what have we to do with its taste, I wonder? Just in the same way I have no doubt that the sweetest of pictures would be extremely disagreeable if we were to eat it. And ranunculus comes from *rana,* a frog or toad, — a strange connection of ideas in this instance, for what has a buttercup particularly to do with frogs? It may be more appropriate in the case of the *Ranunculus aquatilis,* because that plant is born in the water like a frog, and passes its infancy there ; after which it comes up to breathe and flower in the upper air, as frogs come to air themselves in their maturity. A plant may, however, be still more unfortunate than to have its name associated with frogs, or even toads, for there is one very pretty little pinkish flower, common, from April to June, in damp meadows and woods, which takes its name from a minute animal celebrated by the poet Burns, who discovered it on a lady's bonnet at church, when he ought to have been thinking of something else. Few plants are prettier than the common *pedicularis,* with its delicate wax-like flowers and deeply-cut leaves ; and it is a robust plant, too, with a strong perennial root. But what a misfortune to be called *lousewort,* and that precisely for the plant's utility and efficacy against lice ! As men afflicted with very disagreeable names often take care to change them (and they do right), so would the plants, if they were conscious of such ill-luck. Begging the reader's pardon for introducing the hackneyed quotation from Shakspeare about the rose

smelling as sweetly by another name, I would just observe that the rose has been remarkably fortunate in
her name, wherever it is derived from the Latin. It
is perfectly euphonious ; it calls up no association whatever but that of the flower itself, except in the mind of
some learned pundit, who thinks it may have something to do with the Sanscrit word *vrad,* which means
'flexible ;' and wherever either rose or rosa is used in
poetry it always comes in charmingly. Now, without
referring again to the supremely unfortunate *pedicularis,* let me take the case of a particularly magnificent
tree which has occupied us a little quite recently, the
horse-chestnut. I have often wished that awkward com-
pound word could be exchanged for one at the same
time more convenient and better sounding. Imagine
the embarrassment of the poets if the rose had been
called the horse-chestnut ! They would simply have
passed it in silence. It is fatal to the celebrity of a
flower for it to be known by an awkward name, even
though it may smell as sweetly as if some poet had
named it with musical syllables. And why the connection with the horse ? Are horses fond of the fruit ?
Most probably it is only a way of implying that it is
unfit for human food. I might have mentioned, when
speaking of the cuckoo and the use of his name with
the arum, which the people call cuckoo-pint, that another
plant is also dedicated to the same bird, the *cuckoo-
flower,* or meadow-bittercress. This plant is often found
in great abundance in dampish meadows, and I know of
one place near a little stream where the water is entirely

bordered with its beautiful flowers, which in that place are of the purest white, though they are often purplish. Whatever the cuckoo may have to do with this elegant and abundantly flowering plant, it is one of the glories of advancing spring, and where you find it you are very likely to find the marsh caltha not far off, for both of them like damp places. The botanical name *Caltha* is an allusion to the basket shape of the flower, which reminded some one of a little gilt basket, — not that it is much more like a basket than a buttercup is ; however, a name was got for it in this way from κάλαθος. The French name for it, *populage*, is an allusion to its habits. The flower likes damp places as a poplar does, so it was called after *populus*, a poplar ; which is a very singular way of naming a plant, for similarities of structure are much more generally noticed than similarities of taste. As the flower is much larger than that of the buttercup, and equally golden in color, it often becomes of considerable importance in spring foregrounds.

XXXII.

Cones of Pine — The Author audaciously Plagiarizes — Quotation from Sir A. Helps — A Pine-wood — Sycamore-maple — 'Les Bœufs,' by Pierre Dupont — Holly — Flowers of Bird-cherry and Holly.

JUST before the middle of May the pines are beginning to form their cones, which, at a little distance, have a powerful effect upon the color. At this time they are just disengaging themselves from the brown covering, and are of a light and cheerful green ; however, the brown still dominates, especially at a distance. There is scarcely any thing in Nature to be compared with a pine-wood, I think. Now, this sentence which I have just written is not my own, but a piece of downright audacious plagiarism from a very eminent author, who wrote 'Companions of my Solitude,' and whose charming thoughts have become companions to enliven the solitude of many other persons beside himself ; and in that book any ingenious critic, keen to detect a larceny, may find the above sentence printed word for word. I ought, no doubt, to have honestly written it as a quotation with inverted commas, but as the opinion it expresses is just as much my own as his I prefer to appropriate it absolutely. But as one cannot exactly steal a whole paragraph or page, I will now proceed to quote a passage which has always seemed to me one of the most complete expressions of the sylvan influence on the mind of a thinking creature : —

'I remember once when, after a long journey, I was approaching a city ennobled by great works of art, and of great renown, that I had to pass through what I was told by the guide-books was most insipid country, only to be hurried over as fast as might be, and nothing to be thought or said about it. But the guide-books, though very clever and useful things in their way, do not know each of us personally, nor what we secretly like and care for. Well, I was speeding through this "uninteresting" country, and now there remained but one long dull stage, as I read, to be gone through before I should reach the much-wished-for city. It was necessary to stay some time (for we travelled vetturino fashion) at the little post-house, and I walked on, promising to be in the way whenever the vehicle should overtake me. The road led through a wood, chiefly of pines, varied, however, occasionally by other trees.

'Into this wood I strayed. There was that indescribably soothing noise (the Romans would have used the word *susurrus*), the aggregate of many gentle movements of gentle creatures. The birds hopped but a few paces off, as I approached them; the brilliant butterflies wavered hither and thither before me; there was a soft breeze that day, and the tops of the tall trees swayed to and fro politely to each other. I found many delightful resting-places. It was not all dense wood; but here and there were glades (such open spots, I mean, as would be cut through by the sword for an army to pass); and here and there stood a clump of trees of different heights and foliage, as beautifully arranged as if some triumph of the art of landscape had been intended, though it was only Nature's way of healing up the gaps in the forest. For her healing is a new beauty.

'It was very warm, without which nothing is beautiful to me; and I fell into the pleasantest train of thought. The easiness of that present moment seemed to show the possibility of all care being driven away from the world some day. For thus peace brings a sensation of power with it. I shall not say what I thought of, for it is not good always to be communicative ; *but altogether that hour in the pine-wood was the happiest hour of the whole journey*, though I saw many grand pictures and noble statues, a mighty river, and buildings which were built when people had their own clear thoughts of what they meant to do and how they would do it.' *

This is as different as possible from Dante's feeling about woods, but then the English writer knew that he could easily get out of his pine-wood to catch the vetturino again ; and in England, where he had learned to love woods as places to meditate in, they are never large enough to inspire the forest-fear of which I have spoken elsewhere. And yet the pine is not in the spring-time the most cheerful-looking of forest-trees, though it has a wholesome influence on the mind, and fills the air with a healthy and stimulating odor. The sycamore-maple is far more gay, with its long pendent racemes of greenish-yellow flowers. The botanists call this family the *Aceraceæ*, because the wood is sturdy ; and the reader may remember how in that magnificent rustic song 'Les Bœufs,' by Pierre Dupont, the poet begins by particularizing the woods from which the plough and the goad are made, and the wood used in the plough is sycamore :—

'J'ai deux grands bœufs dans mon étable,
    Deux grands bœufs blancs marqués de roux ;
  La charrue est en bois d'érable
    L'aiguillon en branche de houx.'

* 'Companions of my Solitude.' By Sir ARTHUR HELPS. Roberts Brothers' Ed. p. 77.

The holly, that served for the goad, flowers nearly at the same time with the sycamore, but not at all conspicuously, though its flowers are visible. I may just observe what a great difference there often is in pictorial importance between the flowers and fruit of the same plant. In some plants, as, for example, the bird-cherry tree, the flowers are glorious, and the berry of scarcely any visible importance; in others, as the holly, the flowers would almost escape the notice of anybody but a botanist, whilst it is impossible to avoid paying attention to the fruit.

XXXIII.

The Classic Pastorals — Inferiority of the Classical Writers in Passion for Natural Beauty — Superiority of Chaucer to Virgil — Virgil's laconic Way — Chaucer's abounding Eloquence — Virgil never intense when speaking of Nature — Virgil's blending of Human Interest with Nature — How Virgil particularizes — He cared for Nature independently of Personal Ease and Enjoyment — Catholicity of Taste in Virgil — His preference of Olive to Willow — Affectionate Comparison of Species — True Classic Love for Nature contrasted with Wilful Ignorance of False Modern Classicism — Facility of brief poetical Word-painting — A little Virgilian Picture — Virgil's Coloring — Much effect with little Labor — Excessive Brevity of Classical Writers — Their Laborious Corrections — Permanent Interests of Sylvan Life — Virgil's prospective Sense of Duration in Sylvan Things — The Anchorite and the Cicada.

I HAD reserved the reading of the classic pastorals for the full bloom of leafy summer, hoping that in our retirement we might have better access to the thoughts of the poets when the green light fell upon

their pages through the forest-leaves, and every thing ·
around us might illustrate their sylvan imagery. So
when June came I seldom went out without some old
Idyllist in my pocket, and sometimes Alexis read with
me, and often I read alone.

One general result of these readings remains with
me, and that is a strong sense of the inferiority of the
classical writers in the passion for natural beauty, I
will not say to the moderns, who have made a trade
of this passion, just as landscape-painters do, but to
the poets of the early renaissance, who wrote simply
from the heart, and had no idea of making poetical
capital from a business-like observation of Nature.
There is not the slightest comparison, for example,
between Virgil and Chaucer with respect to wealth of
landscape description, either in quantity or passion, —
Chaucer is so much the more opulent and powerful
poet of the two in every thing that relates to external
Nature. And yet when I mention Virgil, I mention
a poet highly distinguished amongst the ancients for
this very delight in Nature ; a poet who certainly did
love sylvan things with a rare degree of affection, and
that not simply for his own physical enjoyment of
pleasant shade or thirst-assuaging fountain, or fruit
delicious in the mouth, but for their own beauty outside of human needs. But how laconically he expresses
this feeling ! how little he dwells upon it ! A few
neatly-ordered words suffice ; the poet thinks he has
said all that is to be said, or need be, and there is an
end. Chaucer, on the other hand, whenever he begins

to talk about his enjoyment of Nature, hardly knows how or when to stop ; he has the abounding eloquence of a warm and earnest enthusiasm, the freshness and variety of his ideas and sensations suggest an equal variety and abundance of poetical expression ; he tries hard to utter all that is in him, very frequently finds that he has not yet succeeded to his mind, and tries again and again, but without effacing the previous attempts, so that there is a string of them one after another.   Hence Virgil may be quoted easily ; there are passages of his, not more than three words long, which afford excellent quotations and good subjects for literary disquisition : whereas to quote Chaucer is difficult in the extreme, for he leads you down to the bottom of the page, and over the leaf, before you have time to pause.   Of course I am clearly aware that a comparison of this kind cannot be made with justice unless we duly consider the reserve which was a part of the classical temper, and the remarkable tendency to think 'it is enough,' which formed habits of work in classic artists so directly opposed to the careless fecundity of the mediæval ones, and to the money-getting productiveness of the moderns.   It is quite evident that if Virgil, whilst retaining this classical reserve, had been imbued with Chaucer's passion for flowers and birds, and spring mornings in the woods and by streams, he would have concentrated the utterance of it into a tenth of the space that Chaucer covered with his facile verse ; but then the utterance would have been all the more intense and powerful for that very concentration, whereas what we have of Virgil's is delicate, but never intense, — I mean, when he speaks of Nature. He is always pleased to be in the woods, and, whilst he is telling the story of this or that poetical shepherd, the landscape is constantly seen by little glimpses behind and between the figures; but it is painted with a quiet affection, no more, and an affection that is immediately satisfied. One thing, however, is in the highest degree delightful in Virgil, and that is the lovely blending of human interests with his observations upon inanimate nature; exactly like the wreathing of leaves and branches about fair or mighty human limbs, that occurs so frequently in the work of the great figure-painters. Thus when Gallus says, in the tenth Eclogue, that he will go and suffer in the woods, the young trees are associated with his passion in a way that could have occurred to no other poet : —

> ' Certum est in silvis, inter spelæa ferarum
> Malle pati, tenerisque meos incidere amores
> Arboribus: crescent illæ ; crescetis, amores.'

' My mind is made up to prefer suffering in the woods amongst the dens of wild beasts, and to engrave my loves upon the saplings : the saplings grow —grow (with them, my) loves.'

This is ingenious, and affectionate also ; and please observe the thoroughly classical brevity of the last four words. Here, however, we have only the young trees in general, and we know that it is one of the marks of true affection to particularize, to distinguish the qualities belonging especially to each of the things or persons that we love. Well, Virgil particularizes also, just like a modern landscape-painter; and I take time to make this observation in passing, that when the pseudo-classical school opposed itself so strongly to the distinction between the species of trees which the modern school of landscape felt to be essential, it would have been easy to reply that their own idol, Virgil, did exactly the same thing in poetry that the new school was humbly endeavoring to do in the sister art of painting. Thus, in the seventh Eclogue, Thyrsis says, just at the last : —

> ' Fraxinus in silvis pulcherrima, pinus in hortis,
> Populus in fluviis, abies in montibus altis :
> Sæpius at si me, Lycida formose, revisas,
> Fraxinus in silvis cedat tibi, pinus in hortis.'

This illustrates at the same time both the two qualities that I have been speaking of, for not only are the trees mentioned specially, but they are connected with a human interest : —

> ' The ash is most beautiful in the woods, the pine in gardens, the poplar by rivers, the fir on lofty mountains ; but if thou camest to see me oftener, beautiful Lycidas, the ash would yield to thee in the woods, the pine in gardens.'

Nor would our analysis of the Virgilian spirit in this passage be complete without the observation, that it affords evidence against the theory that the ancients could see no beauty in Nature except such as was connected with personal ease or physical enjoyment. The allusion to gardens is brief and cursory in the extreme, whilst there is no mention of what are popularly called fruit-trees; but the poet is clearly alive to the beauty of the ash, to that of the poplar, — very different kinds of sylvan beauty, — whilst it may be especially observed that the faculty of perceiving any thing to admire in the 'fir on the lofty mountains' has been supposed to be exclusively modern. Yet, although Virgil had the catholicity of taste which appreciates many different forms of beauty, he had, like all true lovers of Nature, his own little private preferences, which it is interesting to note when an accident of his verse reveals them. For example: he preferred the olive-tree to the willow, —a preference which, when I think of the perfect beauty of willows that have never been mutilated by farmers, I find it difficult to share, though it is possible that a poet living so far south may have had in his mind the peculiar grandeur of very ancient olive-trees, and the value of their pale foliage, which he especially notices, in scenes pervaded by the Italian azure of sky and Mediterranean bays :—

> 'Lenta salix quantum pallenti cedit olivæ,
> Puniceis humilis quantum saliunca rosetis ;
> Judicio nostro tantum tibi cedit Amyntas.'

'As much as the pliant willow is inferior to the pale olive-tree ; as much as the humble lavender is inferior to red roses ; so much, in our opinion, is Amyntas inferior to thee.'

Every lover of Nature has preferences of this kind, and the poet supposes that the gods must have them also ; thus he reminds us that the vine was especially beloved by Bacchus, the poplar by Hercules, the myrtle by beautiful Venus, and '*his* laurel' by Phœbus. But

'*Phyllis amat corylos,*' — Phyllis loves hazels, and so long as Phyllis shall love hazels neither the myrtle nor Apollo's laurel shall surpass them.

This comparison of species is full of affection, and not a narrow affection either ; for though the poet may have had an especial liking for the olive, and probably for the hazel also (there is reason to suppose that Phyllis expresses a taste of the poet himself), he frankly tells us that other trees have been preferred by other personages, and gives each the honor that is its due. This largeness is strikingly different from a bigoted narrowness on this very subject, which is not unfrequently met with in our own time, and of which I have lately given a very striking example. Here is evidence sufficient, though in laconic passages, that the Roman poet had a love for sylvan Nature, which if not so cultivated by attention to minute detail as that of a modern botanist, or a landscape-painter of the botanical school, still paid far more attention to detail than the wilfully ignorant criticism of the false modern classical school, which held the almost inconceivable theory that trees were to be regarded simply as trees, without distinguishing their species. I well know that we are strongly tempted, on the faith of a word here and there, to give credit to an ancient author for much more knowledge and much keener perception than he probably ever possessed ; and that it is one of the commonest illusions of our complex intellectual civilization to forget the simplicity of sight and thought in which men lived long ago, and to attribute to them our own habits and ideas from a respectful unwillingness to acknowledge any inferiority in them: but the exact truth about their ways of thinking is still ascertainable. It is clear that Virgil had much of the sort of vision which belongs to a modern painter. Let us not exaggerate this praise: there is an immense difference between merely writing down the words 'fraxinus in silvis pulcherrima,' and painting an ash-tree well, so as to make us *see* that it is 'pulcherrima.' It is easy to say that a bull has a white side and that the herbage he eats is 'pale;' but it requires an incomparably higher culture of the faculty which perceives color to paint the white bull and the pale herbage in the right tints. However, it may be affirmed with truth that Virgil had the faculty of pictorial sight in the rudimentary state, because he takes notice of the things that painters give their lives to study; and it is perfectly conceivable, that had he lived in our own time he might have become a painter of rustic subjects, equal to Troyon in breadth and repose, superior to him in delicacy. Here, in two lines, is a picture that really reminds one of Troyon, — it was the recollection of these very verses that made me mention that painter just now, — a picture as highly finished as it can be in so brief a space, the subject being a bull with landscape adjuncts, exactly the kind of subject that Troyon painted with so much simplicity and truth: —

> ' Ille, latus niveum molli fultus hyacintho
>   Ilice sub nigra pallentes ruminat herbas.'

> ' He, with his snow-white side resting upon the soft hyacinth, ruminates the pale herbage under the black ilex.'

You have the white bull, the dark ilex, and then the middle tint of herbage, which is called pale by comparison with the tree. 'Black' is merely the popular term for dark, whether dark green or dark purple; it is still constantly used in this way in different languages, especially with reference to trees: thus we have the black poplar, the black forest, the black islands, &c. It is not too much to say that another color is suggested by the simple mention of the hyacinth, and there is a delicate hint of pity for the flower crushed under the weight of the animal; but this belongs to poetry rather than to painting. I do not believe that any artist in words ever painted so complete a picture of animal and landscape with so few touches. You have color (*niveum, hyacintho*), you have texture (*molli*), and you have light and shade (*nigra pallentes*). Whatever may be wanting in the tiny masterpiece is supplied at once by our own memory and imagination, — *form* is only indicated by the mention of the kind of animal and the kinds of plants; but then we remember immediately what is the shape of a bull, of an ilex, and of a hyacinth.

To appreciate the full artistic quality of such a perfect bit of work as this, it is enough to place beside it any piece of common descriptive verse having a similar subject. But whilst thus heartily acknowledging Virgil's peculiar gift, and the art with which he so skilfully used it, a modern critic can hardly escape some feeling of surprise at what seems to him the *excessive* brevity of the classical writers. They said what they had to say so well, that the wonder is they were not tempted to say more, or, if not more on the same subjects, that they did not treat other subjects in the same manner. Their inspiration does not seem to have been frequent in its recurrence, or of long duration when it came. We know that they corrected laboriously, and their corrections, like those of a sculptor on the marble, would result (with their taste) in a diminution of the mass. This being so, it is a subject of special regret that so much of the *Georgics* should have been occupied with mere receipts and advice for the use of farmers.

The interests of the sylvan life are very much the same in all ages, the differences which time has brought about being more in the arms and instruments we use than in the objects of our study or the manner of our enjoyment. The ancients had not our guns and microscopes, but they hunted and botanized after their own more primitive fashion, chasing the same animals, and gathering the same plants. In the fifth Eclogue there is a prospective sense of the duration of sylvan things which expresses itself very strongly in two verses : —

'Dum juga montis aper, fluvios dum piscis amabit,
  Dumque thymo pascentur apes, dum rore cicadæ ;
  Semper honos, nomenque tuum, laudesque manebunt.'

'So long as the wild boar shall love the ridges of the hills, or the fish the streams; so long as the bees shall feed on thyme, or the cicada drink the dew; thy name and honor shall remain.'

Well, here, within so short a distance of the Val Ste. Véronique, there *are* wild boars on the ridges of the

hills, there *are* fish in the clear streams, and the bees
feed on the wild thyme, and the cicada drinks the dew.
So permanent are sylvan things, that Virgil described
prospectively all these neighbors of mine just nineteen
hundred years ago. Neighbors, indeed! though, perhaps, it is not very neighborly of me to shoot the wild
boars, and catch the trout, and take the honey from the
bees ; but my conscience is clear as to the cicada, — her
I have never injured or robbed, not being able to see
my advantage in so doing ; and, therefore, I will call
her 'neighbor' without remorse. As we have been
quoting Latin lately, I may recall what an anchorite of
the desert said with a true affection for this humble
creature, that he had learned in the depth of his solitude, — '*Soror, amica mea, cicada !*' — 'My sister, and
friend, cicada !' I never see one of them without thinking of this, and loving that holy anchorite.

XXXIV.

Theocritus — Greek, French, and English — The real Subject of Greek
Idyl and Roman Eclogue — The Idyllic Shepherds — Their Immorality — A Protest — Nature of the Idyl — Few Landscape Pictures in
the great Idyllists — Method of the Idyllists — Their simplest Art
— Cunning of the Idyllists in describing Things — The pervading
Sylvan Spirit — Virgil and Theocritus compared — Personal Experience of Theocritus — His lively Description of Repose near a Country House — Description by Theocritus — Touches of Reality — The
true Idyllists call every thing by its own Name.

THERE are not many *separate* landscape studies
in Virgil's idyllic poetry; there are fewer still in
that of Theocritus. Greek and Roman remained within
the rigid limits of their art; and perhaps the Greek, by
the quality of his language, even exceeded the Roman in
that brevity that we approach with so much difficulty
when we care to rival it at all. So Theocritus, in the
twenty-fifth Idyl, speaks of the hill-tops with many
springs, πολυπίδακος ἀκρωρείης, which the best French
translation calls *collines aux sources nombreuses*, — how
awkwardly! and which could not be adequately trans-
lated into English without borrowing Tennyson's expression, ' many-fountained,'

' Dear mother Ida, many-fountained Ida,'

which is itself an exotic form, borrowed from the very
Greek word that Theocritus used, taken evidently from
Homer, who uses it in connection with Ida.

But the real subject or motive of the Greek idyl and

of the Roman eclogue, the imitation of it, is not external nature; it is the life of man in Nature, of man as an animal, or lower than any other animal, with pretty hills and foliage for a background, and flower-bearing, grassy lands to play in. It is strange that an immorality so disgusting, so inconceivable by us, should ever have been united with any simple and hearty love of Nature, and it is the stranger that the immorality itself was of a kind completely out of harmony with natural instinct and law: but the truth is, that in the measure of their powers these ancient poets, when they wrote idyls, set themselves to paint animal pictures with rustic back-grounds, the animal being sometimes a bull, sometimes a goat, but more frequently *man.* We have only to read these poems to perceive at once how inevitable it was for the ancients to arrive at the conception of the satyr. The sentimental shepherds whom they celebrate are morally so much beneath what we charitably hope is the common human level, that it is really a relief and a necessary transition to pass from them to the honestly semi-bestial condition of half-animal, in which we see at once that responsibility has been diminished by monstrosity of organization. Had these poets simply taken man as a part of Nature and described his passions naturally, however frankly, we might have read their descriptions with the indulgence that we feel for savages in the South Sea Islands; but their groves are like the Cities of the Plain, and one desires for them, if not the consuming fire, at any rate the oblivion of Asphaltites, — that dreariest, bitterest of seas, whose waters lie for ever, and so heavily — heaviest of all waters — on a vale not morally more impure than the Arcadia of classic imagination.*

I know that morality is not art, and that as we began to talk of these things simply from the artistic point of view, it is a complete change of key to pass into moral criticism. But it was impossible for me to speak of the old idyllic poetry at all without this protest; and now that the protest has got itself fairly uttered I am free to return to art.

The nature of the idyl has been accurately defined by a recent English writer on Greek poetry. 'The name of the idyl,' he says, 'sufficiently explains its nature. It is a little picture. Rustic or town life, legends of the gods, and passages of personal experience, supply the idyllist with subjects. He does not treat them lyrically, following rather the rules of epic and dramatic composition. Generally there is a narrator, and in so far the idyl is epic; its verse, too, is the hexameter. . . . Perhaps the plastic arts determined the direction of idyllic poetry, suggesting the name and supplying the poet with models of compact and picturesque treatment. In reading the Idyls it

---

* Thus I have no hesitation in preferring the twenty-seventh idyl of Theocritus to the twenty-third, notwithstanding the frank license of the one and the decent language of the other. Indeed I think that the twenty-third idyl of Theocritus, and some of Virgil's, are the most essentially and perfectly abominable things, from the moral point of view, in literature. Everybody knows this who has read them, but somehow these authors escape the stigma of immorality because of their sacred character as classics. The worst of modern literature is purity itself in comparison.

should never be forgotten that they are pictures, so studied and designed by their authors : they ought to affect us in the same way as the bas-reliefs and vases of Greek art, in which dramatic action is presented at a moment of its evolution, and beautiful forms are grouped together with such simplicity as to need but little story to enhance their value.' *

Although, as I have already observed, the landscape pictures that can be detached are rare in the great idyllists, they continually *associate*, as we have seen in Virgil, the material of landscape with the human life, which they paint in their little compositions ; and so closely, that if you cannot separate the landscape from the figures, so it is hardly possible, on the other hand, to separate the figures from the landscape. Thus, in his first idyl, Theocritus begins with a pine-tree close to fountains, and speaks of its whispering or rustling, ψιθύρισμα, instantaneously connecting this vague music with the music of a goatherd playing upon his pipe ; whilst the goatherd himself, in answer, connects the sound of water falling from a rock with the song of a shepherd. This was distinctly the *method* of the idyllists, who blended figures and landscape as closely together as they possibly could, often in a way that criticism might fairly blame as being too obviously intentional. The simplest and most natural way of doing this was by merely informing the reader that the little incident narrated occurred in such or such a

* 'Studies of the Greek Poets.' By John Addington Symonds. London : Smith and Elder. 1873.

pleasant place, where this or that species of tree was growing. 'Let us sit down here,' the goatherd says, 'under this elm, before this Priapus and these (carved) Kraniades, where there are a rustic seat and oak-trees.' When the poet describes a vase he takes the opportunity of doing a little leaf-painting at the same time, by twining round the lips of it a garland of ivy mixed with pelichrysum, giving a dainty little touch of color just at the last, καρπῷ κροκόεντι, of saffron-colored fruit. The vase, too, is varnished with 'odorous wax,' the simple mention of which carries the imagination instantaneously to the bees and their labors, and thence to the flowers where the odorous wax is found. Nor is this all; for, in continuing the description of the vase, Theocritus, whilst speaking of the figures upon it, says that near to one of them is a vine laden with grapes, and round about the vase is a wreath of the flexible acanthus. So in Virgil's third Eclogue the two cups, made by the 'divine Alcimedon,' are decorated with carvings of vine and ivy; whilst on two other cups by the same artist, belonging to Damœtas, the acanthus is used for the handles; and in the midst the artist has represented Orpheus *and the forests following him —* 'sylvasque sequentes.' How completely the sylvan spirit flows into every thing here !

Mr. Symonds, whom I have already quoted, thinks that, whilst it is difficult to speak in terms of exaggerated praise concerning the appreciation of scenery by Theocritus, Virgil lacks his vigor and enthusiasm for the open-air life of the country. The sentiment that we find in Virgil appears to be of a different nature. It is not so fresh and lively, but is more indolent and tender ; still, it seems genuine alsŏ. The difference between the two is very like a difference that may frequently be observed between two landscape-painters in our own day, one of whom is remarkable for sketching vigorously in color, and the other for concentrated finish and artistic arrangement of his material in the studio. The two artists may have an equal love for Nature, although the work of the first will seem to have more vitality, and that of the second more accomplished art. Theocritus writes like a man who is accustomed to walk in all sorts of wild places, and who remembers his experiences in such walks. Thus, in the fourth Idyl, Corydon says, 'When you come to the mountain, Battus, don't come unshod ; for on the mountain-land grow ῥάμνοι and ἀσπάλαθοι,' prickly shrubs of Sicily. Evidently this is the recommendation of a practical pedestrian. Then he has the art of finding pleasant spots to rest in; so Lacon says to his companion, 'Don't be in such a hurry, the fire is not at your heels. You will sing more agreeably when you are seated here under the wild olive-tree and those shrubs. Cool water trickles here ; we have grass and a leafy couch, and the grasshoppers chirp close by.' Writing like this takes us out of doors at once, and to the very spot. In the seventh Idyl we have a rich description of a pleasant country-house, and the arrival there : 'Then Lycidas turned to the left' — observe the vivid reality given by this detail — 'and took the road to

Pyxus. But Encritus and I turned towards where Phrasidamus lived, and so did handsome little Amyntas. We reclined rejoicing in deep beds of odorous mastic-leaves, and in leaves just stripped from the vines ; and many poplars and elms swayed to and fro over our heads, and close to us the sacred fountain babbled whilst it flowed from the grotto of the nymphs. And in the shade-giving branches the sun-browned cicadas tired themselves with chirruping, and the ὀλολυγων made its murmuring noise far off* in bloomless thickets of bramble. The larks and goldfinches sang, the turtle-dove uttered her plaintive note, the brown-yellow bees flew round about the fountains, every thing smelt of the rich late summer, of the fruit-time. Pears and apples were beside us and at our feet, and the branches were weighed down to the earth.'

Evidently this description is from memory; it is a lively account of a rest in some house the poet himself must have visited. There is especially one touch, the poplars and elms waving to and fro over the heads of the boon companions, which *must* have been got from Nature. There are other touches scattered about the idyls, which have a like reality. 'I began to love thee,' the Cyclops says to Galatea, 'when first thou camest with my mother *to gather hyacinths upon the hill.*'

Whatever may be the differences between Theocritus and his greatest imitator, one thing they have in com-

---

* The creature is unknown, and the translation of the word can only be guessed at. ∙ M. Remer thinks it meant the green frog.

mon, or perhaps it may be more accurate to say that one quality was preserved in the imitation, and that is, their habit of calling every thing by its own name. It is unnecessary to give examples of this, because every extract that I have made is an example. The weak pastoral poetry of their feeblest and latest imitators is not marked by this masterly precision. Theocritus always had before his mind's eye the image of a tree, when he thought of a tree at all, much too clearly for him to be ignorant of its species. The weak imitator does not see an elm or a poplar, but only 'trees,' which in English have generally the advantage of rhyming with *breeze*, and ' groves,' which are useful because they rhyme with *loves.*

XXXV.

The Aminta of Tasso — His Indifference to Scenery — His Musicaı Verse — Tasso's Treatment of Landscape — His Way of Sketching — Human Interest.

WHEN we pass from the early genuine pastorals to such a pastoral as the 'Aminta' of Tasso, we very soon find out that we have left sylvan Nature behind us. We have shepherds, and satyrs, and pastoral costumes, and an abundance of pretty talk, but we are no more in the fresh air of Theocritus than if the Tuscan poet had studied nothing but a classical dic-

tionary. He does not really care in the least about the
scenery of his poem ; occasionally a tree is mentioned,
or the woods, or a rivulet, or a little lake, but curso-
rily, in the temper of a figure-painter who dashes in a
bit of background with what may happen to be upon
his palette. The *words* of course come in well and
musically, as words : '*l'onde*' rhymes prettily with
'*fronde.*'

> ' Ho visto al pianto mio
> Risponder per pietate i sassi e l'onde ;
> E sospirar le fronde
> Ho visto al pianto mio ;
> Ma non ho visto mai,
> Nè spero di vedere
> Compassion nella crudele e bella.' *

These verses are quite typical of Tasso's treatment
of landscape. He may use it for rapid allusion, but will
not dwell upon it an instant longer than is necessary for
his immediate purpose, and recurs to human passion as
a workman who has glanced out of window applies himself again to his own business. So in the second scene
(Act I.) Aminta tells, very exquisitely, that pretty story
about the bee stinging, and how Filli, who was stung
on the cheek, was cured by Silvia's lips ; after which he,
Aminta, who had not been stung by the bee, pretended
that he had been, and so got a sort of kiss from Silvia,

---

* ' I have known the stones and the water answer my complaint
from pity, and I have known the leaves sigh to it; but I have never
found, nor do I ever hope to find, compassion in her who is cruel and
beautiful.'

who did not know that she was kissing him ; by which
act of innocent charity Silvia inflicted a deeper wound
than any bee could have inflicted.   This little scene
takes place '*all' ombra d'un bel faggio,*' under the shade
of a fine beech-tree, and in the course of the narrative
Aminta compares Silvia's sweet words to the murmuring of a slow rivulet that makes its way amongst
little stones, or to the noise of a light breeze under
the leaves.

> ' E le dolci parole, assai più dolci
>   Che 'l mormorar d' un lento fiumicello
>   Che rompa il corso fra minuti sassi,
>   O che 'l garrir dell' aura infra le frondi.'

But the poet instantly passes from these light
touches of landscape-sketching to the real subject of
his thoughts : 'Then I felt in my heart a new desire
to bring this mouth of mine nearer to her mouth.'

> ' Allor sentii nel cuor nuovo desire
>   D' appressar alla sua questa mia bocca.'

And when Dafne mentions a pond and an islet, it
is only to tell how Silvia looked at herself in the water
whilst she was dressing her hair and adorning it with
flowers.

XXXVI.

The French Imitation-Pastoral — Le Brun — Le Brun's Good Intentions — The Modern Genuine Pastoral — Lamartine's 'Laboureurs' — Troyon and Rosa Bonheur — Millet and Jules Breton — George Sand — 'La Petite Fadette' — Landry and Sylvinet — A perfect Bit — Difficulty of treating Rustic Subjects — A Satirist of Florian.

WHEN you come to the French imitation-pastoral, the indifference to landscape is pretty nearly absolute. You have '*rochers*' and '*bois*' and '*forêts*,' of course, but not the faintest sign that the writer has ever walked in the woods with his eyes open. The following lines from Houdard de Lamotte are a fair specimen of the sort of landscape-painting you have to expect : —

'Aux plaintes de Daphnis les Nymphes s'attendrirent ;
Dans le creux des rochers les échos en gémirent ;
Comme aux accords d'Orphée on vit du fond des bois
Les lions attendris accourir à sa voix.'

The most curious thing about the French pastoral writers of the eighteenth century is that they do really seem to fancy themselves students of Nature. Le Brun wrote a poem on 'La Nature, ou le Bonheur Philosophique et Champêtre,' and in the first canto invokes the wood-gods and the nymphs : —

'Et vous, de la Nature immortelles compagnes,
Vous, déités des bois, vous, nymphes des campagnes,
Laissez-moi parcourir vos bosquets ombragés
Que l'art contagieux n'a jamais outragés.'

13

Here are decided intentions of taking walks in the woods, but they come to nothing; and the poet does not get beyond a very external interest in agriculture, which leaves him at liberty to soliloquize at great length upon things in general.

It was only after the mania for imitating Virgil and Theocritus had *completely* spent itself that the genuine modern school of pastoral art arose. The feeling which inspired Theocritus exists in our own day, but now, when it is genuine, it *never* expresses itself in the form that was natural to him. Most commonly, a modern poet who has this inspiration gives utterance to it by means of color upon canvas, making his idyl really *visible*, according to the derivation of the word from εἶδος and εἴδω, and he who cares for this kind of poetry may find good pages of it in the annual exhibitions of pictures. Sometimes our modern writers in verse or prose describe rural things with idyllic grace and sweetness, yet hardly ever with idyllic concision; and it is for this reason chiefly that a painted idyl, which produces its effect instantaneously on the spectator, is nearer to the original conception of the εἰδύλλιον. I should like very much to quote some of the best modern work in writing, but it is almost impossible to do so without invading one's space too much : such quotations are like the young cuckoo in a small bird's nest; they grow and grow till they push the native progeny aside.

'Les Laboureurs' of Lamartine is a very good specimen of the *genuine* modern rustic poem. Here is one

extract, spoiled, or nearly so, by being cut too short.   It
is quite a picture : —

> 'Laissant souffler ses bœufs, le jeune homme s'appuie
> Debout au tronc d'un chêne, et de sa main essuie
> La sueur du sentier sur *son front mâle et doux ;*
> *La femme et les enfants tout petits, à genoux*
> *Devant les bœufs privés baissant leur corne à terre,*
> *Leur cassent des rejets de frêne et de fougère,*
> *Et jettent devant eux en verdoyants monceaux*
> *Les feuilles que leurs mains émondent des rameaux ;*
> Ils ruminent en paix pendant que l'ombre obscure
> Sous le soleil montant se replie à mesure,
> Et, laissant de la glèbe attiédir la froideur,
> Vient mourir, et border les pieds du laboureur.
> Il rattache le joug, sous sa forte courroie,
> Aux cornes qu'en pesant sa main robuste ploie
> *Les enfants vont cueillir des rameaux découpés*
> *Des gouttes de rosée encore tout trempés ;*
> *Au joug avec la feuille en verts festons les nouent,*
> *Que sur leurs fronts voilés les fiers taureaux secouent*
> *Pour que leur flanc qui bat et leur poitrail poudreux*
> *Portent sous le soleil un peu d'ombre avec eux.'*

This is just as truthful as the best bits of Virgil, and
it is a charming rustic scene.   I have *Italicized* what
seem to me the best and happiest touches.   We see
that this is strictly the same rustic inspiration that
animated Troyon and Rosa Bonheur, yet sweeter and
tenderer than theirs.   Millet and Jules Breton, two
poets who have worked in color, have much more
human. sympathy than the two illustrious animal-
painters just mentioned, and are nearer, but in their
own original way, to the temper of the literary artists.

But by far the greatest of all modern writers on rustic subjects is George Sand. She alone has found the means of conciliating a perfectly rustic tone of thought with the exigences of accomplished art. You may read her 'La Petite Fadette' in any farmhouse within sixty miles of the place where it was written, and the peasants will understand you and be grateful; you may read the same book to the most learned critics in polite literature, and they will feel the freshness of Theocritus, the consummate art of Virgil. When Landry is seeking his twin-brother Sylvinet by the brook-side there occur the most exquisite paragraphs, finished like portions of a poem : —

'Chacun sait pourtant qu'il y a danger à rester au bord de notre rivière quand le grand vent se lève. Toutes les rives sont minées en dessous, et il n'est point d'orage qui, dans la quantité, ne déracine quelques-uns de ces vergnes qui sont toujours courts en racines, à moins qu'ils ne soient très gros et très vieux, et qui vous tomberaient fort bien sur le corps sans vous avertir. Mais Sylvinet, qui n'était pourtant ni plus simple ni plus fou qu'un autre, ne paraissait pas tenir compte du danger. . Il n'y pensait pas plus que s'il se fut trouvé à l'abri dans une bonne grange.'

Landry finds his brother by the brook-side, and then comes one of the most perfect bits in the whole story. See how delicately finished it is, and yet how full of Nature, and how free! It is precisely in the early Greek idyllic manner, the unaffected manner of Theocritus : —

'Il se mit donc à siffler comme s'il appelait les merles pour les faire chanter, ainsi que font les pâtours quand ils suivent les buissons à la nuit tombante. Cela fit lever la tête à Sylvinet, et, voyant son frère, il eut honte et se leva vivement, croyant n'avoir pas été vu. Alors Landry fit comme s'il l'apercevait, et lui dit sans beaucoup crier, car la rivière ne chantait pas assez haut pour empêcher de s'entendre : "Hé, mon Sylvinet, tu es donc là ? Je t'ai attendu tout ce matin, et voyant que tu étais sorti pour si longtemps, je suis venu me promener par ici, en attendant le souper, où je comptais bien te retrouver à la maison : mais puisque te voilà, nous rentrerons ensemble. Nous allons descendre la rivière chacun sur une rive, et nous nous joindrons au gué des Roulettes." '

The difficulty of writing well about rustic subjects is twofold. Either the writer may be untrue, as Florian was by a false refinement, or he may be too realist, too *terre-à-terre*, like a vulgar painter, and be excluded from all access to the ideal. Our knowledge of Nature feels itself insulted by the first, and our sense of artistic *convenance* by the second. The two faults, of utterly opposite kinds, were very cleverly united in the same song by a writer who felt the absurdity of Florian and the crudeness of the realism that is entirely without an ideal. He makes a poet go into the fields with his head full of Florian's notions, and enter into a conversation with a shepherdess of the least imaginative type. What *he* says is the 18th-century pastoral, with its false ideal ; what *she* answers is the gross modern realism that has no idea whatever. In the *chanson* the male speaker has entirely the worst of it, yet before the tribunal of a competent art-criticism she also would be condemned as unfit for the world of art — that world which has laws of its own about truth, where truth is studied earnestly, yet never uttered without reserve.   Here is one stanza : —

'HE.

' Permets qu'à ton corsage
Je place ce bouquet,
À tes pieds ce feuillage,
Sur ta tête ces bluets !

SHE.

Monsieur, tout ça m'ennuie,
Moi qui n'ai qu'mes sabiots,
S'il vous en prend l'envie
J'vous les casserai d'sus le dos.'

XXXVII.

The Nightingale — His wonderful Voice — His various Emotional Expression — His Music is also Poetry and Eloquence — The Charm of the Nightingale's Singing — Byron — The Opening of 'Parisina' — The Nightingale sings on a height — Chaucer's Love of the Nightingale — Goldfinch and Nightingale — A Poet's Paradise — Tradition amongst the Peasants — Buffon's Description of the Nightingale's Song — The Talk of the Birds — The Secret of the Bird-Language.

AS an eloquent speaker dislikes interruption, and never attempts to display his eloquence when he cannot be sure of silence round about him, so the nightingale says nothing in the daytime, when a thousand other voices and noises of all kinds would interrupt his melodious utterance, but reserves it for the silence of the night, when he alone is king of the forest, and he may fancy that all other creatures are listening.   His song was too original and too beautiful to be mixed with the vulgar noises of the day, and even the glare of sunshine would have been too violent an accompaniment; but when the woods lie dark in the broad shadows that are cast by the midnight moon, and only a leaf glitters here and there as it trembles in the soft, noiseless breezes of the summer night, then, on some thin high branch, the nightingale sits and sings alone. And what wonderful singing it is! Many a human reputation has been overdone, but this reputation of the nightingale, great as it has been in all countries that are favored by his performances, and even in other countries, too, by hearsay, has never yet fully prepared any sensitive person to hear him for the first time without both delight and amazement. The wonder ever remains that a creature so small and weak, so little gifted with the graces of outward appearance, a little, thin, gray bird that only weighs half-an-ounce — the weight of a letter — should possess a voice as strong as the voice of a prima donna at the Opera, and at the same time so marvellously sweet and pure. But not alone for its strength and its purity is the song of the nightingale astonishing. Its variety and flexibility are more astonishing still. No musician ever better understood the value of *piano* and *pianissimo*, of *forte* and *fortissimo*, no musician ever developed a *crescendo* with more sure and delicate gradation. And then the clear, shrill pipings, the long brilliant shakes, the sudden sharp strokes of sound like the crash of a violinist's bow upon the strings, the tender passionate cadences fading away .

into the night air and dying slowly in a prolonged agony
till they grow so thin and faint that you know not
whether yet they have wholly ceased or not! The bird
runs over the whole range of emotional expression, from
the intoxication of loudest triumph that can be heard as
far as the shouting of a strong man, down to the sighing
of an airy voice that seems like the lamentation of an
inconsolable spirit. Often there is an evident artist-
pride in consummate executive accomplishment, often
the bird plays upon its own marvellous instrument as a
musician plays the flute or the violin, seeking for the
most varied and original effects, and rejoicing in them
when they are found. Again, the song of the nightingale being his only utterance, it is not music simply
as music is for us, but also poetry and eloquence. The
nightingale is not merely a musician playing on an
instrument, he is a singer as we say that the poets
themselves are singers. No one who listens can doubt
that he expresses an original emotion. The abundant
variety of his song is evidence that it is not simply
mechanical, and the pauses that he allows himself are
not merely to recruit from physical weariness, but much
more to seek a fitting expression for the emotion that
is beginning to succeed to that which has just been
expressed. If the reader thinks that it is too much
to claim for this the character of poetry, since there
is no conscious exercise of creative intellect, he will
scarcely deny to the bird a gift like that of some musician who in the late evening sits at his piano, and
in a long series of unpremeditated improvisations gives

expression to his feelings as they arise. He, too, in a certain sense, is a poet, though not in words. And the true ineffable charm of the nightingale's singing is not in the quality of the sound, exquisite as it is, but in the wonder of the communication from the little bird to us. 'What!' thinks the human listener, 'can the bird feel all these mighty emotions? can he feel such glory of triumph, such tender melancholy, such languor of passion?' Man, as he listens, quite easily falls under the spell. The very hour and season conspire together against him. It is summer in its richness, it is night in its beauty and calm. The heart is hushed and sub-dued, the eyes are quite ready to moisten at any suggestion of melancholy, or the imagination to be aroused by any awakening voice. The voice comes mysteriously from an unseen being, the quiet of the night is filled and flooded with it, we are bathed in the sound as in moonlight, and then all our great human feelings are played upon by that tiny creature as an organ is played upon by the organist.

Some of the very sweetest lines in poetry have been suggested by the nightingale. Byron, from his residence in southern climates, where the song of the bird is bolder and more varied than in England, was familiar with it, and has celebrated it in two of his best-known and most beautiful passages. There is nothing in all poetry more exquisitely finished than the opening lines of 'Parisina.' Byron was always happy in his openings, but this one comes upon the reader with a sudden sweetness, that makes him feel in an instant the delicate firm touch of the master's hand. What a way of telling us that it is late evening!

> ' It is the hour when from the boughs
>   The nightingale's high note is heard ;
> It is the hour when lovers' vows
>   Seem sweet in every whispered word ; `
> And gentle winds and waters near
> Make music to the lonely ear.
> Each flower the dews have lightly wet,
> And in the sky the stars are met,
> And on the wave a deeper blue,
> And on the leaf a browner hue,
> And in the heaven that clear obscure,
> So softly dark, and darkly pure,
> Which follows the decline of day
> As twilight melts beneath the moon away.'

In this passage the ' nightingale's high note ' is the dominant note of the whole composition, nor is there any more perfect example in the poetic art of the immense importance that a true master can give to a single line.   The bird is only mentioned once, and then with the utmost brevity ; but that ' high note ' once sounded, fills the whole exquisite description in the succeeding verses. Byron seems to have been particularly impressed by the height from which the voice of the bird announced itself ; and here, no doubt, is one of the elements of its effect ; just as it is in the bell's note from a cathedral tower, or the Muezzin's voice from a minaret.*

---

* Not to multiply quotations, I have omitted the beautiful passage near the beginning of the ' Giaour,' but may remind the reader of the well-known line, —

'His thousand songs are heard *on high.*'

Chaucer, always so alive to every thing that could add a charm to the woods and fields where he delighted to wander, paid great attention to the songs of birds, and to the nightingale especially. He tells us in 'The Flower and the Leaf' how eagerly he listened for this bird, although many others were singing in a way that ought to have gladdened any one : —

> 'And eke the briddes songe for to here
> Would have rejoiced any earthly wight,
> And I that couth not yet in no manere
> Heare the nightingale of all the yeare,
> Full busily hearkened with herte and with eare,
> If I her voice perceive coud any where.'

There is a charming description, in the same poem, of a conversation between a goldfinch and a nightingale ; the goldfinch singing first when he had eaten 'what he eat wold,' and the nightingale answering him with so merry a note that all the wood rang suddenly. Then comes one of the most *naïf* passages in all Chaucer, when he tells us how he wanted to get sight of the nightingale, which at first was not easy (as any one knows who has tried) ; however, he managed it at last, and then felt so gladdened by seeing what he wanted to see that he fancied himself in Paradise : —

> 'Wherefore I waited about busily
> On every side, if I might her see ;
> And at the last I gan full well espy
> Where she sat in a fresh grene laurer tree,
> On the further side even right by me,
> That gave so passing a delicious smell
> According to the eglantere full well.

> Whereof I had inly so great pleasure,
> That, as methought, I surely ravished was
> Into Paradise, where my desire
> Was for to be.'

Beautifully, however, as the poets may have sung of the nightingale, I doubt whether it ever occurred to the most inventive of them to imagine such an exquisitely poetical reason for his choice of the night-time for singing as the simple peasants about the Val Ste. Véronique have handed down by a believed tradition. Some peasant-poet must have had this original fancy, and then been pleased with it, and told it to his neighbors, whose poetic sense preserved it with that inability to distinguish between history and fiction which always marks the uncultivated human being. They say, and believe, that long ago the nightingale sang in the day-time like other birds, but that once in a warm night of May, when the vine was growing quickly, a bird of this species went to rest upon a vine and fell asleep there; and whilst he slept the tendrils grew very fast, and as they grew they twined about his tiny legs and held them, so that when morning came he could not get away, though his comrades came to help him. The poor bird died in this miserable situation, and his comrades were so impressed by what they had seen that they dared no longer go to sleep at night, but watched in fear of the same sad fate, and sang to keep each other awake. Even now, in the early summer, they utter the same notes of warning, and what they say is this : ' *La vigne pousse — pousse — pousse —— vite vite*

vite vite vite vite vite ! ' When a peasant tells this he always pronounces *pousse — pousse* — very slowly, and in a low voice, as if he were telling you a secret that deeply concerned you ; but when he comes to the *vite vite vite* he breaks into louder and higher tones, and finishes in a hurried presto.

The finest and most complete description of the nightingale's song that I ever met with is in Buffon. It is remarkably accurate, and full of the closest study, whilst the mastery of language displayed in the literary workmanship is quite inimitable, so that after reading it no other author would venture to attempt any such piece of work with the hope of excelling it in the same way. The most astonishing thing from the critical point of view, in this masterpiece, is that, although Buffon wrote in a language which is remarkably poor in words that express varieties of sound, we never feel this poverty in the least when reading it. The entire passage is too long to quote, but the following extract from it is sufficiently independent to be detached : —

' Il commence par un prélude timide, par des tons faibles, presqu'indécis, comme s'il voulait essayer son instrument et intéresser ceux qui l'écoutent ; mais ensuite prenant de l'assurance, il s'anime par degrés, il s'échauffe, et bientôt il déploie dans leur plenitude toutes les ressources de son incomparable organe ; coups de gosiers éclatants ; batteries vives et légères ; fusées de chant où la netteté est égale à la volubilité, murmure intérieure et sourd qui n'est point appréciable à l'oreille, mais très propre à augmenter l'éclat des sons appréciables ; roulades précipitées, brillantes et rapides, articulées avec force et même avec une dureté de bon goût ; accents plaintifs cadencés avec

mollesse ; sons filés sans art mais enflés avec âme ; sons en-
chanteurs et pénétrants,' &c.

Then follows a very sagacious observation on the
artistic utility of those intervals of silence which the
nightingale employs so well, and which answer, in his
singing, to the spaces of smooth wall in architecture, to
the spaces of blank paper in an etching.

After the month of June the nightingale sings no
more, but cries and croaks — a lamentable change for the
worse ; and more than that, a loss of all that we care
for in the creature.   After that the bird is forgotten by
those whom he once enchanted, and dwells in perfect
obscurity under the shadows of the deep woods that
were filled by his marvellous melody.   Happier, however, than men who have been famous and are famous
no longer, he lives on in a prosaic way, without re-
gretting the wonderful nights when his voice was
supreme beneath the moon, and all things that had
ears must listen.

There is a popular superstition in the Val Ste.
Véronique, and in the country for some miles round,
that every bird repeats some phrase of its own in distinct French words, which we should all hear and understand if we were only clever enough.   It is believed
also that certain wise and elderly persons in the villages
do really understand the language of the birds, and they
seem to be disposed to profit by the popular illusion, which
they are at no pains to dispel by disclaiming the knowledge imputed to them.   Very probably this superstition
may have had its origin in mere tales of infancy.   Some

parent' may have pretended to know the language of
the birds to amuse or govern his children, and afterwards the tradition of this may have remained. The
same pretension is to be found in Oriental story. But
there is one peculiarity about it in the neighborhood of
the Val Ste. Véronique, which is this. He who knows
the bird-language is forbidden by the popular superstition to communicate it to any one until he lies upon
his death-bed, when he may teach it to one member of
his family; who, of course, is bound by the same law.
Now as it generally happens that a man lying upon
his death-bed has other things to think about than the
transmission of bird-lore, the consequence of course is
that the knowledge of it is conveniently attributable to
people who have not transmitted it. 'My father knew
their language,' a peasant-girl will tell you, 'but when
he came to die he did not teach it us.' In this way
a pleasant and permanent mystery is maintained, and
it is still believed that one or two ancient men and
women know the bird-lore, and may possibly communicate it when they come to die, if any one is there to
receive it.

XXXVIII.

The Ash — Cantharides — The Elder-flower — Elder-flower Wine — Elder-tree — Honeysuckle — Forget-me-Not — Coloring of the For-get-me-Not — Dislike to certain Trees — The Robinia — Robinia and Birch — Branching of the Robinia — Odor of the Flowers of the Robinia — Wild Thyme — Beloved by Hares and Bees — Honey-suckle — Creeping Bugle — Veronica — Galium — Goldfinch — This-tle — Lime-tree.   ʹ

THE ash comes into full leaf in June, and is one of our finest and most artistic trees. The country people about the Val Ste. Véronique have a proverb to the effect that it neutralizes poisons : —

'Dessous le frâne venin ne regne.'

Certain insects have also an especial belief in the salubrity of the ash, or at least in its suitableness to their own constitutions. Those remarkable insects, the cantharides, fix upon it as a lodging for their colonies. The Val is sufficiently far south for this to happen occasionally, and when it does happen the effect is most curious. The trees are entirely covered with the glossy green insects, which emit such a pungent odor that it is almost impossible to remain under them or near them.

A much more agreeable, yet rather heavy and in-toxicating fragrance, is that of the elder-flower, which is abundant towards the middle of June. In grape-producing countries the wine made from this flower is always unknown, but in the north it yields its properties by infusion, and the product, after fermentation, is used as a substitute for champagne, often by very rich people. As is generally the case with substitutes, there is little real relation between the original wine and that which is made to replace it. Elder-flower wine is not champagne, nor any thing like it, but it has great claims to consideration on its own merits; and although no poet has ever sung its praises, they certainly ought to be sung, and not coldly spoken only, as in this pedestrian prose.* The closeness of the relation between taste and perfume is rarely more manifest than in this beverage, for to drink it is to drink perfume, the perfume of an elder-bush in June. I may ·add that the heaviness in the natural fragrance is maintained in the somnolence which the wine induces, for he who has indulged in it is sure to be overpowered by drowsiness unless he resists with all his might, or counteracts the sleepy drink by some awakening stimulant.

The elder-tree sometimes grows high enough to be of some importance in the near landscape, and its white corymbs of flowers are visible at a great distance. The way in which these corymbs are carried on the tree is one of its chief beauties, their flat surfaces being in so many different positions, but always in obedience to a regular law of growth; the foliage, too, is elegant and gracefully borne.

* Elder-fl)wer wine is at least mentioned in a very well-known Scottish ballad, 'The Laird of Cockpen :' —

> 'Mistress Jean she was making the elder-flower wine,
> Now what brings the Laird at sic a like time?'

The honeysuckle begins to flower a little later than the elder-tree. When the elder is all covered with its corymbs the honeysuckle flowers are opening, a bud or two here and there entirely out, the rest not yet. Their pink and yellow are pleasant with the peculiar tertiary green of the older leaves, one of the best sober greens in landscape. The new leaves are brighter and cruder.

A flower strictly contemporary with the elder, and of some importance from its quantity, notwithstanding its extreme minuteness, is the forget-me-not, the *Myosotis* (called so because its leaf is like the ear of a mouse). The effect of the color of this tiny flower is amazing when you consider how little there is of it ; but this is due to a principle well known to modern painters, even *too* well known, — the principle of stippling with pure color in minute touches. Here is one of those instances in which Nature herself does this. If the flower were wholly blue it would still act in the foreground, when abundant, as a stippling with pure color, but the principle is carried still farther. There is a central eye of yellow entirely surrounded by sky-blue, and the effect of the flower is due in great part to the purity of the central spot. Even the least observant are struck by the forget-me-not, and how much of the popularity of the flower is due to its bright coloring may be guessed if we suppose it green like its mouse-ear leaves. No lover would have paid much attention to it then.

I alluded in a preceding chapter to the intense dislike which some people feel for particular trees. Amongst the trees which have bitter enemies may be mentioned the acacia, or, more correctly, the robinia. It was brought into France from Canada by a botanist called Robin, in the reign of Henry IV., and has thriven so well that you find it all over the country. The remarkable rapidity of its growth is a great temptation to its use as an ornamental tree ; but now come the objections. Its enemies dislike it because the leaves grow late in the spring, and some people cannot endure the odor of its flowers; which to me, however, is very agreeable, especially when it comes on the soft, mild, evening air of June, and is thus wafted from a little distance. Other objections are that the stem is ugly because so deeply furrowed, and that the thin, light foliage gives but little shade. I confess that there is almost a contradiction in character between such a rude stem and such delicate leaves and flowers, or at least a very striking contrast, and I admit that the shade given is not comparable to that of the lime-tree or the horse-chestnut ; still it may be answered, that we feel the delicacy of the leaves all the more from the roughness of the furrowed trunk, and that the robinia gives as much shade as the birch, whose beauty is generally appreciated. The branching of the robinia is rather straggling and wayward, so that the twigs do not compose so well together as those of the ash or birch ; but even this is interesting as a special characteristic, for if all trees threw their branches out in exactly the same manner we should be wearied by their monotony. There is a great deal of *imprévu* in the branching of the robinia ; no painter would invent such branching unless

he had studied it in Nature. Its spring colors, light
green leaves, and white flowers, are gay and pleasant.
As for the odor of the flowers, there are people who
detest the perfume of the rose, so that it is difficult
to please everybody.

Most people like the fragrance of wild thyme. There
are often great quantities of it in dry, stony places, where
its tiny dull-green leaves make an agreeable sober foreground color, not harshly interrupted by the modest
violet of the flowers. Its strong perfume is due in part
to the presence of camphor in the plant. It is beloved
of hares and bees, and the scent is so refreshing that it
will revive a weary or fainting person. It is constantly
used by the clever French cooks to give flavor to their
dishes. The poets have loved it since classic times, and
with reason, for there is a great charm in the union of
its modest appearance with so sweet and healthy a perfume. It is one of the humble plants which form the
variegated carpet of the earth ; a plant to be crushed
under hoof and foot, yet so strong and spreading that it
is never seriously injured, and in return for much ill-
usage only yields its fragrance the more abundantly.

The later weeks of June are remarkably rich in
flowers. The honeysuckle is then fully out (at least in
the Val Ste. Véroniqne). We have the creeping bugle
in abundance, with its fine blue corolla; the germander
veronica, with its veined flowers of tender blue ; the
crosswort galium, the 'slender galingale' of poetry, with
yellow flowers, honey-scented ; the emollient mallow ;
and the harsh thistle with its purple glories. It is

curious that the thistle, which we so generally associate with donkeys, should have given, in one language at least, its name to that sweet singing-bird which, according to Chaucer, had a singing conversation with the nightingale — the goldfinch ; in French, *chardonneret*, from *chardon*, because it frequents the thistle. The plant may also be associated with the fine arts, as its spiky forms are peculiarly rich and interesting in certain kinds of decorative drawing and silversmiths' work. They are excessively difficult to draw, from the complicated perspectives of the prickly wings on the leaf-margins. Few artists have ever drawn a thistle thoroughly, probably from a feeling that any complete rendering of such a plant would lead to hardness in execution.

Of the large plants which flower late the lime-tree deserves special mention, for its agreeable qualities as a shade-giving tree, and its pleasant color and odor. Few trees are more intimately connected with human life than this. It is so constantly used to shade private and public walks, that most of us have recollections associated with it. The lime has also its heroic traditions. It has never supplied masts for war-ships like the fir, nor material for their strong hulls like the oak, but it was used in ancient times for bucklers ; and its bark must have had a sacred character, as it was worn by sacrificing priests. The flower of the lime-tree is gathered in great quantities for medicinal purposes, and administered very extensively in France as an infusion.

XXXIX.

Gray Coloring after Heat — Blue Sky turns to Gray — French Landscape-painting — Monotony of Sunshine — Favorable to Work — Abundant Light — *Ennui* of Sunshine — Despondency caused by it — Oppression of Sunshine — 'Mariana in the South' — The Black Shadow — Auguste Bonheur's Interpretation of Sunshine — Changes in the Condition of the Eye — Sunshine of Different Degrees — Streams in the Val Ste. Véronique — Dreary Scenes on Southern Rivers — The Loire — Its Affluents — The Great Bridges — The Herds — Processions for Rain — Oppressive Heat — Sudden Coming of a Thunderstorm.

TOWARDS the end of July, if the year has not been exceptionally wet, the landscape of Eastern France loses its freshness, and acquires that rather dull and gray look which often astonishes English critics in the works of the most faithful French landscape-painters. From the artistic point of view I cannot think that this gray look is altogether a misfortune, The brightness of the spring color is quite gone, much of the herbage is dried by a sun that is almost African in its severity ; but what the landscape loses in gayety it gains in sobriety, and the tints, quiet as they are, often go very well together, and richly deserve study. The greens all become tertiary greens, but there is great variety in them, and it is just the variety which a cultivated colorist is sure to pay great attention to,

whilst a crude one will as surely neglect it. As an accompaniment to this dulling of all the greens, the sky
changes from the clear blue of early summer and the
dark blue of the first heats to a sort of gray, which is
very well known to the inhabitants of southern climates
— the dark gray of the hot weather. This particular
kind of gray is never to be seen at all in northern countries. It is a real sky-color, not cloud-color; but it is
far, indeed, from the blue which we most commonly
associate with the open heaven. I have often matched
it very carefully in oil and water color, and always
with renewed astonishment at the quantity of red and
yellow that it requires. These gray skies of the intensely hot weather are often most accurately rendered
by the French landscape-painters, which makes northern critics affirm that they cannot color.

There are long weeks of monotony in the fine
summers, that may be appreciated for their practical
convenience by landscape-painters who work from Nature, as the same effect of gray sunshine recurs day
after day; but their influence upon the mind is rather
a tranquillizing than an exciting influence. The monotony of sunshine is like any other monotony; it tends
to lull the mind into a condition of fixed routine, in
which activity is still possible, yet repeats itself as the
days do. Through the long summer, which seems not
merely long but endless, we do always the same things
at the same hours, moving with the quiet regularity of
the shadow on the sun-dial. When the physical con-
stitution is inured to heat, there is no season of the

year more favorable to regular work. The intense light does not weary the eyes, — it is astonishing how easily they endure the solar glare, — and it is easy to provide an artificial shadow. Then the mind, being entirely undisturbed by any considerations about the weather, settles into a routine of habits, and pursues its objects with a tranquil simplicity of purpose which is sure to lead to some tangible result. There is light enough, and there is time enough for every thing : thus, with plenty of work and a sustained energy, a man may pass through the long monotony of the southern summer without weariness, and even regret the conclusion of it when it breaks up at last in thunder ; but if once the *ennui* of sunshine seizes you it is very terrible and very difficult to contend against. Then the constant gray-blue of the sky becomes hateful, the well-known forms of the surrounding landscape, of which nothing is relieved and nothing veiled, sicken you like the mechanical repetition of a tune on the barrel-organ : day after day you look vainly for the change that will not come, and you sink at last into a kind of despondency, which looks upon the condition of the world as hopeless, a globe whose wretched inhabitants are slowly roasted before a steady central fire from which there is no escape. This temper has been accurately described, or rather the feeling of it has been conveyed to the reader, by Tennyson in 'Mariana in the South.' Over and over again, in the poem, recurs the oppression of sunshine, the wearisome monotony of light. She dreams of native breezes and runlets babbling down the glen, but awakes to the 'steady glare' of the south : —

> 'She woke: the babble of the stream
>   Fell, and without the steady glare
> Shrank one sick olive sere and small.
>   The river-bed was dusty-white ;
>   And all the furnace of the light
> Struck up against the blinding wall.'

In the last stanza but one the same note recurs : —

> 'And flaming downward over all
>   From heat to heat the day decreased,
>   And slowly rounded to the east
> The one black shadow from the wall.'

This last touch of the black shadow is a repetition of one given in the opening of the poem, where the black shadow is the very first thing mentioned. It was rightly chosen for two reasons, since not only did it prepare the reader for the black shadow dwelling steadily on a hopeless life, but it also truly depicted an effect of glaring sunshine upon landscape. Here, again, is a very common error of northern criticism. In the north the black shadow does not exist, because the sun is not glaring enough to produce it, and northern criticism denies the truth of it when adequately interpreted in painting. The poet is not scientifically exact in calling the shadow black, as a painter in studying from Nature will find it to be gray or green, purple or brown, according to its situation ; but as a poetical artist Tennyson chose the right word, for it is the word which conveys the idea of darkness best, —

'dark' not being dark enough. It would be easy, too,
to prove that a painter who conveys the impression of
the black shadow paints it falsely. Auguste Bonheur
may be mentioned as an example. He paints southern
sunshine truly so far as the impression on the spectator
is concerned, falsely as to imitation of particular tints.
In very intense sunshine the eye adapts itself to cir-
cumstan·es, and for its own protection contracts so that
a glaring thing, such as a white ox, shall not hurt it.
Now, if you can look at a white ox at all in the glare of
a Burgundy July, even the lighted side of an oak-tree
will seem dark to you, and a cast shadow on foliage
will seem what in popular language is called 'black.'
Auguste Bonheur renders this effect with great truth,
but necessarily in a much lower key than Nature's.
And now comes the one important consideration which
reconciles art with Nature, and is always overlooked by
writers on these subjects. The eye looking at Nature
in glaring light, and the eye looking at a picture in
the quiet light of a gallery, is not in the same state ;
but a picture of sunshine painted on Auguste Bonheur's
principles bears the same relation to the open pupil
in a shaded room that the natural scene bore to the
contracted pupil in the brilliant sunshine out of doors.
The rule which affirms that if you match shades by
holding the palette-knife up to Nature you will get right
relations of color, is true only of figure-painting and
still-life, when the model is carefully placed in a gallery light. In open sunshine such a practice would
induce an artist to paint in too high a key, so that he

could not convey the sense of darkness in shadow and local color, which is one of the peculiar effects of really intense light. Thus Turner, working in a high key, expressed the sunshine of England; but his system, good as it was for the pale northern landscape, was inadequate to the expression of the southern summer, with its apparently dark dull greens and grays, and shadows far darker still.*

The chief misery of a long hot season — the want of water — is entirely unknown in the Val Ste. Véronique, where the pure little streams rush over their clean granite beds with as much vivacity as if it had been raining the day before. They are fed by springs in the upper hills, which never fail in the hot weather, and the consequence is a perennial refreshment of the valleys for several miles; but if you follow these babbling rivulets farther down, you observe the gradual loss of their early freshness and brightness, till finally they are absorbed in the river of the plain, and in great part lost by evaporation. Nothing, even in winter scenery, is drearier than the bed of some broad southern river after the torrid months have dried it. The Loire, amongst French rivers, most abounds in dreary scenes of this kind. For hundreds of miles you may follow broad tracts of burning sand, or hot white pebbles through which the stream finds its way tortuously, often

* This seeming darkness of certain tints in intense sunshine is chiefly, no doubt, due to contrast. As a matter of *fact* (not of human sensation), Tennyson's 'black shadows' must be lighter than a white object in dull daylight. But art ought always to go by impressions and sensations rather than scientific facts.

breaking into several different channels, of which not
one is navigable; whilst the occasional trees along the
banks are too far from the water to get the slightest
benefit from it, and their foliage is burnt to the sem-
blance of a premature autumn. The most important
affluents in such a time often cease to flow altogether,
and consist of nothing but a long series of stagnant
pools, which infect the air, with hot stones or baked
mud between them. At such a time the great bridges
seem nothing but lines of useless arches built long ago
for some forgotten purpose. Leaves wither, flowers
fade, the pastures are scorched, and animals droop and
languish. Yet, even here, might the art of a true
landscape-painter find motives, like that of the poet,
in the very desolation of the persistent sunshine, which
has its own melancholy like the gloom of the north,
and, like it, cannot be borne without resignation. The
starving herds resign themselves to a condition of Nature beyond their power to alter; the peasants go to
the priests and ask them to pray for rain, or get up
some procession. At length, in some ancient city, the
cathedral doors are opened wide, and out of the cool
pleasant gloom within comes forth into the fierce heat
of an August afternoon a mitred bishop, all gleaming
with gold and jewels, behind a heavy shrine carried on
eight priests' shoulders, with little windows in its gilded
sides, through which you may see the brown bones
of a saint who died long ago, and a long procession
winds slowly chanting about the quaint old streets.
Then the evening comes with its short twilight, and the

night without a breath in the motionless hot air. The day dawns just like yesterday and the unnumbered days before it. Will there ever be any change, or has the sea forgotten to send her clouds for the refreshment of the land? Is the sea dry like the rivers?

> ' Tout est morne, brûlant, tranquille ; et la lumière
> Est seule en mouvement dans la nature entière.'

Suddenly in the fiery sky rolled a black cloud, like volumes of smoke from a mine, and out of the cloud came a ball of fire that struck an ash-tree close to the house and split it, and sent fragments of the wood in every direction like scattered lucifer-matches. Half a second afterwards came a sound, not like thunder with its reverberations, but like a deafening explosion. The next day every leaf on that ash-tree was shrivelled and brown, and the tree died. Then began the usual series of thunderstorms, and every night the landscape was illuminated by the flames of farm-buildings in the distance, and every morning brought news of loss or ruin, of crops destroyed or animals too frightened to move burnt together in their stalls. So after the steady flame of the sunshine comes the far more terrible flame of the unavoidable lightning, and all night long the peasant, awake and anxious, goes watching about his barns.

XL.

The Harvest-time — What our Bread costs — Merriment in Harvest — Strength of the Girls — A Picture by Jules Breton — Jules Breton's Poetry — Alfred de Musset — The 'Chanson de Fortunio' — Rossetti —·'The Blessed Damozel' — Stalks of Wheat — Weight of Wheat needed in the World — Buckwheat.

THERE is a time of the year, varying in date with the climate of different places, which is felt by all to be the richest and mellowest time, and that is when the wheat is garnered. The reapers go down from the hill villages into the fertile plains, walking in bands through the sultry night, when not a cloud obscures the starry sky, and the broad yellow harvest-moon comes up in the east to light them. Many a league do they march, singing the old harvest songs, and at sunrise they are at work already in the ripe wheat, and their sickles are set to the harvest. Oh the toil and the endurance that are paid for the bread we eat! From dawn to dusk, in the full blaze of morning, noon, and afternoon, the reapers reap without ceasing, except their little half-hours for food, and in the late evening they load the harvest-wains. All that time they have to bend to their toil, with the heat of the earth in their faces and the heat of the sun upon their backs. Their food is poor indeed, and the wonder is how it supplies the waste of sweat and toil. And yet they all delight in the harvest-time, and keep to their work gaily with many a merry jest. The strength of the girls is surprising; often a girl will lead the line and keep up to her work quite steadily, which confirms the theory that women were made for labor. One of these strong girls was the subject of a picture by Jules Breton; but in his picture she has done with reaping, and sits apart from her companions, who are dancing, for they forget their fatigues in the dance. She has reasons of her own for not joining them; very likely some feeling of jealousy or disappointment; perhaps a certain youth may have invited another maiden, and now, according to peasant custom, is engaged to her for the whole evening. Jules Breton writes admirable verses, and in a little poem of his, which has been published, I find some stanzas which may refer to this very picture : —

'Dans la poussière ardente et les rayons de flammes
Joyeusement, les mains aux mains, dansent les femmes,
Mais la plus belle rêve, assise un peu plus loin.
Elle est là seule . . . .'

No wonder that painters like the harvest-time, it is so rich in color, and in the association of human life and labor with the bountiful gifts of Nature. The toil that it brings is sweet and healthy toil, and the only laborers who are really to be pitied are the few weaker ones whose strength is hardly equal to the work. For the rest it is a time of merriment and gladness, a change of scene and of society for the laborers who come from a distance, and the pay is far higher than in

ordinary times, which also disposes the heart of man
to gayety.

Wheat is almost sacred from the great service it
yields to man, so that it is not surprising that the poets
should speak of it with an especial tenderness and
delicacy.   Thus Alfred de Musset, in one of his most
exquisite little songs, the 'Chanson de Fortunio,' compares the fairness of a fair lady to wheat, and with
how pure a touch !

> ' Si vous croyez que je vais dire
>   Qui j'ose aimer,
> Je ne saurais pour un empire
>   Vous la nommer.
> Nous allons chanter à la ronde
>   Si vous voulez,
> Que je l'adore, et qu'elle est blonde
>   Comme les blés.'

And when Rossetti describes the *Blessed Damozel*
in heaven, he can think of no more delicate comparison
for her hair than to say that it was like ripe corn : —

> ' Her hair that lay along her back
>   Was yellow like ripe corn.'

A stalk of wheat is not a very strong thing ; it can
only just bear the weight of a very little bird, and even
that seems wonderful till we reflect how light a small
bird is, and how perfectly it is able to balance itself ;
and yet on these slender stalks what an enormous
weight of bread-making material is carried !   Many a
great ship is deeply laden with it, many a granary-floor
is covered till the great oak-beams visibly bend beneath

the load! And what tons upon tons of it does the world need! There are more or less acceptable substitutes, but always far inferior to the wheat that gives white bread. One of these, buckwheat, a cultivated polygonum, is now in much favor with the peasants, and ought to be with artists also, on account of its wonderfully rich color. It is called *sarrasin* in France, because the Moors took it into Spain, whence it came northward. It grows easily on soil too poor for wheat, and you may now see many little fields of it up amongst the rocks in the poorer and wilder districts. Early in September it is in the full richness of its color, the stalks being of a beautiful red, that is easily heightened when there are warm tones in the general light, which often happens at that season of the year.

XLI.

Suapwort — Use of Soapwort — Horsemint — Common Mint — Wild Carrot — Vervein — Polygonum — Change — Dock-leaves, their Color — Hornbeam — Juniper — Bracken — Heather — Cherry — Moun-tain-Ash.

LET us take a last look at the wild flowers before the season for them is quite over. We never could have omitted all mention of that handsome plant, the common soapwort, or *Saponaria*, which in August is prodigal of its large flowers, pink or nearly white, in dense corymbs at the summit of the stem. Every house-wife in country places where the plant grows, and where people are simple enough and sensible enough to accept a benefit directly from Nàture without going to a shop for it, — every housewife so situated well knows that to put this plant into her washing-tub is as good as a lump of soap. It grows abundantly by the streams here, so those two great aids to cleanliness, soap and water, are given by Nature together. The saponaria is not only useful but beautiful: a stately, handsome plant, that holds quite an important place, especially on the little islets in the streams; but the pale tender color of its flowers is not so conspicuous as the brilliant yellow of the senecio, for example, which abounds at the same season. However, it is not merely for brilliancy that a plant may have pictorial value: sometimes the very opposite of brilliancy may be the reason why a judicious artist would care for it. There is horsemint, whose pale cottony leaves are very valuable as a cool gray green. It makes great masses in some places, and has much the same qualities as the mullein, except as to the flowers ; for whilst those of the mullein are of a fine lemon-yellow, the tiny flowers of horsemint merely make a sort of pale purplish gray. The flowers of common mint are much more visible, and have some effect in quantity. The large white umbel of the wild carrot is extremely common at this season, but cannot be said to add much to the beauty of foregrounds, except perhaps by giving a certain lightness. We must not omit that sacred plant, the vervein, which the Romans used in their religious ceremonies, and which in war-time was carried by heralds as the white flag of truce is now. The Druids had a great respect for it also, and only culled it after a sacrifice. This plant appears to make a great fuss at starting near the ground with very big leaves, to end meagrely at the top, where the twigs and flowers are so thin and small. The tiny pale violet flowers are, however, effective in the same way, though not to the same degree, as those of the forget-me-not. Sometimes they fill a ditch, for hundreds of yards, with their innumerable constellations.

One of the most beautiful and important of all aquatic plants is the amphibious polygonum. Its rosy flowers stand up boldly above the surface of the water, whilst its long green leaves float upon it. This is a good plant to study for pictures that have a pond or a stream in the foreground, as it detaches itself well, and the flat leaves give a good horizontal surface, whilst the erect flower supplies a vertical object of the greatest use for contrast. There is a good contrast of color, too, between the flower and the leaf.

It would be tiresome to prolong this into a mere catalogue, and the limits of these sylvan talks are nearly reached. Vegetation never stands still, but there is a time when it appears to pause, before the change towards decay. Yet even then the change has already begun, and you have only to look around you to find evidences of the coming destruction. In meadows and pastures the docks soon take their rich deep red of leaves and fruit, the stalks being yellowish streaked with red, and quite harmonious ; they are a most important element of landscape. The curled dock makes especially magnificent color, with its dark-red stalks and leaves. Some of the leaves of hornbeam turn *pale* yellow, and others dark red. You have them pale yellow, dark red, and fresh green, quite on the same branch or twig. The juniper turns red altogether, much resembling the tint known to painters and colormen as. light red ; but this happens capriciously, as it seems, to one plant, whilst others in the same place remain quite green as in summer. At the same time the bracken is just beginning to turn yellowish brown at the tips and edges of the leaves. The crude violet purple of the heather is entirely gone, and in its place we have a sad brown in the flowers. The leaves of the wild cherry-trees are beginning to turn red, and the robinia leaves are turning pale yellow. But where in all Nature is there such a red as the vermilion berries of the rowan-tree, or mountain-ash, the *sorbier des oiseaux?* There are such prodigal quantities of it, too! I know a little village churchyard, with a tiny old gray church, and just along the wall there grows a row of rowan-trees that look like the trees in the garden of Aladdin when the fire of sunset is upon them; and there is a place near a mountain village where the road winds between an avenue of them, — a sight to see in the autumn!

XLII.

Sunset-light on Thistles — Fruits not generally Conspicuous — The Rowan — The common Cornel — Elder-berry — Blackberry — Small Polygonum — Ferns — *Persicaria* — Wild Hop.

I SPOKE just now of vermilion berries bathed in the flame of sunset, and will add another observation about sunset-light.   One of the finest sights in Nature is a field of thistles in September, with the level rays of a golden sunset striking across and catching the down of the heads.   The light is detained by them, and in them as it were, so that each thistle-head becomes a distinct source of light ; not with glittering reflection like the ripples on water, but with a charming softness, as if the rays were entangled in meshes of floss silk.

The reader may think, that after saying so much about flowers I dismiss fruits very summarily ; but it so happens that fruits (I use the word, of course, in the large botanical sense) are, as a general rule, less visible than flowers, and in these chapters we have talked almost exclusively of what is visible.   Some fruits are conspicuous, like those of the rowan-tree lately mentioned ; and the black, bitter fruit of the common cornel, or dogwood, is visible enough at the beginning of autumn in the hedges, the smooth leaves turning pale as the fruit ripens.   The elder-berries are out at the same time, berries from which a wine is made greatly inferior to that from the flowers of the same tree. It may be mentioned as a little detail worth remembering for foreground color, that the fruit of the blackberry is red before it turns black. The leaves of the bramble are, however, more important than the fruit, as they have quite a peculiar way of changing color in autumn. Many of them turn bright red quite suddenly, whilst quantities of others will be spotted with dark purple. The isolation of the red leaves may be of use to an artist who wants an intense color in small quantities. A very valuable cause of color in some situations is the small polygonum, which, with its red stalk and leaves just turning yellow, produces the most beautiful dark gold in mass. The ferns begin to take autumnal color rather capriciously ; it seems to seize upon some leaves to the neglect of others, and these leaves will be entirely affected by it, passing from dark brown near the root to yellow at the end. One of the latest flowering plants is the fine polygonum called *Persicaria*, often nearly two feet high, with a red stalk and spikes of rosy flowers ; but the stalk strikes the eye more than the flowers do. A very familiar plant, the wild hop, has an appearance at this season which bears some resemblance to flowers. The scales of the spike become enlarged so as to entirely conceal the fruit; and these dry scales are visible in September as a pleasant light brown, the leaves being still green.

XLIII.

Ferns — Robinia — Oak, Birch, Ash — Poplar — Chestnut — Cherry and Pear — Pear — Hornbeam — Beech — Willow.

A S we get deeper into autumn the changes of vegetation accelerate. The ferns turn red and yellow to begin with, to end in a uniform dry light red ; generally the change is completed about the middle of October. Some trees turn yellow in places, a leaf or two at a time, like the walnut ; the robinia does the same : indeed, in the robinia it is not by leaves but by leaflets that the process begins. Oak, birch, and ash, begin by showing yellow leaves here and there, like a sudden attack of disease ; but, considered as a whole, an ash-tree passes from green through pale yellowish-green to yellow. The poplar yellows all over gradually. Chestnuts at this time are much denuded of leaves ; those which remain are green, or brown, or yellow, about one-third of each, and the yellow ones are often brown about their edges. Cherry and pear-trees give most of the red in the woods, the latter often reaching a bright scarlet, which tells with great effect in the distance. Some pear-trees turn darker than others, and there are often both vivid red and fresh green together on the same tree. So in hornbeam ; you have pale yellow leaves and leaves of reddish gold, whilst the rest are fresh green. In beech there are three colors, — light red, yellowish red, and green. A few days later the pale yellow tinge of hornbeam is entirely gone, and has given place to a rusty brown. Meanwhile the willows remain still perfectly green.

XLIV.

Angelica — Leaves of Angelica — Bramble — Blackberry — Scabious — Honeysuckle — Tufted Hair-grass.

OF foreground plants, the angelica may be mentioned for its important size. The leaves are but little seen, being for the most part low down upon the stem, but they become a very pale green, and turn whitish or yellowish, often also inclining to purple. At the same time the angelica becomes brown in the umbels, because the fruit is ripening fast; in doing which it turns from green to brown. A little later, the leaves turn pure Naples yellow. Once more, for the last time, we must mention the bramble, now most rich in color with deep crimson or bright vermilion, passing to russet and green, and the abundant black fruit for a rich dark at the bottom of the scale. When the morning mists of October clear away and the bright sunshine succeeds, as it does regularly about eleven o'clock, all the blackberry leaves glitter in the bright light, and many of them show a colored transparence like jewels. At the same time they are often covered with threads of gossamer, on which are hung millions of minute drops, each of them clearer than a diamond, and with a sparkle of light inside it. Even so late as this you may occasionally find a flower in all its perfection — the scabious, for instance — which preserves for us the memory of summer. A few honeysuckle flowers may be found in October, although the plant is generally in berry. The tall grasses become very beautiful at this season; the tufted hair-grass may be mentioned specially for the remarkable way in which it catches the light. Under the sun it seems full of warm yellow light, almost as if it were luminous by a light of its own; indeed the sunshine seems to get entangled amongst it as in the down of a thistle, and this often gives great splendor to a foreground, but the effect is to be seen only when you are looking towards the sun.

XLV.

HERE, perhaps, it is well that these notes should come to an end ; for we began them with the late autumn, and have now completed our cycle. Our year of retirement, our *sylvan year*, is drawing to its close, and we leave the Val Ste. Véronique to return to the outer world. We always begin by expecting too much from the time that lies before us, as if the experience of the past were not there for a warning, with its long list of schemes unrealized, its losses (especially of time), and its disappointments. When I came with Alexis to our lonely house in the valley, I expected more from this space of calm and peace than it appears to have yielded now that it lies behind me in a retrospect. ' A year,' I thought, ' will do much towards the healing of my sorrows ; and in a year I can learn much, and acquire a beneficial influence over Alexis.' But what is a year in the life of a mature man ? All the old impressions remain just as vivid after it as before ; and the more painful they were then, the more vivid they are now. Still the study of Nature has been good for me, and it

is agreeable to have renewed or increased one's acquaintance with the sylvan world. My plans for doing
something in science, and art, and literary study, were
larger than my powers of realization in so limited a
space of time: however, they have constantly and not
unprofitably occupied me. The paternal scheme, with
reference to Alexis, has been farther from any perfect
realization than the others. I had counted upon his
companionship in my pursuits, and hoped that I might
be able to teach him a good deal without his suspecting
that he was being instructed; but he very soon found
this out, and by calling every thing a lesson compelled
me to fix regular hours for study, exactly as if we had
been master and pupil at a school : in fact, he called
them 'school-hours,' and asked for his liberty at other
times, or took it. He had full holiday on Thursday
and Saturday, on which days I was in no danger of
being disturbed by him, for he never made his appearance, but went great distances on foot with my keeper
(who had been known as a famous poacher under the
nickname of 'the Weasel'). In a word, I discovered
that my didactic propensities must be greatly restrained
if I did not wish to frighten this young bird away into
the woods altogether. On the other hand, it was impossible to suspend his education for twelve months.
In this perplexity I took a neighbor (who lived ten
miles off) into my confidence, and he recommended
a private tutor for the young gentleman. The plan
seemed feasible, and the more so that there were so
many spare rooms at the Val Ste. Véronique : so one

day a young abbé arrived, who knew, I suppose, what every abbé knows, but who was utterly incapable of conversation, and replied always in monosyllables, with a modesty that was perfectly irritating. My dinner-table had been tolerable with Alexis, when I did not put him out of humor by attempting to convey instruction to his mind; but it was not tolerable with the abbé, and the long spaces of silence must have been as uncomfortable to him as to me, for he made a request that he might be served in his own apartments, — a relief both to him and me. He had not been accustomed, however, to solitude, so that the silence of the big house, where we never heard any thing but the whistling of the wind, or the cry of a bird or wild animal in the forest, ended by preying upon his mind; and one day, pale with terror, he declared he had seen a ghost, and announced his sudden departure. From a malicious look of Alexis, I suspected that he knew more about the ghost than he chose to tell; however, the abbé left us with an unearthly expression on his otherwise not very interesting physiognomy, and when he was gone I attempted to resume my former office of pedagogue. My young pupil, however, affirmed that it was now the long vacation, when nobody learned any thing; and no sooner had the shooting season begun than he got himself invited to a château twenty miles off, where, with a merry party of young gentlemen, he did nothing but shoot from morning till night. I was vexed with him at first for his indifference to learning, his insensibility to the melancholy events which had happened in our family, and his pleasure in escaping from my own paternal society ; but a little reflection soon set me right on these points. His was not the age when learning of any kind is a solace or a pleasure, nor does the fortunate elasticity of youth accept any bereavement, however terrible, as a sufficient reason for perpetual sadness ; whilst as to the charms of my own society, I quite understood that a lad, who for nine months had sat at table opposite to a grave old face like mine, might wish to see younger faces and merrier. However, I confess that what Alexis learned during our time at the Val Ste. Véronique was not of a very intellectual nature. He picked up a good deal of natural history from the keeper, and acquired something of the knowledge which distinguishes Red Indians, — at least in Cooper's novels ; and he educated his legs, for he became an excellent pedestrian. All this is excellent in its way ; but another year of our wood-life would turn the boy into a half-savage, and unfit him for any other society than that of his dear friend, the Weasel. So our experiment of sylvan retirement is not likely to be repeated, except for briefer spaces. We may, in the future, permit ourselves the enjoyment of sylvan weeks or months ; but this long stay in the Val Ste. Véronique will remain alone in our memory as — THE SYLVAN YEAR.

INDEX TO "SYLVAN YEAR."

THE

UNKNOWN RIVER.

An Etcher's Voyage of Discovery.

BY

PHILIP GILBERT HAMERTON,

AUTHOR OF "THOUGHTS ABOUT ART," "CHAPTERS ON ANIMALS," "ROUND MY
HOUSE," "A PAINTER'S CAMP," ETC.

TOM.

BOSTON:
ROBERTS BROTHERS.
1882.

PUBLISHERS' NOTE.

In reproducing an edition of " The Unknown River" without the illustrations, the publishers have not thought it important to make any changes in the text. To the general reader their absence will not lessen the charm of the narrative, and those who prefer the more expensive edition with the etchings can gratify their tastes.

TO

THE REV. HORATIO N. POWERS, D.D.,

ONE OF THE MOST VALUED OF MANY KIND FRIENDS
IN AMERICA,

I DEDICATE THIS VOLUME.

PREFACE

TO THE AMERICAN EDITION.

———

IN the revival of the too long neglected art of etching, we who in England and France have tried to recover the right use of the needle have had to contend against many difficulties; and little of what we have hitherto done can be considered more than tentative and experimental. Etching, however, has this advantage over line-engraving, — that the comparatively rapid and spontaneous nature of the process, and its purely artistic and intellectual aims, obtain indulgence for many imperfections which would not be tolerated in a craft professing great mechanical finish. In etching, the spirit of the work is of more consequence than manual accuracy; and I have therefore allowed several plates to be published in this series, in which the manual work is rude, because they expressed my meaning, though in a rough way.

Nearly all the plates in this series — indeed, the whole of the landscape subjects — were etched directly from Nature, often under circumstances very different from the convenient surroundings of an engraver's table at home, with rain pouring over the plate, or daylight rapidly declining, joined to serious apprehensions about passing some dangerous rapid before I could get to a village inn, or find shelter beneath the thatch of some humble hamlet nestled in a nook of the wooded and rocky shore. Hence they are literally no more than the notes of impressions which an artist takes in his memorandum-book. As for the two or three subjects in which the author himself appears, it may be remarked, that, as he could not *pose* and draw at the same time, there was a peculiar difficulty in these attempts, which the author, from want of practice in figure-drawing, could scarcely be expected to overcome. A friend of mine, who is a figure-painter by profession, kindly made one or two slight sketches as helps; but, as the artist in question belonged to the severest French classical school (with which, as an artist, I have no affinity whatever, though as a critic I admire much of what it has accomplished), his sketches were conceived in a temper so opposed to mine that they turned out to be of no use for this particular purpose. Dog Tom was introduced at the urgent request of an unknown correspondent whose love of dogs touched the author in a tender place, and made him, somewhat rashly, turn animal-designer for the occasion. American critics are therefore requested to remember that the figures and dog are thrown in, as it were, simply for the reader's amusement, and not with any ambitious artistic pretensions.

However, such as they are, it has been the good fortune of these little plates to please many people in Europe, and amongst them a few more than ordinarily fastidious and capable judges. This may be attributed to the fact that in etching them the artist worked without the least reference to criticism of any kind, in the simple enjoyment of one of the pleasantest artistic expeditions imaginable. Indeed, although working very hard the whole time, I was under the delusion — it may be strictly said, *labored* under the delusion — that the voyage was a perfect holiday, a belief that was greatly encouraged by an absolute indecision as to which plates should be published and which de-

stroyed.   Another piece of luck was, that I had
no time, nor acid, to bite the plates there and then,
and so innocently fancied that they were all very
pretty (an etching done according to the old negative process always looks pretty when it is first
drawn, because the lines glitter charmingly on the
black ground), and felt agreeably encouraged, the
evil hour of disappointment being put off until my
return to home and the printing-press, which told
the painful truth with a frankness equal to that
of the most unpleasantly honest *dilettante* in
England.

It may interest readers who share the author's
boating propensities to know that the voyage was
undertaken in a canoe fabricated by his own hands
of paper, on a light skeleton of laths.   The whole
of the voyage was accomplished in this fragile
craft; but it is only honest to add that she became
leaky before it was over, and was condemned as
unriverworthy at the end.   Not that I think, even
now, that paper is a bad material for canoes, but I
had not then (1866) hit upon the right material
for gluing it.   I employed the *enduit Ruolz*, which
takes about twelve months to harden, and I had
not patience to wait the twelve months; so the

sheets or bands of paper did not really adhere, and the water oozed between them after a while. The proper gum to use for fastening paper so as to resist water is simply a strong solution of shell-lac in spirits of wine. I have a canoe at present and two small punts which are made of thin wood, lined with paper, applied with shell-lac. When a leak shows itself, it is stopped at once with a bit of paper and a touch of the solution, which dries immediately. An English oarsman tells me that for the last two years he has used bits of calico with the same solution in an old wooden canoe, which remains serviceable, thanks to the shell-lac. One result of the voyage narrated in this volume was the invention of a machine which is a punt by day on the water, and a hut by night on shore, large enough to stretch a hammock in. The American reader will no doubt pardon an allusion to these fancies, and believe them compatible with serious work in other ways. If it is boyish to like boating, in all its forms (as some grave and wise men seem to imagine), I hope to remain puerile yet a little longer. The cold sapience of age comes on rapidly enough to all of us; and it is not a misfortune to be able still to feel an irrational delight in a canoe when she glides in safety, and an imprudent indifference when she upsets.

The verses at the beginning of this book were written during the late war, in anticipation of an attack from the Germans, which took place shortly afterwards; and I witnessed the combat for many hours on the banks of the river, between Garibaldi,. who defended Autun, and a strong body of Bavarians who attacked it, — not exactly the moment for descending the river in a paper canoe! Another chapter was added that day to the long history of that ancient city by the Arroux; and as I watched the flight of the shells in the clear December air, and saw, beneath the moon, the fiery tongues darting from the mouths of the enemy's guns, I thought of many a former siege in times when war was less noisy and less bloody, but more cruelly protracted. How little I imagined, when writing the chapter about Augustodunum in this book, that I should see an army in battle-array drawn up against it, — a dark, thick line of Germans, with cannon glittering at intervals! Yet once again the Roman wall rang in echoes to the war-trumpet, and once again the river was stained with blood!

The wild rain drives in gusty showers,
  And past the moon the storm-clouds fly.
  The river, rising, hurries by
The gray 'old city of fair towers.'

The bayonets gleam in all her streets :
  All hearts are anxious, homes are sad —
  Oh, when shall victory make them glad,
And light the faces that one meets ?

O River ! once so fair and clear,
  Now dark as death thy currents flow ;
  They may be reddened — who can know ? —
Before the closing of the year.

O River ! made for my delight,
  I see upon thy wintry flood
  A floating corpse — a streak of blood,
And flames reflected in the night.

October, 1870.

THE UNKNOWN RIVER.

CHAPTER I.

ON a bright afternoon in autumn I lay on the green bank of a little stream. The stream was so little that my dog Tom cleared it at one bound, as in the eager excitement of a wildly impossible chase he rushed after flying game. Of course he never yet caught a bird on the wing, but his faith in the practicability of such an achievement does not seem to be in the least shaken by the discouraging lessons of a constantly recurring experience. Only a peregrine falcon, strong-winged, sharp-taloned, could follow and slay those partridges; but Tom dashes after them through and over all manner of obstacles, hoping, by perseverance, to attain his object, like the man who ran after the express train.

Tom is a dog of immense energy when out of doors, and the most listless indolence at home. He will run a hundred miles in a day, or swim fifteen, but he will not walk across the room without the most elaborate preparation in the way of stretchings which he believes to be necessary; and when the little distance is at last accomplished he falls down with a grunt as if extenuated by fatigue. Another peculiarity of his is the wonderful difference in the state of his affections, for when in the open air he is in the highest degree grateful for the least word or gesture of his master, and very demonstrative himself; whereas in the studio, where he passes too many tedious hours, he has scarcely ever been known to acknowledge a caress even by one movement of his tail. He is by race a setter, and seemed destined to a sporting career, but, as his master's fowling-piece has not been used for some years, Tom's instincts are quite undisciplined; and though in outward appearance the finest setter in the whole neighborhood, so that all sportsmen stop and look at him when he passes by, he is a lamentable instance of the consequences of a neglected education, and almost any dog of the same breed is professionally his superior, if only he has passed through a proper course of discipline.

We digressed into this talk about Tom after saying that he jumped over a brook. The brook murmurs over the pebbles about a hundred yards lower down, and we hear the refreshing sound coming on the faint, cool breeze; but the brook is very calm and quiet just here, and washes its sandy banks with silent regularity, taking the earth away grain by grain, an unceasing agent of waste, and author of endless change.

There is no rest to faculties wearied by labor like rest by a quiet stream, on a beautiful afternoon in summer. If you distribute your work wisely, and are fortunate enough to have work of a kind that may be done at your own hours, you will take care, when the days are long,

to reserve some considerable part of the afternoon as
sacred to utter idleness, and, if a quiet stream is within
an easy distance, there you will go and rest. Most men
under such circumstances take a rod and fish, but it does
not always happen that there is any thing which the dignity of manhood may avow an interest in catching. The
man who rents a salmon river in Scotland, or even the
Englishman whose trout stream is well preserved, may
go. forth with the implements of the angler and a con-
sciousness of noble aims. But can anybody past boyhood pretend to take an interest in catching minnows,
unless, indeed, he be a Frenchman who has just landed a
goujon, and is vain of the exploit?

It is curious how capable we all are of seeing people
and things every day of our lives without being once
prompted to ascertain any thing further about them,—
whence they come, whither they go, what their past has
been, or what may be reserved for them in the future.
The inhabitants of great cities, being satiated by the continual sight of innumerable persons and things, have this
indifference in the most strongly developed form, but it
may be observed in the country with regard to what is
most commonly seen there. For instance, brooks and
streams are very commonly met with in all northern
countries, and therefore very few people ever give a
thought to the geography of them, or have any thing
beyond a very vague and general notion of their course.
The inhabitants of the region through which the stream
passes usually know it at bridges and fords, and farmers
know it where it eats away the land, and where, in times

of flood, it is most likely to leave a deposit of sand and pebbles ; the angler, too, may have followed it for a few miles, and some professional landscape-painter or amateur may have explored a few of its most picturesque parts. But no man living knows the whole stream, and so there is always a great mystery about it ; and any one who cares to follow its course faithfully may enjoy all the keen delights, and feel all the unceasing interest, which belong to a true exploration.

In this especial sense our little river is indeed unknown, and as I lay idly on its bank on that bright autumn afternoon, it occurred to me clearly for the first time that the river came from far, and went yet farther ; that it was not confined to the fields about my house, and that this little scene was not a solitary gem, but one only of a thousand links in a long chain of various and unimagined beauty.

Why had not this been equally clear to me years before ? Why do we dream ever in one place, or travel by the same weary old roads, when infinite beauty and novelty are open to us ? It is because the beauty and the novelty are so *very* near to us that we miss them, and often so cheap that our pitiful small dignity despises them as something puerile. When we are weary of the monotony of life, and the whole human organism longs for the refreshment of change, we would go to the end of the earth, and, in order to defeat our purposes as completely as possible, carry our habits with us. We are accustomed to railways and newspapers, to bitter ale and sweet tea ; and we seek these things, and a thousand others that habit has rendered necessary, wherever on earth we go. And yet change more refreshing and novelty more complete are here within one day of slowest travel, than in journeys to Berlin and Vienna; for the truest change and best novelty are not in length of travel, but in the abandonment of habit, and especially in the zest of free and personal discovery.

There is an unfortunate belief that this glorious pleasure and passion of the discoverer are not now to be enjoyed in Europe. It is supposed that since every State in that region has been explored by many travellers, and even more or less accurately surveyed by the makers of maps, there is nothing new to be found there. The reason for this appears to be a confusion between the genuine pleasures of the discoverer and the satisfaction of his pride. Of course there can be nothing to boast of in discoveries such as those here narrated, but there is much to be enjoyed. The explorer of a nameless European river need not hope to be remembered like Livingstone or Speke, but he may set forth in the full assurance of finding much that is worth finding, and of enjoying many of the sensations, deducting those connected with personal vanity, which give interest to more famous explorations. It is necessary, however, to the complete enjoyment of an excursion of discovery, that the region to be explored, whether mountain or river, or whatever else it may be, should not have been already explored by others, or at any rate not with the same objects and intentions. A geologist has a certain satisfaction in marching, hammer in hand, over a tract of country not yet conquered for geology; and an artist likes to sketch in secluded valleys where it is not probable that any artist has been before. On the same principle a traveller who is fond of boating has an especial pleasure in descending some stream of which it may be safely presumed that nobody ever descended it in a boat. In this especial sense there is much yet to be done in the way of exploration, even in the most known countries.

No sooner had these ideas formed themselves in the writer's mind, than the little stream by which he was lazily reclining acquired a new importance; and the low music of its shallows, instead of being, as formerly, the lullaby of Mother Nature, became an awakening call to action, and a promise of joyful change. A thousand scenes rose rapidly before his mind, and the pipe which had languidly yielded half an hour before the tiniest puffs of smoke to the fragrant air now gave dense clouds, in which the smoker saw endless visions. He saw the deep, calm pools under the rich, overhanging foliage where the currents fall asleep together, like tired children that have filled the fields with their merry noise, till weariness fell on their swift limbs, and hushed their happy voices, and laid them in silent sleep under the soft green leaves. He saw the rapids dashing into white foam amongst the rocks, and the kingfisher glancing above them like a sapphire-flash in the sun. He saw the picturesque farms and cottages by the unfrequented shore, the gray, deserted castles, the antique cities, — the remains of a thousand years. And then came the majesty of the effects of Nature, the splendor of the sunset and the promise of the dawn, the mysterious poetry of summer twilight, and the long hours alone beneath the moon.

By this time it became impossible to remain quiet in that place any longer. Tom was called back from his vagrant courses and taken into his master's confidence. Tom listened with the utmost attention whilst the novel project was explained to him, and, although he may not have clearly understood its details, he perceived at least that action of some kind was meditated, and eagerly expressed his willingness to take a share in it.

CHAPTER II.

DURING the last few years the noble old art of etching has been revived by many painters. Some of my friends have practised it with distinguished success, and their example led me to recur to an art which I had first attempted in boyhood, and then neglected for many years. Of the means at my disposal for the illustration of the projected voyage none seemed better than etching, as it is the only kind of engraving which can be done directly from Nature, and the only engraving, too, which has enough of the spirit of liberty to harmonize with such a state of mind as that of a wandering canoist. It accepts laborious finish when the artist has time for it, but it also allows of rapid sketching when he is in a hurry. So it was decided that the voyage should be written, and that the illustrations should be etched from Nature on the way.

All the plates being prepared at home in my own etching-room (nearly sixty of them), I laid them on small drawing-boards, four to each board, and, by means of two very small screws to each plate, fixed them to the board so as to resist any jolting that they might be exposed to. There was no necessity to pierce the plates with holes to receive the screws, since, by placing the screws near the edge of the copper, the screw-heads held the plates firmly enough. I had previously tried many experiments for the carriage of plates, but none succeeded so well as this. If the coppers had been all of *precisely* the same dimensions, they might have been carried in a grooved box, such as photographers use for their glasses ; and this, no doubt, would have been a considerable economy of space, and would, at the same time, have saved the weight of all drawing-boards except one.*

Having screwed my sixty plates to a quantity of small drawing-boards, I slipped these boards into several grooved boxes ; each box provided with a lock and key. I then calculated the probable length of the voyage, and, having locked my boxes, sent them to inns at different distances down the river, to await my arrival. Thus I was never obliged to carry more than one box of plates at a time. It is unnecessary to go into the detail of my other preparations, which were of the kind now so well known to canoe-men, and to all who take an interest in canoe-travelling.

Here.is the little village from which the expedition started. The canoe had been transported thither in a cart, and as we arrived in the evening it was not considered advisable to begin the voyage till the following day. So I dined at the little inn, and after dinner went out to walk in the village by the shore of the narrow rivulet I was to embark upon on the morrow.

It was a clear, bright moonlight night (the etching, it

---

* It is necessary, however, when plates are carried in a grooved box, without being fixed to a drawing-board, to revarnish their edges before biting.

may be well to observe, is intended to represent a moonlight), and I wandered first about the river, and then in a small valley between precipitous little hills. I was in the heart of the Morvan, a highland district in the east of France, almost unknown to tourists. The river to be explored was the Arroux, that passes by the antique Augustodunum, and flows to the historic Loire. Nobody had explored it yet, and all the hazards of the enterprise rose before me as I leaned over the low parapet of the one-arched bridge at Voudenay.

The stream flowed under the bridge, after a curve like a snake in the grass, a silvery snake glittering under the moon. It came from a rustic mill, and the monotonous noise of the mill-wheel was the only audible sound, except the wash of the swift current on its pebbly margin. Beyond the bridge the stream looked dark and treacherous (for the moon was behind me then), and it went and buried itself in a black wood. This was all that could be seen of it from Voudenay. It was very narrow, and wilful and swift, and it hurried away into the black wood as if it had some deadly unavowable work to do there, somebody to stifle and drown in the awful shade of the forest.

What would this adventure bring me to? No man knew the river, no man had ever known it. Its course was full of dangers. A thousand strong boughs were waiting for me, stretching their gnarled and knotty arms across the stream. There were festoons of briers and thorns, there were deep black pools hidden under the intricate branches, there were roots in the river, and lower down I had to expect sharp rocks also. But could I not swim? Yes, in *water*, but not amongst stones and snags. Better the angry waves of the ocean, than these treacherous, suffocating snares!

There was just so much of apprehension as sufficed to give interest to the adventure. It amounted to a certainty that I should be upset (probably more than once), and have to struggle for dear life, but it was not so certain that I should struggle for it unsuccessfully. I returned to the little inn, and had a long talk with a set of peasants, and then went to bed in a room that looked out upon the river, the moonlight falling on the counterpane. The night was exquisitely calm, the peasants left the inn, and all the house was still.

I have accustomed myself to do with what suffices for the peasantry, and can therefore lodge in the poorest country inn or cottage without any painful sense of privation. This is a valuable accomplishment for an explorer of unknown rivers, who may have to lodge very simply from time to time. Thus, my first night I slept in the same room with a farmer's boy, my second with a wheelwright, and my third with the family of a poor miller; but I always had a bed to myself and clean sheets (though coarse). A sleepy traveller needs no more.*

We are afloat at last on the little river, which loses its terrors in broad daylight. I am in the paper canoe, and Tom is swimming behind. If that is the way he intends

---

* I much prefer the independence of a tent, but in this voyage it did not seem practicable to carry a tent and provisions.

to follow me during the whole voyage he will incur much
useless fatigue. Why does not Tom simply run along
the bank? he would go twice as fast, with a tenth of the
fatigue. I stop the canoe and reason with poor Tom. I
explain all this to him both verbally and by signs, but
his only answer is to look at me imploringly, and lift up
his wet old nose, and splash with his fore-paws, and put
one of them timidly on the edge of the canoe. I remove
the paw, and use one word of menace: the sensitive
creature takes an expression of extreme sadness; I have
wounded his feelings. I speak more kindly, and explain
that the only objection is to his bigness; that he is dearly
beloved, but unhappily too big; and that the canoe can
never carry both of us. The kind tones encourage him
again; this time he puts both paws on the canoe, and is
within a hairbreadth of upsetting her. My only chance
of getting the great, heavy, clinging paws off is to hit
their owner a smart rap on the nose with the paddle.

The narrow stream winds rapidly between banks of
gravel, and four little boys are running along the shore,
keeping pace with the swift canoe. Poor Tom cannot
swim quite so fast, and has been left behind for several
turns of the river, but now he comes galloping like a
racehorse across the fields. Nothing could be easier
and more agreeable than the voyage has hitherto been,
but the stream, already very rapid, runs faster and faster,
and is evidently carrying me into a dense grove of trees,
which will probably be long, and which may offer very
serious difficulties. The worst of these very narrow
rivers is that there is not room to use the paddle, and

you are carried along by the impetuous current with a
very slight chance either of stopping yourself, if rushing upon obvious peril, or of defending yourself against
the branches.

Here we are amongst the willows, carried rapidly
down a little sylvan tunnel, three or four feet wide and
about a yard high. It is wonderfully beautiful, if one
had only the time to appreciate its beauty ; but the current is so strong and impetuous, and the turns are so
numerous, that there is hardly time to think of any thing
but the management of the .canoe. The little boys are
behind somewhere ; I hear their loud chatter in the distance, and a yelping bark from Tom informs me that
he is yet alive, though I know not whether in water or
on land.

The first insurmountable obstacle is a young tree,
lying quite across the stream. It has not been cut down,
but the water has eaten away the earth about its roots,
and it has fallen across the current. If the place had
been a little more open I might have hauled the canoe
on shore and launched her a little lower down, but here
the dense underwood makes that manœuvre impossible.
Here come the little boys! I have a long and strong cord
in the canoe ; I tie a stone to one end of it, and throw it
over a branch to a boy on the other side, telling him to
tie it to the top of the fallen tree. Then, with the branch
for a fulcrum, I and the little boys on my side pull very
hard, and gradually the little tree rises and rises till the
course is clear. After overcoming other difficulties with
the help of the little boys, who were exceedingly useful,

I came to a place where the river was less impetuous, and where I had leisure to admire its beauty. The canoe was floating pleasantly through a rich wood of oak and chestnut with here and there a group of graceful poplars. It was a constant succession of scenes like the one given opposite, whose exquisite loveliness it is not easy to convey by Art.

CHAPTER III.

THE etching which illustrated the end of our last
chapter was done on the copper from Nature at
a little place that seemed convenient for lunch. A few
square yards of firm sand-bank lay between the dense
underwood and a deep pool, and this sand-bank was
covered with short grass. The canoe was drawn up
here, and her owner took out the materials for luncheon,
and made what would have been a solitary meal, if Tom
had not come up in great glee, doubly delighted at finding his master on *terra firma*, and all the signs of a
festival spread out around him. Tom loves his master
dearly, but his affection for beef and mutton is at least
equally strong; and it is probable that the happiest
hours of Tom's existence are such hours as this, when,
in addition to the excitement of travel, and the free ex-
penditure of his immense energy, he has the satisfaction
of dining with his master on terms of something like
equality. All the little boys had now been left behind
except one, and he, unfortunately for his own interest,
was on the other side of the stream. I wanted to get
him over and invite him to lunch, and crossed for the
purpose in the canoe ; but the canoe only held one person, and the youth did not sit steadily, so that before we
were two yards from the shore a capsize seemed inevitable, and I put back. After luncheon the voyage was re-

sumed; the nature of it will be best gathered from the etching.

There are two little villages in the region where I was now voyaging, about a mile apart, and bearing the same name of Voudenay; so, to know one from the other, the inhabitants have called them Voudenay-l'Eglise and Voudenay-le-Château. My first day's voyage was from one of these villages to the other, total distance *one mile*. The reader may laugh if he likes, but that is about the proper degree of speed for an artist on his travels.

After dark, as I wished to get a few miles lower down the stream, I determined, as the moon did not rise till rather late, to continue the voyage by lamp-light. The canoe was provided with a carriage-lamp for the purpose, which was fixed in the forepart of the deck, and it was found quite possible to pursue a very intricate and sometimes even perilous navigation by the help of this artificial light. Where the narrow river was most thickly shaded on both sides by dense vegetation, the branches meeting immediately overhead, and festooned with overhanging creepers, the lamp-light gave a strange beauty to the scene; and as the canoe floated somewhat rapidly down this little green corridor, it seemed like a voyage in fairyland. Every tiny leaf and spray, every slender thread of stalk, came for one moment out of the blackness of night into the full brilliance of the lamp-light, then passed into the darkness behind. An endless succession of this inexhaustible loveliness made the night voyage one continual enchantment, and I was not sorry to have seen a river under an aspect so strikingly new. There exists, unfortunately, an especial difficulty in rendering the peculiar beauty of these effects in etching ; and, knowing this, I have not wasted time in the attempt. The art of etching cannot reserve white lines of sufficient thinness and purity to give the effect of lamp-light on delicate sprays and grasses. The effect would be broadly given, and it would be possible enough to reserve white lines, but not with the fineness necessary to do full justice to the kind of delicacy which, in subjects such as these, would become the particular aim of the artist. Nothing struck me so much, in this delightful little voyage with the lamp, as the exquisite tenuity of the smaller plants as they came out with tiny leaves and stems against the black void of night. This might be approximately interpreted in wood-engraving, which most naturally works in white lines, but not so well in other processes. It was found that this voyaging by night added considerably to the interest of the exploration, for the mystery of the unknown was still more strongly felt when all that lay before us was in absolute darkness, and only became suddenly illuminated as the lamp approached.

He who attempts the exploration of a river not reputed navigable must be prepared for passages of such extreme difficulty that it may be necessary to remove his canoe altogether from the water, and drag her over the dry land. The morning after the voyage by lamp-light I had a good deal of such work, so much that at length I lost patience and hired a spring-cart in which both the vessel and her owner were transported by a fast-trotting horse to a place four kilometres lower down, whilst Tom galloped along the road with a sense of freedom much greater than any which he had enjoyed amongst the tangled vegetation of the river's bank.

When the boat was launched again, the stream took quite a new character. Instead of flowing with a current of equal breadth, and almost equal rapidity, it now alternately slept in calm pools and rushed hurriedly over short pebbly shallows. It is difficult, in words, to convey any idea of the variety of these beautiful pools, except by simply saying that they are various. If there were eighty of them, or a hundred of them, or however many there may have been, there were just as many new and admirable pictures. The shallows, too (though in passing rapidly over them we had not time to think of much but the safety of the canoe), were by no means the least interesting portions of the voyage, especially when they turned mysterious corners, and opened out new glimpses down the stream. At length we came to a pool so very long and so very tranquil that it seemed as if it would never end. The canoe glided over its glassy surface for many a long minute, and, just as the explorer rested on his paddle and the little vessel had gone forward alone so long that the impetus was dying gradually away, something unwonted was reflected in the smooth water; and, instead of the accustomed intricacy of boughs and fluttering of innumerable leaves, the voyager saw great stones as of a feudal castle, and surely on the green shore there stood a great ruin!

Whoever wishes to enjoy the sight of some noble ruin should come upon it in this unpremeditated way. One-half the delight of it is in the surprise. When you have been told at starting, by a guide-book, that 'at three miles from your inn is such a castle, now ruinous but formerly belonging to the Counts of, &c.,' and read the description of it in detail, you will either be quietly pleased or provokingly disappointed; but you will never feel the gladness of a delightful surprise. How noble look the gray old towers when the mind has been occupied all day with Nature and forgotten the history of man! What a welcome interruption to the perpetual sylvan harmony!

This ruined Castle of Igornay has towers, round and square, and a great court-yard, now full of the picturesque of a French farm. It has true machicolations, and must have been a strong place formerly. I found a young miller at the mill, who was more intelligent than lads of his class usually are, and a diligent reader of the newspaper. All the recent events in Italy and America were familiar to him, and he asked me a hundred questions. As it was cold, he made a blazing fire for me, and when I left helped to carry the boat, so as to avoid the mill-weir. There are some shallows just below Igornay, so the young miller waded and dragged the boat after him, with me in it, till we got into deeper water; would not hear of my wading, though I told him I was accustomed to it, and it would do me no harm. I paid him with nothing but thanks.

Few hours of travel have ever been more delightful

than those which now followed. A misty morning had ended in an afternoon of brilliant sunshine; the river was seldom less than three or four feet deep, and it turned continually, every turn offering some new and beautiful picture. The splendid autumn trees burned in the glowing light against the pure blue of an unclouded sky, and their long reflections trailed in glimmering gold on the calm surface of the quiet, sequestered pools. In such delightful scenery as this two or three miles a day seemed only too rapid travelling; I longed continually to tie the boat to some tree, and etch whilst any light remained. Soon, however, the stream narrowed again, and an impetuous current rushed under closely woven boughs, and between many awkward snags. Many a place seemed impassable, but the stream was too swift and too narrow to admit of any going back, and there was nothing for it but to shut one's eyes and dash at the branches with the paddle lying useless on the deck. Once the boat was jammed between a root and a tree where the stream was strongest, but I got through by pulling at the tree with both hands. As for landing, it was out of the question; *there was no land to be seen*, nothing but branches, — branches everywhere, overhead, before, behind, to the right and to the left, with an impetuous current under them, strong, swift, and deep. Then I heard a roar of water amongst rocks, and, in an instant, turning a corner, found myself at the foot of a steep hill, thickly wooded as far as I could see; and where the water had eaten into the hill the rocks were bare, a long row of them, and there were stones in the stream, over which it boiled with white foam. However, there was paddle-room, and I was really far safer than five minutes before under the branches. Whilst happily congratulating myself on my escape from so many difficulties, I turned a sharp corner ; a long branch lay athwart the stream from side to side, two feet above the water; the boat passed under it, but I could not diminish myself sufficiently to pass under it too, so was upset in an instant, and fell in head first.

CHAPTER IV.

THE shipwreck that ended the last chapter occurred just at sunset. After a night's rest in a poor cottage, the voyage was resumed in the brilliant light of a new and cloudless day.

The river was still most dangerous, slipping furtively and fast through the thickest underwood, turning sharply in unforeseen ways and places, like a panther in the dense jungle.

At last, after being hurried down a narrow channel, with about as much freedom of will as the train in an atmospheric tube, we came suddenly out upon a great open pool. This was the confluence of the Arroux and the Drée, and the Arroux had doubled his substance by this alliance.

Before it, he had been a wild young rivulet of the most imprudent and impetuous character; after it, he had times of leisure, and lived in visible dignity, an important occupier of land. Imagine a constant succession of large and beautiful pools linked together by rapid babbling shallows on which the canoe darted gayly and swiftly without grounding. The pools were deep, with sloping bottoms of the finest sand, perfect bathing-places every one, and every one a picture.

After many windings, one curve of the beautiful river disclosed a noble city, rising far off on the slope of a lofty hill, blue in the haze of the bright afternoon, with massive walls and many towers. It is old Augusto-dunum, once the sister of Rome and her rival, since then strong in the middle ages with all the picturesque strength of turret and battlement, now narrowed till within the vast enclosure of the Roman fortifications the market-gardener grows his vegetables, and the farmer ploughs his fields. Still by the quiet river the Roman wall stands rugged, rich branches hanging over it, heavy and full, and striving to reach the flowing water. And the Roman gate still augustly receives the traveller as he crosses the bridge over the Arroux, its gray arches and pilasters borne high over the mighty portals with a little statue of the Virgin between them, record of the faith of the middle ages, and a gas-lamp to prove that the modern time has come.

A great and wonderful Roman city, one of the noblest in the Roman world, stood here on the banks of the Arroux. In the circuit of her walls were more than two hundred towers. She had a great amphitheatre, and innumerable temples, and theatres, and baths. The soil to this day is full of fragments of precious marbles from the luxurious Roman dwellings. For a thousand years the earth has been yielding a harvest of antiquities, still inexhaustible ; columns, and statues, and bronzes, and pavements of Roman mosaic. And when the glorious Roman city, SOROR ET AEMULA ROMAE, was utterly ravaged and destroyed, there arose upon her site a mediæval city, smaller, yet not less beautiful, so that a king of France called it his 'City of Beautiful Towers.'

But the mediæval city has disappeared almost as completely as the Roman. The classic amphitheatre is razed to the ground ; of the mediæval cathedral (a great edifice of the purest Gothic) there remains *one* arch in a garden. The present cathedral is a church which stood under the shadow of the old one. A few fragments of the mediæval city remain here and there, — the house of Rolin, chancellor of Burgundy, now a carpenter's shop, a tower of the old Donjon, and here and there a few houses of the thirteenth or fourteenth century. Still Autun is a picturesque and quaint place, full of endless subjects for an etcher.

If there is any thing in the history of the past that can move or interest the present, the past of this strange city cannot leave us cold. Who could float here on the Arroux, close to the Roman wall, without thinking of all that has happened here, by the shore of this now peaceful river ? A simple catalogue of the vicissitudes of this city, unparalleled in the succession of her misfortunes, reads like some marvellous poem. The story of all her sieges has a Homeric grandeur.

First she was ravaged by Tetricus. After a resistance of seven months she was punished by the conqueror of Tetricus, Aurelian. Ruined by German hordes in the third century, she was sacked again under Diocletian. For twenty-five years she lay prostrate in her ashes, and the lands about her were untilled. She was punished again by Constantius after· the defeat of Magnentius. She was besieged by Chonodomarus and Vestralphus ; and after that by the Vandals ; and after that by the Bur-

gundians ; and then by Attila, who massacred the inhabitants and reduced the whole place to ashes. Childebert
and Clotaire ruined the city on the flight of Godmar.
The Saracens sacked Autun ; the Normans sacked it in
886, and a few years later Rollo pillaged it again. After
the battle of Poictiers the English came and burned part
of the city. Admiral Coligny came and burned a pri-
ory and the palace of an abbot, pillaging the abbey.
Towards the end of the sixteenth century Autun was
beseiged by the Marshal Daumont, and her archives
used for gun-wadding.

There are great incidents in her history : the martyr-
dom of St. Symphorien, the visit of Bishop Proculus to
Attila. The reader may remember the great picture by
Ingres, of the young Symphorien led by the Roman
lictors to execution, his mother encouraging him from
the wall. And if Symphorien sacrificed himself for his
faith, Proculus did the same for his fellow-citizens. He
went to Attila's camp to entreat him to spare the city,
and Attila beheaded him.

A memorable circumstance, in another way, was the
visit of Constantine to Autun. Constantine had raised
the city from ruin and despair; rebuilt her edifices, re-
established her schools. Finally he came in person with
his court. The expression of the people's gratitude
moved him to tears. He forgave them five whole years
of taxes.

The saddest history connected with the city is that of •
poor Queen Brunehault, early in the seventh century.
She wished to place her grandson (she had four) on the

throne of her son Tyherri, who was dead. Clotaire II. had the four sons arrested. The queen herself was arrested near the lake of Yverdun, and taken to Clotaire's camp in Burgundy. Three days of torture ended by a derisive promenade on a camel through the camp. Her grandsons were slaughtered before her eyes; then she herself was tied to the tail of a wild horse. Her body was brought to Autun and laid in a marble tomb.

But the grandest and noblest action of all that shed lustre on the antique city is the refusal of the Count de Charni to execute the massacre of St. Bartholomew. There were eight hundred Calvinists in the place, and the order came to slay them; but the advocate Jeannin recommended the *Bailly*, de Charni, to disobey the royal mandate, and they spared the Calvinists, to their own eternal honor. In his disobedience De Charni had the boldness to tell the king that he wished to leave him time to reflect upon orders issued in anger; and the Chancellor, on reading De Charni's letter to his majesty, observed: '*C'est un juge de village qui nous préscrit notre devoir!*'

The bishops of Autun, when newly appointed, used to make a solemn entry into their city. They had an episcopal residence at Lucenay (an exquisitely beautiful little place amongst the hills), and the new bishop left this residence in state. But he did not enter Autun at once. First he stopped at the monastery of St. Andoche, without the walls, and the abbess was obliged to entertain him and all his retinue. Near the convent there was a country-house called Genetoie, and the proprietor of it was obliged to give the bishop hot watei for his feet, an obligation much less heavy than that which fell upon the abbess. The bishop went to Genetoie to await the arrival of the chapter. When they came he presented himself at the closed door of the cloister, and was refused admission twice, answering each time that he was the bishop of Autun. The third time he was admitted, and took the oath.

The accompanying illustration shows all that remain of the house of Genetoie as it appeared when islanded by the flood of 1866.

CHAPTER V.

THE bishops made their entry into the city by the bridge of St. Andoche, but one of them went out of it again by the other bridge, and his carriage-wheels rattled on the road to Paris ; and in Paris he took up a new trade which he practised with the most distinguished success. Can you fancy Talleyrand as a bishop going about gravely in violet, and giving his precious benediction ? All the portraits I ever saw of him represent him in court dress, and nothing is more difficult than to rid one's self, even temporarily, of an association. The converse difficulty is that of imagining Pius IX. as an officer of dragoons. Had it been possible to see the two together, in the garb of their first professions, who would have guessed which was to become a famous pope, and which an equally celebrated diplomatist ?

When Autun was left behind, the river went for half a mile in such a stately manner that anybody would have given it credit for being navigable in the most serious sense of the word, — navigable for vessels laden with much more valuable merchandise than the materials of an unpopular art. In this long, quiet reach the lads from the college came to practise themselves in swimming, and this led me to think about three youths who may have bathed here not so very long ago, but whose history was at least as romantic as that of the

Greek and Roman heroes they read about in their text-
books at the college. One of these youths was called
Neapoleonne de Bounaparte,* and the two others were
brothers of his. Napoleon did not remain quite four
months at the college of Autun (the fact is unknown to
all his biographers), but his brother Joseph stayed here
as many years. Napoleon's little cell (the colleges had
cells in those days) still existed two or three years
since. It was positively known to be one of the five or
six that remained, but which there was no means of
ascertaining.

At length the towers of Autun, which showed themselves in glimpses during the windings of the river, and
completed in this way a hundred pretty compositions,
disappeared finally behind a spur of hill clothed with a
dense pine forest. Once more the canoe floated on a
quite lonely river without evidence of human labor or
habitation, except now and then the smoke of a distant
farm, or the cry of the drivers of oxen, generally the
name of each animal, sung out with a musical cadence.
It was pleasant to get into the perfect country again,
though Autun scarcely seems a city, and the Arroux
flows past it undisturbed by human interference except
when the strong brown-skinned horsemen ride up to
their waists in the water, and the fishermen cast their
nets.

Westwards rose the blue mass of the Beuvray, where
recent investigations have fixed the site of a city older
than Augustodunum, the Bibracte of the Gauls. But

* So entered on the college books.

Bibracte is almost without a history. Cæsar went there, and said that it was a great stronghold, and took provisions from it for his army, but left us scarcely a word of description. Bibracte can never have been more than a great fortified hill-village, or Gaulish *oppidum*, composed of very rude huts, huddled close together, and protected by solid walls built in the strong Gaulish way, with logs nailed together with huge nails, and earth and stone between them. Floating down the river in the evening I saw the last flames of sunset die behind the Beuvray, and the majesty of its purple crests was enhanced by its ancient strength. What is on the hill-crest now? On the site of the buried city is a forest of old gnarled beeches, and in the midst of the forest stands a little camp of huts, where an antiquary passes his summers, with a band of faithful men. Even now, I thought, in the evening, he is standing on some brow of rock, and looking over the boundless plains. He can see the lands beyond the Loire, and the whole course of the river that I am obscurely exploring. And when the twilight comes, and his evening walk is over, he will go to his wooden hut and sleep amidst his trophies. A pleasant, enthusiastic, absorbed life he has of it up there! He tells me that there is danger in the delight of it, the danger of a too complete abandonment to the enjoyment of glorious Nature and the dear antiquarian dream. He has a charming house in the city, with its *salons* filled with pictures and its museum with antiquities, and only a rough hut up there on the mountain; but every year as the summer comes he longs for the little hut, and the free range of the wild forest, and the fresh, high air, and the silence and the calm, and the healthy days of toil, and the lonely evening walks about the hill, and the vast, illimitable horizons. Whoever has once known this passion for wild Nature never, whilst health lasts, can lose it. There comes upon him every year, first a vague uneasiness, then a craving and longing for something, he knows not what, and then he begins to dream at night of regions beautiful and wild. The streets of the town, even the spacious country-house, begin to feel like prisons, and he wants to get out into the forest, or on the mountain, or float on flowing rivers and tossing seas.

In consequence of having etched the little plate which the reader has just seen, I had to paddle some miles after sunset, and did not reach the next village until darkness had fairly set in. The river, fortunately, presented few of those dangers which had been so frequent in the earlier part of its course. There were a few rapids here and there, but not dangerous rapids, and now and then one of those disturbed places called ' *remous*,' produced by sudden alterations in the form of the river's bed, often at a considerable depth. On the whole, however, the river was safer here than anywhere else on its whole course until it reached the plain of the Loire, and this will be readily understood after a few words on the geology of the district. The basin of Autun is a wide valley hollowed in the rock, formerly a lake-bed, and afterwards filled to the brim with alluvial deposits. It is through these deposits that the river cuts its serpentine course, and so long as it has to do with nothing but soft loam, and sand, and little rounded pebbles, the navigation is safe and easy. But when we come to the thick granite *lip* of the great basin, we shall find that the stream suddenly takes a new character. It is a lowland river in the basin of Autun, a highland stream for twenty miles as it crosses the rocky edge of the basin, and after that a lowland river again as it meanders through the plain of the Loire. This accounts for my getting safely to the inn after dark; a little lower down all night-travelling was out of the question.

But at the inn there was not a bed to be had, so I went to a country-house on the other side of the river, belonging to a rich land-owner whom I did not know personally, but who had an encouraging reputation for hospitality. Going to beg a night's lodging at a private house where you are unknown requires more assurance, I think, than any thing I ever attempted.

The master of the mansion was absent. The butler put his head out of a bedroom window and heard my petition. The butler was a very decent fellow; he dressed himself and came downstairs, and kindly heard all I had to say. For a moment I believed the difficulty overcome, but unluckily the favorable impression which I had succeeded in making on this man's mind availed me nothing, for the supreme authority was the house-keeper. She put her face out of a window, an ugly visage whose thousand wrinkles were strongly illumined by a candle in her skinny hand, and one glance assured me that she would be inexorable. Nothing could be more decided than her refusal.   And they talk of the tender-heartedness of women !

How and where I passed that night shall be a mystery. How do vagrants and vagabonds pass theirs ?

This castle is the Castle of Chaseux, a picturesque old ruin by the river-side, in a charming situation.   The effect is more picturesque in the etching than in the reality, because he who only sees the drawing does not realize the curiously small scale of the towers.   They are decidedly the tiniest towers I ever saw in any castle of feudal times ; but they looked larger, no doubt, when they had their pepper-box roofs.   For the rest the place is not without grandeur, and it has some literary interest as an occasional residence of Madame de Sévigné with that cousin of hers, Roger de Rabutin, Count de Bussy, commonly called Bussy Rabutin.   How she could ever forgive him his offences against decency, and his slanders against herself, is one of the mysteries of the womanly heart.   I never had the curiosity to read any thing of Bussy's except a few of his brevities.   One does not care to plunge into dirty water ; it is enough for me that Bussy shocked Louis XIV. (not an eminent model of virtue) to such a degree that the indignant monarch first put him into the Bastile, and afterwards banished him to his estates in Burgundy.   Here, at Chaseux, he spent part of his seventeen years of exile ; and it is one of the most extraordinary instances of the irony of fate, that the portrait of this wretched noble, who disgraced his family and his age, actually now hangs in the little village church where he heard mass, — hangs over the altar, and does duty as a saint. The dress and accessories have been repainted, to suit the present destination of the work ; but the worldly, seventeenth-century face looks still out of its flowing wig, between the tall candles on the altar. And the priest kneels, and the people bow, and the incense rises before it !

CHAPTER VI.

THIS etching is intended to represent one of those effects of twilight on the river which are amongst the charms of a lonely voyage. You see the great masses of the magnificent trees, but you hardly see the dark ground they stand upon, and it is not easy to tell where the water ends and the land begins. For the full enjoyment of such an hour as this, the scenery should be previously unknown to you, that the sense of mystery may be felt in its fullest intensity ; but, on the other hand, there ought not to be any apprehension of danger. It is *after* a day of peril and adventure that you most enjoy the peace of the solemn gloaming, when the reaches of the river sleep in their glassy calm, and the heron lifts himself languidly on the breadth of his great gray wings.

The heron is not mentioned by accident or put in for the sake of a poetical effect. He *was* there. He passed the canoe like a winged shadow, and then rose in the calm, pure air. Just then came a great flock of rooks, and, as they were flying about four hundred feet above me, the heron attained nearly the same altitude. The impertinent rooks attacked the noble bird (fit game for peregrine falcons !), and they plagued him and insulted him till he knew not what to make of it. But he presented his sharp, long beak to his assailants, and after teasing him for a quarter of an hour they left him to take his lonely way in peace.

Danger a-head ! O captain ! hearest thou not the roar of the rapid ?

It was time to cease gazing up into the unfathomable blue ; it was time to get a firm seat, and grasp the paddle well ! No more enjoyment of the poetry of the twilight, only a wish for the 'light of common day,' wherein all sweet illusions fade.

It was a great rapid amongst boulders, the largest of which were as big as the room you are sitting in, dear reader. They were scattered to the right and to the left, and one or two ugly fellows apparently barred the way. The channels were narrow and deep, and the water hissed and twisted amongst them like serpents. A yellow glimmer from the evening sky shone on the swift currents, and said, 'I show you all their complexity — select ! '

After another rapid, apparently much less dangerous than the first, and in reality (as often happens) much more so, the author arrived at Étang, a little old village, with two fine bridges and a railway station just built. There were some good subjects for etching in this place, especially the old houses near the river.

A relic of great interest for me (who have a peculiar weakness for tents and encamping) is preserved at the house of a rich man in the neighborhood of Étang. It is a fragment of the famous pavilion of Charles the Bold, which fell into the hands of the victorious Swiss, after the battle of Granson. The faded glory of its

magnificent embroidery recalled the costliest of all the
countless tents that ever trembled at the blast of trum-
pets ; and such is the power of great associations, that
the last rag and remnant of a splendor which dazzled
men's eyes four hundred years ago gives poetry to the
house where it is preserved, and to the very landscape
that lies around it.

Étang possessed, at the time of my visit, the ugliest
church (and this is saying a great deal) ever erected in
the eighteenth century. Preparations were, however,
being made for rebuilding it in a better form ; and, as
the new church was to be rather larger than the old one,
it was necessary to make new foundations in the surrounding graveyard. This disturbed numbers of crosses
which marked the graves, and these crosses were thrown
all together into a corner. The graves themselves had
to be cut through, and, as the workmen simply dug the
new foundation without troubling themselves about the
bodies, they often cut them in two ; so that many a dead
man had his legs amputated, or his head cut off, in a
manner quite unforeseen by his friends and relatives
when they interred him near the old church wall. The
writer witnessed some incidents of this kind which were
not much to his taste ; and when the new church stands
in the glory of its Gothic arches and groined vault, and
windows of brilliant stained glass, if ever he visits the
place again he will never be able to see the stately walls
of the fabric without thinking of the mutilated remains
on each side of their deep foundations.

Two fine hills are visible from Étang, not mountains,

but true hills of noble aspect, with rocky heights and deep ravines. One of these is the Beuvray, mentioned in the preceding chapter as the probable site of Bibracte ; and exactly opposite to the Beuvray, on the other side of the river, is the hill of Uchon, which may not have been the site of a Gaulish place of strength, but which still carries on its rocky height the tall fragment of a mediæval castle, once of considerable extent. I determined to explore this hill in detail, and gave a whole day to it, with two guides, — a village schoolmaster, who kindly offered his services, and a fine boy who was one of his best scholars. The first thing to be seen was a rocking-stone, a natural curiosity of sufficiently frequent occurrence to need little description here. This stone, commonly called ' La Pierre qui croule,' or by abbreviation 'La pierre croule,' is nearly at the crest of the hill, in a large wood. Without the help of my guide I could not possibly have found it. As in the case of other rocking-stones, many attempts to remove it from its pivot have been made by stupid peasants, who have harnessed oxen to it with ropes ; but the stone, which weighs nearly thirty tons, has always resisted all such attempts to deprive it of its peculiar virtue and pre-eminence. When set in motion, its movement is so regular and sure that it cracks nuts without injuring the kernel ; and as the schoolmaster was provided with nuts for the occasion, and we had a boy with us willing to eat them, I had the opportunity of verifying this.

The ' Pierre qui croule' is close to a deep ravine ; and near it, on the summit of the hill, were many magnificent groups of rocks. Wherever a plough could be driven, even on the very summit, the land was cultivated, and the cottages of the peasantry were scattered amongst the rocks in the little fields. The hill has an industry of its own, that of sabot-making, due to the neighborhood of the forest. I and my companions called at a cottage which was a workshop of *sabotiers*, and were very kindly received. As I was very thirsty, I begged the *saboticrs* to give me a drink of water, which one of them immediately did, in a perfectly clean but most extraordinary cup, — a new sabot. I had some rum in a flask, and offered a drink to all present ; on which the four workmen and three visitors provided themselves with sabots, and, having half filled them with water, passed the flask to flavor it. A little incident occurred then, which amused and delighted me by its quaintness and originality. It was proposed to *trinquer*, to klink,* and the seven sabots were solemnly struck against each other in token of good-fellowship. They were not the most elegant of cups, and they did not ring very musically when struck ; but, after drinking out of glasses all one's life, it may be an agreeable novelty, for once, to drink out of a wooden shoe.†

---

* The old Shakspearian word.

† What added to the fun was, that, in addition to the schoolmaster and boy, a friend of mine accompanied me, who is a dignitary of Autun (not mentioned in the text for that reason), and it was highly comic to see his dignity condescend to such a drinking-vessel. Some time afterwards, an old gentleman who had heard of this incident, but did not know the name of my companion, told the story, with the remark that 'no eccentricity could astonish one in an Englishman, but the wonder

Uchon is the quaintest little hill-village that I ever met with in my travels. Perched on the very highest and steepest part of the hill, not safely on the summit, but on the slope just below it, the village commands a view of immense extent. There is not a place of equal height for sixty miles before it, and the eye ranges to the illimitable plain of the Loire. It is just the site for a feudal castle, and accordingly we find the last remnant of one, — a tall fragment of wall, leaning, like the Tower of Pisa, over the narrow road, with a fine Gothic fireplace high up its side where the floor once was, and where the lady sat in her lofty chamber, and looked out on the world below. The most curious thing at Uchon is the church, which simply follows the slope of the ground, the floor in the interior being as steep as the hill-side on which the edifice is built. As the altar is at the higher end, the effect produced is really fine, and might be worth imitating artificially.

The walk was enlivened by a continual conversation with the school-master, who was even more intelligent than his usually intelligent class. Amongst other interesting things, he mentioned several words which, so far as he had been able to ascertain, were peculiar to the place. Two of these were especially interesting, — the verb *douler*, to suffer (Lat. *dolere*), and the substantive *vialet*, a foot-path (diminutive of *via*).

The writer, in his descent of the mountain, was in

that state of excitement peculiar to landscape-painters
when they find themselves in a place full of good material for study. The foregrounds were excellent, especially the magnificent old trees, and the groups of oxen
and peasants in the steep little fields composed in a
charmingly accidental way. The worst of it was, that,
being anxious to resume my voyage, I had not time to
etch upon the mountain; and the next etching I did was
at noon on the following day, when I had landed in a
quiet place for lunch, and the canoe lay idly on the
water.

CHAPTER VII.

THE river now flowed through very majestic sylvan scenery, equal in some places to the finest parts of the Thames, and curiously destitute of every thing that we in England are accustomed to consider especially French in character. The banks were often rocky, and the foregrounds rich in heather and fern, with immense quantities of broom. Out of this rose gigantic oaks, that would have done credit to any park in England. Here is a sketch of the trunk of one which I found to be fifty feet in circumference.

This noble tree was in every respect one of the most perfectly and equally developed I ever met with. Sufficiently isolated for its growth not to be in the least interfered with, and yet at the same time not too much exposed to any prevailing wind, its massive column rose straight upwards, and its enormous branches (themselves equal to considerable trees) spread equally in every direction. I have only given the trunk here because the attempt to represent the whole tree always failed to give any notion of its vast dimensions. Its crown of foliage, too perfect and too regular to be picturesque, was like a sylvan world erected on a pedestal. At some distance the tree did not strike one as being particularly big, probably on account of its beautiful proportions, and the not inconsiderable size of its neighbors; but once under the shade of the great branches, the spectator suddenly becomes aware of the weight and size of the enormous limbs, and then makes deductions concerning the strength of the trunk that can support them. The impression is completed by making the tour of the trunk. The whole tree is perfectly sound, and neither lightning nor human hand has ever lopped off one branch.

An impression prevails in England that the French are indifferent to sylvan beauty, probably because wood is their principal fuel, and therefore an immense destruction of young trees takes place yearly in the forests, whilst the peasants amputate the arms of the older ones. They often, however, preserve fine timber for ornament as we do; and I learned without surprise that the fine oaks, of which the giant just described was the chief and king, enjoyed, in consequence of a decree of the owner of the soil, absolute immunity from the axe. Many trees in the same neighborhood, especially the old chestnuts, must count their age by centuries; and the beeches that crest the Beuvray, though not finely developed, owing to the altitude of their situation, give every evidence of antiquity. The park of Monjeu, an estate belonging to the Talleyrand family, near Autun, is full of magnificent timber even yet, though much was destroyed by the imprudence of a man of business, who, in the owner's absence, sold it to a contractor. The haste with which this unfortunate contract was annulled, at a heavy loss, so soon as M. de Talleyrand became aware of what had been done, is a proof that he valued the timber for something more than its mere salableness. But the best evidence that the French are not indifferent to the beauty of their trees is, that scarcely a single town, however insignificant, is without its public avenues, in which the trees are encouraged to attain their fullest possible development. What English town, of equal population, has any thing comparable to the magnificent avenues that encircle Sens?

The navigation during this part of the voyage was more agreeable to the traveller himself than likely to prove interesting when narrated. Here and there the rocky bed of the stream produced narrow passes of a trifling degree of difficulty, and after them the river widened into long and tranquil reaches, over which drooped the heavy-leaved branches, dipping their extremities in the deep water that reflected them. At length, when these were gilded by the refulgence of sunset, the sound of a mill-wheel became audible in the distance, and that pleasant rush of water that may indicate either a rapid or a weir. Then a village church came into sight, and finally a few roofs of picturesque mossy thatch, which turned out to be the whole village.

The church was one of those simple old Romanesque edifices which abound in this part of France. The architects of to-day have broken with the Romanesque tradition, and, in order to get more imposing effects of height and size, have adopted a very plain kind of lancet-Gothic. But for a little village church I think nothing can be so well adapted as the Romanesque, with its tiny apse and aisles, and its general air of snugness, completion, and solidity on a most unpretendingly small scale. A little Romanesque church never seems to need any thing more ; but a very plain, tall, lanky, modern, Gothic church, with its invariable gawky tower at the west end, looks hungry and uncomfortable, as if the architect had been pinched in his financial conditions, which he very generally is, and at the same time obliged to give as many square yards of wall as possible for the money.*

The church of this little village of St. Nizier had been closed at the Revolution, and never opened since. The inside was full of straw, and my canine companion rolled his wet hide upon it in a manner which appeared to indicate that he would consider it very eligible bedding if we stayed all night there. Seeing no sign of any thing like an inn amongst the half-dozen cottages which constituted the whole burgh, I felt greatly inclined to accept the dog's suggestion ; but, although the church was an ample and sufficiently comfortable bedroom, one could not hope to find any dinner there, and I looked about the small cottages if haply there might dwell therein some man or woman skilled in the preparation of food. Now a certain observant villager, seeing me thus in quest of something which I had not found, came

---

* One of these churches was erected lately in a certain commune, and when the plans had been made I asked the priest what sort of architecture had been determined upon ; but neither the priest, nor the *maire*, nor any other notable of the place, could tell me, the fact being that, though the plans had been presented for their august approval and honored therewith, they did not know the difference between one sort of architecture and another.

with much courtesy and proffered me his services ; and it turned out that this villager was in a position to be particularly useful to a traveller, for he was at the same time innkeeper and mayor, a man capable at once of nourishing the stranger, and casting over him the ægis of political protection. He lived in a small cottage whose worst defect, in my view, was that of being alarmingly damp. It had been submerged in a great flood which had happened a few weeks before, and the walls were still full of moisture that oozed out from the plaster on every side. However, here I stayed two nights, and contended against the damp by means of a blazing fire and warm bedding. The place was rather amusing, foɪ the inn was at the same time the village shop, and my bed was in the shop itself ; so I had ample opportunities for studying the inhabitants of the place. As all the villagers went to bed about sunset they did not disturb my privacy in the evening ; but they began their shopping at such an uncommonly early hour in the morning, that it was rather a perplexing matter how and when to go through the business of dressing. The most amusing plan seemed to be to lie quietly in bed and watch them ; but this, though agreeable to a sluggardly mind, did not especially advance my own projects. One thing struck me very much, and that was the total absence of any visible stock-in-trade ; yet notwithstanding this apparent deficiency every article in demand always came forth at once.

The innkeeper was a man of some culture, and both could and did read, which is more than can be said of most French villagers of his class. I found books in his house which interested me exceedingly, especially 'Charton's History of France,' which is carefully illustrated from authentic memorials of preceding centuries, not with fancy compositions invented by some artist of our own. My host was doing what he could to increase the free library in the village, already considerable enough to be a great treasury for a poor student. He took me to see it, and I certainly had not expected to find a library in a place where there was not a tiled roof, nor even a priest.

Every one who has travelled (unless he be a downright gourmand) will probably have remarked, that it is not the places where we have fared most luxuriously, which usually leave the most agreeable impression upon the mind. At the fine places we expect too much, I think, and are almost always either disappointed or within a very little of being so. I have heard a whole carriage full of men do nothing but grumble and swear as they drove home after a most extravagant Greenwich feast, and I have seen the same men quite happy and contented with a slice of beef and potatoes. In this latter frame of mind, which expects nothing, and is always satisfied with what fortune sends, did the present writer stay his two nights at St. Nizier ; and he left it with a pleasing impression, as he walked down, paddle in hand, towards the rocky shore, his canoe being borne with great ceremony behind him by the mayor himself and one of the most active and influential members of the Common Council. Nevertheless, it may be acknowledged that the beautiful scenery lower down the river was not a whit the less attractive for the fact, that a renowned French cook kept an hotel somewhere in those more favored regions, — an hotel where a man might not only eat, but *dine.*

CHAPTER VIII.

A FTER St. Nizier the river became even more picturesque as it proceeded. Rushing swiftly and
merrily between willowy islets it carried the traveller
along with very little consideration for his private tastes
and preferences. The only possible exercise of choice
was at the moment of selecting the channel; after that,
retreat was simply out of the question, and all that could
be done was to keep as clear of accident as might be.
A river voyage has been compared over and over again
to the course of human life, and no wonder, for the
simile holds good in the minutest details, especially in
such a voyage as this. How very important, for example, and at the same time how very difficult, it is to
choose the right channel when several lie before you of
which you are about equally ignorant! If you have
made a mistake, if you have chosen the wrong profession
or the wrong wife, then there is nothing for it but to try
to get along as safely and creditably as you can, and
avoid an upset if possible. If the mistake has been made
it cannot be unmade, but skill and courage may still often
save a man from its most disagreeable consequences.
There are lives which must be as easy as it would be to
paddle down the broad Loire with the ordnance map in
your pocket, which shows the safest way everywhere;
but these existences lose in interest what they gain in

safety: and the most interesting life to live, like the best
river to explore, is one in which the course is not known
in detail beforehand, but constantly calls for the exercise
of skill and judgment, and is even to some degree
affected also by pure hazard.

The tiny hamlets on the shores of the river were often
very beautiful in their way, or, at least, very picturesque,
and quite unspoiled by any modern perfections and reg-
ularities of brickwork or of roof. Many of the best of
these hamlets are of great antiquity. I know one where
the cottages have not received any important addition,
and have not been repaired in any other sense than that
of simply replacing parts as they decayed, for the last
four or five hundred years. And the life in them has
followed the same unswerving tradition. The language,
the religion, the customs, of the inhabitants remain almost precisely what they were in the Middle Ages. The
oxen are yoked to the *char* as they were centuries ago ;
the *char* itself is a precise copy of that used by remote
ancestors ; the ploughs and other implements of agriculture are untouched by modern improvement. We
know little of the lives that are led in these out-of-the-
way cottages and hamlets, because it is so difficult for
us to get rid of London and Paris, of literature and science, and modern thought and reflection ; so difficult
to realize what a life must be which neither London nor
Paris influences in any perceptible way whatever ; a life
quite beyond the range of literature, inaccessible even
to the cheapest of cheap newspapers, ignorant of every
thing which makes us men of the nineteenth century

instead of the fifteenth or the tenth. This simple patri-
archal existence will not, however, endure very much
longer; the light of modernism is breaking in upon it
already here and there, through chinks in its ancient
walls. It is difficult to find a place which is forty miles
from a railway, and the railway brings its influences with
it. A youth leaves the parental cottage for some distant
place, and when he comes back gives his parents some
rude notions of geography. The region through which
flows 'the Unknown River' is so near to the Alps that
their white crests may be seen occasionally from the
summits of these hills; yet the peasants are not aware
that the Alps exist. Once, however, a young man went
to work at Grenoble, and he came back and told the
people in his village that there were high mountains on
which the snow never melted, even in the heats of summer. This is the way a little knowledge comes to them;
it comes personally, by oral communication, not by
books. A soldier comes back from Mexico, and tells
them that Mexico is beyond the sea. I was greatly
astonished at the little hamlet, here faithfully represented, to hear a man of saddened aspect speak of
Boston. 'What Boston?' I asked, wondering how he
should know of any Boston unless there were such a
place quite near to him in France. 'It is of Boston
in the United States of America, that I am speaking,
sir,' answered the man of the sad countenance, astonishing me more and more, for what French peasant
knows that the United States exist, or the Atlantic
Ocean either? So then he told me his tale, and as it

is both a pretty tale and a true one, I repeat it here for
the reader.

It is simple and short enough. He and his wife were
very poor indeed, almost destitute, and so, though they
loved each other much, she went out as a nurse to Paris.
In Paris she entered the service of some rich Americans,
who, when they returned to their own country, offered
her terms so tempting that she crossed the Atlantic with
them. Year after year she sent her earnings to her hus-
band, and year after year he laid by the hard-won gold
until there was enough of it to buy the cottage he lived
in, and a little field or two ; enough to keep them in independence all their lives. He took me into the cottage,
and showed me his wife's portrait (blessings on photog-
raphy, that enables a poor man to have a portrait of the
absent or the dead !) and kissed it tenderly in my presence, and said how hard the long separation was, and
how he looked for her return. As he said this the tears
ran down his cheeks, and he showed me the bright good
walnut furniture in the cottage, and the fields by the
river side, and said that all this comfort was *her* doing,
all this wealth *her* winning. She had learned to write
on purpose that she might write to him, and month after
month her kindly letters came, cheering him under the
long trial of her absence. It was four years since she
had left the cottage, and for these four lonely years the
father had been like a widower, and the children had
grown around him. And now the months went ever
more and more slowly, as it seemed, when he wanted
them to go faster, for this very autumn she was to sail

and come to enjoy the peace she had created. May the ship that brings her paddle prosperously across the wide Atlantic, and the good woman find her way in safety to her own cottage, and to the loyal heart that yearns and waits for her so wearily!

> ' Fair stands her cottage in its place
>   Where yon broad water sweetly, slowly glides ;
> It sees itself from thatch to base
>   Dream in the sliding tides.'

The character of the river became more and more strikingly picturesque as it advanced towards the Loire. Promontories of rock jutted into the stream, which took sharp curves under steep and richly wooded banks, and went to sleep in out-of-the-way corners, where it made wonderfully perfect and tranquil harbors for the canoe. Sometimes there would be a ruin on some height, which though on a small scale was not without grandeur, and afterwards the rich meadows and woods descended to the level of the water. Then came a long decline where the water rushed over a thousand dangerous crests of rock, and after that a pool so long and sleepy and quiet that it seemed as if the river had finally made up its mind not to flow any more, but to lie for ever in that place like a fish-pond. However, when it *did* awake and start again, it started with such freshness and energy that the interval of rest had evidently done it good, and it went gambolling amongst the rocks in a manner which, if not absolutely alarming to the canoist (one never confesses to feelings of serious alarm) did at least call for the best exercise of his skill.

In this manner we came to one of the very loveliest

places I ever saw in the course of all my wanderings, a place where a rich avenue came down to the water's edge. I left the canoe and walked up between the stately trees. When the long avenue came to an end I found myself in a noble demesne with a little lake, and an island in the middle of it. On that island once stood a noble feudal castle, where royal guests have been entertained; and the castle lasted, in all its strength, till the last century, when a great fire gutted it from roof to basement. It would have been a noble ruin, but the marquis, its proprietor, in sheer anger at the accident, utterly effaced every vestige of the stronghold of his ancestors; so that literally not one stone remains upon another. An exquisite old gateway, of the loveliest Renaissance work, with sculpture as delicate as that of Melrose, has been re-erected at a little distance by the present owner, who inhabits a simple modern house. He intends to build a new castle more worthy of his ancient name; but an ancestral mansion, once destroyed, can never be replaced. Even an ancient avenue may be replaced in time: young trees will grow old, and they succeed each other naturally in generations; but the real feudal castle is one of those things that neither man nor Nature restores when once it is destroyed and lost. We may build an imitation of it, but not the thing itself; the spirit that created it has departed, never to return. There was something terribly childish in the anger of that old marquis! The flames had destroyed the woodwork; and so, in a pet, he finished what they could not achieve, and levelled all his towers!

CHAPTER IX.

A CERTAIN critic in the 'Athenæum' has lately accused the author of this little narrative * of 'intense egotism;' and not very long since somebody complained that he talked too much about his dog. Now, in the present chapter, if the story of the voyage is to be faithfully narrated, there ought to be a thrilling account of a perilous and extraordinary shipwreck ; but if the writer is neither to talk about himself, nor his dog, nor any thing that is his, how is he to tell the tale ? The truth is, that if you listen to critics you will never publish any thing. One critic dislikes the egotistic bits, another hates all landscape descriptions, another cannot endure any allusion to past history, another feels bored by any thing resembling philosophical reflection, a fifth scorns the repeater of an anecdote, and so on; till, if you try to please them all, simple abstinence from writing is the only thing possible for you. On the other hand, if you eliminate one of these elements in order to please one critic, the others immediately complain that it is wanting. It is a fact, that a very eminent publisher complained to me a little while since that there was not enough about myself in a MS. I sent him, and too much about Julius Cæsar and the Gaulish System of fortifica-

* These chapters were first published in the *Portfolio; an Artistic Periodical.*

tion. Now it so happens that the present chapter might be dedicated plausibly enough to Julius Cæsar, for he crossed the Arroux at this very place in his chase after the Swiss; and no doubt it would be more modest, and more scholarly, to give a learned little dissertation on that event than an account of my own shipwreck. The only objection is, that most readers would skip the speculations about Cæsar.

It was already rather late in the evening, and I was sketching by the river-side at Laboulaye, and smoking the pipe of consolation. The high-road passes not far from the river at that place, and my dog-friend, hearing the sound of wheels, went to see what sort of a carriage was passing by. Soon after the carriage stopped, and I heard the sort of bark which a dog gives when he meets an old friend, — a bark of joyous congratulation.

It was a fat doctor of my acquaintance, who was driving towards Toulon-sur-Arroux in the cool of the evening. It is his nature to be sociable, and he is a hater of solitude. He had recognized Tom at once, which is easy on account of the dog's uncommon size and beauty, and so knew that I could not be far off. Then he admired the canoe. — Would I take a passenger? He would be delighted to go with me to Toulon if I would give him a berth. — Could he swim? — Swim! not in the least, but he would risk the adventure nevertheless. — Well, but then he would most likely be drowned. — He did not care if he were.

Solitude is very pleasant, but students of landscape get rather too much of it perhaps, and at times one will incur a risk for the pleasure of a genial companion. So it was settled that the doctor should send his servant on to Toulon with his carriage, and that we should see how the canoe would behave with both of us. Amongst my stores I had a waistcoat containing India-rubber air-bags, to be worn whilst descending particularly danger-ous rapids; so I made the doctor put this waistcoat on, and inflated the air-bags, till he looked like a pouter pigeon. All being ready, we got into our places very steadily, sitting face to face ; and I took the paddle, making my passenger promise to turn neither to the right hand nor to the left. He quietly lit a cigar, and sat as coolly as if he had been on a safe ship and a deep and tranquil sea.

The river here was a series of rapids and deep pools, where the swirling water was always trying to get you under the steep walls of rock. It was necessary in several places to cross a rapid to avoid being caught between great boulders, and we had very near shaves for it once or twice. The coolness of the doctor all this time was admirable to behold. He smoked his cigar qui-etly and sat with perfect equilibrium, so that I had no trouble with him of any kind except for his weight, which was considerable indeed. I praised his self-pos-session, and he answered that he had perfect confidence in my skill. I said I could not promise to get us through such a succession of dangers without an accident. 'In that case,' he replied, 'I am satisfied that you will do what can be done, and am content to take the consequences.' 'But, if we capsize, you may be drowned in spite of the waistcoat,—the current is tremendous.' 'I'm not afraid of death,' he answered with unfeigned courage.

He had hardly spoken the words, when, in attempting to cross the rapid to avoid an ugly piece of polished granite, about the shape and color of a whitened skull, I found it could not be done without uncommon effort, and broke the paddle in trying. Of course, after that, the upset was inevitable. The doctor did not stir, but smoked tranquilly still, not uttering a single word; the canoe was carried against the granite, broadside on. She rose upon it a foot or two, then slipped to the right a little, the stern dipped, the water clasped me round the waist and filled the well, and she (slowly as it seemed) capsized. Just as she went over, but not before, I saw the doctor throw away his cigar. Once in the water I found myself hurried along irresistibly, but soon got my head clear, and hoped, by surface swimming, to escape contusions on the knees. In this way I got down the rapid quite safely, and was hurled at last into a deep pool, where, after the first plunge, I felt comparatively at ease. Finding it impossible to land on the rocky side, I allowed myself to float into an eddy, and was quietly carried out of the central current into a sort of tiny haven or bay, where I landed.

It then became necessary to think about the doctor. He was not far behind. Like myself he had been carried down the rapid, and was now bobbing about in the great pool, thanks to the inflated waistcoat. But he had not the slightest notion about directing himself, and had got into a *cercle vicieux*, in a whirlpool that turned him

round and round. Seeing that he would probably be
carried out of the pool into some other rapid, I thought
it time to set about saving him, and called out that he
was not to grasp me, but simply lay his hands on my
shoulders. When I approached him in the water (rather
cautiously at first), he behaved with the same coolness
he had displayed in the canoe. He laid a hand on each
shoulder so lightly that I hardly felt it, and I towed him
easily into port.

He began by expressing polite regrets ; but these were
interrupted by the arrival of the canoe, bottom upwards,
and many articles that had been in her. There was the
box of etchings, which I swam for first, and many another
thing. Luckily, I secured the canteen, and the doctor
prescribed brandy for both of us. After that, we hauled
the canoe under the copse, and left it.

After walking about half an hour through a dense
wood and over very rough and broken ground, we came
to the river again, where it spread itself into a little lake,
and at the lower end of the lake there was a weir and a
mill. We looked miserable creatures, both of us. We
had lost our hats, and the miller's wife took us for
beggars. But the doctor entered exactly as if the
place belonged to him, and declared that we must have
a change of raiment. Now, considering that we were
constructed by Nature on totally opposite principles —
resembling each other as the Tower of London resembles the Clock-tower at Westminster — it is obvious that
the miller's clothes could not fit both of us. When
we were dressed in this disguise, the doctor filled the

miller's suit to overflowing, and looked like an overpacked carpet-bag, whereas the present writer had the appearance of a village school-boy who had suddenly outgrown his habiliments. At first the miller's wife viewed us with suspicion, but the doctor made himself so agreeable that the cloud disappeared from her countenance, and the light of it beamed upon us kindly.

By this time it was dark, and our hostess took clean, coarse sheets out of her polished presses, and laid them on two of the four beds that were in the room. But the doctor wrote a few words on a slip of paper, and sent it to Toulon by a little boy, and in a while his carriage came up to the mill with the boy in it, and under cover of night we made our entry into the town, still in our borrowed clothes. The worthy innkeeper was just going to bed when we arrived, but the active little *marmitons*, in their white jackets and caps, set to work with alacrity at their tiny charcoal fires and shining copper-pans. And we sat down, in our queer costume, to the best of suppers, with wonderful appetites and joyous laughter. And so pleasantly ended our shipwreck ; but it might have ended not so pleasantly as that. One thing is certain, without the inflatable waistcoat the doctor's patients would have benefited by his advice no more.

As this chapter has been written from the beginning in open defiance of criticism, I may as well sin to the very end, and speak of the faithful hound that followed me. He needed no inflatable waistcoat, but came dancing down the rapids like a cork, and never left us. He is the most indefatigable of swimmers; mile after mile did he follow the canoe, like some tame, affectionate seal. And is he not to be mentioned, — he, the unwearied follower, the brave defender, the faithful companion and friend? No one dare approach the canoe when he is there; and shall he not sup with us after our shipwreck, and be honorably mentioned here?

Ce qu'il y a de meilleur dans l'homme, c'est le chien.

CHAPTER X.

THIS little etching gives a tolerably good notion of the present condition of those fortifications which, in the middle ages, were the citadel of Toulon-sur-Arroux.   The etching was made some time since ; had it been executed during the last few weeks, I should have run considerable risk of being ill-used as a Prussian spy.   For it is not safe, in this month of September, 1870, to draw so much as the wicket-gate of a cottage garden anywhere in France, whether you are a Frenchman or a foreigner ; and, if the latter, your chances are so much the worse.   It had formed part of my plan to republish this series of papers with additional etchings on a larger scale, and I began these additional plates in the month of July, intending to revisit the scenery of the whole river, and select about a dozen of the finest subjects.   I had done a few of these when the great spy-mania took possession of all French minds, at least in the lower classes, and there arose such a hubbub about my doings over an extent of country thirty miles in diameter, that it would have been absolute madness to let myself be seen with any thing of the nature of drawing materials about me.   So the larger etchings were brought to an abrupt termination. The reader, who is by this time familiar with the slight and purely artistic little plates which have illustrated these chapters, will be amused at the notion that they can be supposed to be of any imaginable utility to Von Moltke and the Crown Prince in their brilliant invasion of France; but the peasantry in these parts have made up their ingenious minds on the subject, and, as to arguing with them, one might as well try to argue with a tribe of hostile savages. Like the country people in England, they confound drawing with surveying, and believe that artists are men employed to make maps. Who employs them? that is the next question; and the answer, of course, is, 'The King of Prussia.'* When I made these little plates at Toulon, I was enjoying one of the blessings and privileges of peace. He would be a bold man to-day, who would sit down and draw a citadel anywhere in France, even though it had been dismantled for the last three hundred years.

Here, again, is the bridge. If any one drew that bridge to-day, it would clearly be that the Prussians might pass over it. But in those happy times of peace the peasants felt rather flattered that a 'map' should be made of their bridge; and the more knowing ones suggested that, since the present writer made such good maps of bridges, he would do well to make one of the new railway-bridge at Étang, which was of iron, and perfectly straight, and had been pushed from shore to

* In the good old times, before Bismarck was heard of, *travailler pour le i vi de Prusse* used to mean working without any probability of payment. In that sense, undoubtedly, the present writer, like most artists, has worked a good deal for the King of Prussia. But tell it not in Gath, repeat it not in the villages of Burgundy!—a pleasantry of that kind, in these times, might cost the jester's life.

shore all in a single piece, just as you would put a plank
over a rivulet.

Toulon is a very quaint little town, with a rather picturesque market-place on a hill-top, and the streets sloping down on all sides to the river and the surrounding
country.   On the top of the hill is the old citadel, of
which one tower serves for the tower of the old church.
The population of Toulon has diminished of late years,
but the church, which used to be considered quite large
enough for the place (a quaint old Norman-looking
edifice), has not satisfied the ambition of the present
incumbent, who saw big churches rising in all the neigh-
boring villages, and thought he might as well have a big
church too.   So he raised a subscription and built one ;
but a certain pillar of it was unfortunately erected immediately over an old well, and the covering of the well
gave way, and the pillar went down into it, as a steel
ramrod used to go down the barrel of a rifle before these
breech-loading times.

In lonely travel the great secret of avoiding *ennui* is
to take an interest in the people as well as the scenery.
Any one who is on the look-out for characters is always
sure to meet with them.   For instance, I found a doctor
at Toulon who smoked without ceasing when he was
awake, except when he laid down his pipe to take his
knife and fork.   He was an old man, in perfect health,
and still in full professional practice.   This last fact may
seem incompatible with incessant smoking, and would,
no doubt, be so in London ; but in a tiny town where
everybody knew the doctor, he was indulged in his habit

by everybody. I spent a good many hours with him, and during the whole time he was doing one of two things, either smoking his pipe or filling it. He had read most of our best authors in the original, having taught himself English alone, with the help of nothing but books. He had a capital little English library at home, and had read every volume in it : all Scott, all Dickens, all Shakspeare, Byron, and many others. His pronunciation was, of course, as bad as our pronunciation of Latin ; and I felt, on hearing him read a little, as an old Roman would feel if he could go to Oxford and hear the men there deliver Latin orations. However, in this instance there was nothing to laugh at, because there was no pretension ; and the doctor knew our literature better than many Englishmen do, and understood it, and loved it. He had never heard an English word pronounced by a native before he hit upon me, so that I was a real *trouvaille ;* and he was extremely kind to me, and invited me to breakfast, pointing out a charming harbor for the canoe at the end of his garden, as a temptation to future voyages.

But the best character in Toulon was the *maire* of the place, Monsieur B., an artist of reputation in a much more useful line than any etcher. I fear that no plate of mine will ever give Monsieur B. half as much pleasure and satisfaction as the *plats* of his cooking gave to me. He keeps the hôtel where I stayed, and he made me a little portable *dèjeûner* to take with me every morning when I set out to work. French cookery is always either exquisite or abominable, and his was of the former.

Monsieur B. is a very celebrated man indeed. People write from a distance to order a dinner, and then travel to Toulon to eat it. Unfortunately, he is also celebrated as the most irascible man in the country; which, considering the generally explosive character of French tempers, is saying a good deal. As that man must be a wonderfully perfect Sabbatarian who can win fame in Scotland for his observance of the day of rest, so that Frenchman must be irascible indeed who can make himself famous for his irritability. His powers of voluble invective surpassed all that I had ever heard in the way of scolding, and their effect was immensely enhanced by the most scientific modulation of tone. His loud voice disturbed me in the early morning as he scolded a boy-cook for having used a pound of first-rate butter, reserved especially for pastry, in cooking yesterday's dinner. Now the misapplication of the butter was commented upon in a restrained and subdued *piano*, with deep concentrated rage; and now it passed with a rapid crescendo to *forte* and a terrible *fortissimo*, that made the very windows rattle. When a servant is to be reprimanded, the first observations are made in the utmost moderation, and if only Monsieur B. could stop there, he would deserve the credit of being a reasonable though vigilant master; but the sound of his own voice exasperates him, and even when the culprit offers no reply, his fault is described to him over and over again, every time with increasing vehemence, till at length the floodgates of invective are opened wide, and the torrent rolls and roars.

Yet nothing can exceed Monsieur B.'s politeness to his guests. In the midst of his loudest furies, he will turn aside and speak to you with a serene countenance and gentle voice, whilst over the door of the dining-room is the inscription : —

'*Rien ne doit déranger l' honnête homme qui dîne.*'

CHAPTER XI.

THE admirers of beautiful scenery are often somewhat narrow, and even bigoted, in their admiration. It has been the fashion, for the last half-century,
to enjoy mountain scenery very much, and to undertake
long journeys in search of it ; but the proof that this love
of Nature is rather the love of a certain kind of exhilaration, to be had best in mountainous districts, is that most
people still remain perfectly indifferent to the beauty of
the plains. They can understand that you have reasonable motives for going to Switzerland or the Tyrol, but
what can you see to care for on the Loire? 'Mere poplars, you know, and that sort of thing,' say the few who
have visited the river that Turner loved. Therefore I
feel a little apprehensive that the sympathy of many
readers, which has gone with me whilst I had to speak
of rocks and rapids, and heathery hills purple in the
evening, may leave me now that I come to the broader
waters and less romantic landscapes of the plain.

And yet, when the last rapid had been passed, and
the river spread into sleepy reaches, only occasionally
interrupted by the gentle murmur of a safe and sandy
shallow, over which the canoe glided like a boat on
some languid stream ; when the sun at evening, instead
of suddenly and prematurely disappearing behind the
wooded heights, sank slowly in the immensity of the

clear heaven, till he set on the far horizon as he sets on the summer sea, — there came upon the spirit of the voyager such a sense of boundless space and free breathing of balmy, illimitable air, as he never knew in the narrow gorges where dark hills and dense woods overshadowed him.

Every scene of Nature has its own character, and its own charm. The plains have not the sublimities of the hills, nor the guarded seclusion of the shaded valleys, and we miss the weird shapes of the gray rocks that breast the stream where its flowing is strongest; yet it is glorious to see all the blue sky in the daytime, and all the stars at night. And the river seems to gain a certain dignity too, with its assurance of perfect peace. It has space for all its waters, and knows restraint no more. The graceful trees only adorn its borders, but do not arrest its course. If it winds in beautiful curves, it does so from deliberate preferences. It would be easy, as it seems, to go straight to its distant bourn, but to go indirectly is yet a little easier; so it turns for its own pleasure, and visits here a village, and there a solitary farm, where the oxen stand knee-deep in the evening.

The gradual growth of a river might be illustrated by drawings of its bridges. First you have the trunk of a single tree, rudely flattened on the upper side by strokes of a peasant's axe, and supported by two rude abutments of unhewn granite blocks. A little lower down the stream has become too wide for the single trunk to cross it ; so now you have two trees that meet on a rock in the middle. After that you come to the first serious attempt at construction: a wooden bridge for foot-passengers only, the cattle and cart traffic still passing through the water in a shallow ford a little below. Then comes the first stone bridge, a single arch, if the people are rich enough to afford a piece of accomplished engineering; but, if the village masons have done the work, more usually two or three tiny arches, that a stray cow might possibly pass under, and which are pretty sure to be choked with water in a flood which will wash over the rude parapet. As the river widens it passes near some town or city, and then we find the stately stone bridge of careful masonry — three arches, perhaps — where the high-road enters the town. After that the number of arches increases, till at last you meet with those long and stately constructions, whose fine perspective attracted Turner so much when he illustrated the rivers of France.

The accompanying sketch, which represents the bridge of Gueugnon, gives evidence that the Unknown River has quite grown out of the romantic and tumultuous period of its existence, and become a sober stream capable even of rendering service to navigation, if it were worth while to deepen a few shallows here and there. Indeed, from this bridge to the Loire the river is classed amongst those which, if not positively navigable, might easily be made so.

Gueugnon is rather an industrial place, as may be guessed from the smoky chimneys in the etching, which belong to some ironworks, where they make wire, and sheet-iron for tinning. Here the traveller found an iron canoe, flat-bottomed, and extremely even uncomfortably narrow. She must have been terribly crank; but that is a defect the body accustoms itself to so easily, that, after a fortnight's practice, one sits in a crank boat as easily as in a stiff one. There is usually a certain amount of jealousy amongst boat-builders, and the mechanic who had made the iron canoe spoke very disparagingly of mine, which I took with British coolness; merely inquiring whether he had ever descended the rapids in his invention, which was entirely without a deck, and would have certainly gone to the bottom like a lump of lead after half a dozen waves had washed into it. The crowd around us seemed to consider that the best proof of the quality of my own vessel was her successful voyage down the wildest parts of the river. After that, the inimical mechanic became suddenly very amiable, and conducted me over the ironworks, explaining every process most politely. The reason for this amiability became evident at last ; for just as I left him, and thanked him, he proposed to build me an iron canoe which should be made exactly according to my own fancy, and have a deck, and every thing I had a mind to. In a word, he was a shipbuilder (on a very small scale) touting for orders. Had the present writer been a permanent resident at Gueugnon, it would have been rather a tempting proposal, as there is no employment in the world more congenial to his feelings than superintending the construction of a boat.

There is a great weir at Gueugnon, which offers a slope of most excellent masonry very like a great rail-

330 The Unknown River.

way embankment, and when the water flows over it in one smooth sheet, it would be delightful to glide down it in a canoe. Unfortunately, however, there are rude stones at the bottom, which would give the adventurer a most unpleasant reception. I got amongst these stones in the dark, and had plenty of trouble with them, — the last inconvenience of that kind in the course of the voyage.

There was a comfortable inn at Gueugnon — well, comfortable is perhaps hardly the word for any French inn of that class ; but these things go by comparison, and, after lodging in peasants' cottages amongst the hills, it seemed quite stately and luxurious to sit at dinner in the evening with two candles in tall candlesticks on the table, and an attentive waiter at one's elbow.

The etching opposite shows the way in which I used to have to seek for a lodging when belated ; and it was always disagreeable to me, mainly on account of the necessary yet almost impossible explanations. How can you make a peasant understand your purposes in an artistic excursion of any kind ? How, especially, can you make him understand such purposes when complicated with the amusement of canoing ?

On a fine night it was positively more agreeable to sleep in the canoe, in the manner represented at the close of the chapter. Since then the author has invented much more luxurious arrangements ; * but it was not

* This alludes to a contrivance by which a hut and a punt are united in one construction. During the day, the punt, which is of wood, contains a second punt of tinned iron. The iron punt is divided into

unpleasant to make a bed of rushes, and sleep soundly and softly, covered up to the chin with waterproofs to guard one from the dews of the night. Many a poor soldier in the present war, forced to lie on the bare ground, often stony and muddy, would consider these contrivances a luxury. It was something, too, before going to sleep, to look up at the moonlit clouds and the stars in the depths between them.

several compartments, in the largest of which sits the canoist. All the other compartments are closed. Two of them are kept accessible by movable lids; one of these is used for provisions and the other for clothing. That for provisions contains eight boxes fitted to each other carefully, in which may be kept the different requisites for a week's voyage, and a complete cooking apparatus. That for clothing contains a change of dry clothes, a hammock, &c., and bedding. When night comes the boat is drawn up on the shore, and the tin punt removed from the interior of the wooden one. Two light frames are then fixed upright in the wooden punt, and the tin one is easily lifted upon these frames. A double curtain is then fixed all round, and we have a hut with a wooden floor, a metallic roof, and canvas sides. In this hut the hammock is easily suspended.

This contrivance has been completely realized in every detail, but I have never had an opportunity of using it, because, during the summer of 1870 there was no water in the rivers, and since the beginning of the Prussian War it would be madness to show one's self in any such mysterious-looking invention, as it would set all the peasants perfectly mad. In times of sanity and peace it seems to me that nothing could be better adapted for a tour such as that described in these pages. It is unpleasant to have to leave work undone in order to go five or six miles lower down a river to seek for a lodging. Many etchings were left unfinished for that reason in the excursion here narrated, and have consequently been thrown aside. Many subjects remarkably suited for etching had also to be passed without illustration when the weather was not mild enough for a bivouac.

CHAPTER XII.

ON leaving Gueugnon, in the cool of a bright autumn
evening, I saw a magnificent piece of black oak
which had been disengaged from the bed of the river
during the great inundation, and thrown upon the high
shore. The whole trunk was complete, and measured
seventy feet in length by forty in girth. I cut it in
several places with a penknife and found it as black as
ebony. How many centuries it had lain in the river's
bed I know not, but, judging from the color and condition of the wood, which was all black bog-oak of the
finest quality, the tree must have lain beneath the flowing water as long as the black oak in the deepest bogs
of Ireland. What noble chambers might have been
furnished out of it! what rich inlaying of parquets
and wainscot would it not have supplied!

The landscape now began to wear an aspect of uncommon sadness and desolation. The river divided
itself into many straggling currents in a wide desert
of sand and pebbles. A low, yellow precipice of the
same material hid all the fields from my sight, as I sat
low in the canoe on the level of the dreary gray water.
How mournfully, too, the water seemed to murmur
down its tortuous, divided channels! For miles and
miles there was nothing to be seen except a great
château on the top of a bare slope, a long, ugly, melan-

choly building, enough to make one miserable to look at
it, and think that any one could be condemned to live
in it.

When I came near this château, the twilight was
already very far advanced, and I landed to eat a little
supper. The land was bare of trees, a desolate expanse
of uncultivated soil, where a herd grazed in the distance.
Suddenly I wondered not to see Tom galloping towards
me, as he generally had done at these improvised meal-
times on the shore. I called and whistled for him long
and loudly, but in vain, and during all that remained of
the voyage I saw his affectionate face no more. This
caused me some anxiety, and rather spoiled my pleasure,
but I trusted that he would find his way home again.
On my return I made inquiries, and found that he had
first returned to the inn at Gueugnon, after losing me
in the tortuous channels of the river, and stayed at the
inn till *déjeûner* the next morning. After his meal he
suddenly disappeared, and the innkeeper could give no
further account of him. The same evening, however,
he arrived at my house, a distance of fifty kilometres,
where he rushed to his kennel at once, and fell down in
it like lead, exhausted. The next day he was all right
again. But it was a severe run, for no doubt he had
made the fifty kilometres a hundred, and followed the
river's brink in the thick underwood ; often, I dare say,
swimming against the stream. I never knew such a
persistent swimmer. He never had the sense to follow
the canoe on the bank, but would always swim behind
it, however cold the water or long the distance. It was

this which had separated him from me. Being rather
pressed for time in the late evening, I had pushed on
too fast for Tom.

The voyage had been a lonely one from the beginning,
but it seemed doubly solitary after the loss of my com·
panion. I had never been able to do with him in the
canoe, — he was much too large and heavy for that, —
but every time I landed, either to make an etching or
eat a dinner — and I never did either afloat — Tom had
always joined me, and so the long solitude had been
made less difficult to endure. I humbly thank Divine
Providence for having invented dogs, and I regard that
man with wondering pity who can lead a dogless life.

The dreary hours and the dreary landscape both came
to an end at the same time. The moon rose, trees began
to reappear on the river's brink, the scattered currents
met together again, and there were vistas of prolonged
perspective. I remember one especially, a scene of
most perfect and extraordinary beauty. For a length of
about a thousand fathoms the stream was straight as a
cathedral aisle, and at about half the distance there was
a transept on each side, that might have been designed
by art. All along, the shores were shaded by the richest
foliage. Boughs hung gracefully till they dipped their
golden leaves in the glassy water. Tall poplars rose at
intervals, like towers, to mark the far perspective. It
was midnight. A pure semi-transparent mist filled the
still and silent air, and above in the clear heaven shone
the round and brilliant moon. Not a sound was to be
heard but the alternate dip of the paddle, which I used

as gently as might be, for it seemed wrong to break so beautiful a mirror. At last I toiled no more, and the little boat glided on and on with its own motion, as if drawn by invisible spirits. During the whole voyage I had found nothing so exquisite as this, nor has any other impression fixed itself so perfectly in my memory.

That scene was too ethereal to be etched ; but next day I drew this bridge, partly because it was the last bridge on the Unknown River, and partly as a memorial of the great and disastrous flood. In these terrible months of 1870, when a thousand bridges that spanned the fair rivers of France have been ruined to check the progress of an invader more to be dreaded than any inundation, men pray that the rains may fall and the waters rise till the streams are all torrents and the plains all inland seas.

After this bridge, the scenery of the shore began to assume the large aspect that belongs to the stately Loire. A steep bank rose in the distance, clothed with vines and crowned with a group of buildings clustering round convent-towers. The current became swifter, as if the Unknown River were hastening to its end ; it curved rapidly once or twice, then suddenly behold an expanse of broad water before me, flowing westwards, and, before I had time quite perfectly to realize the change, the canoe was carried out upon the Loire.

And so the voyage came to a successful end, and for the first time since first his waters flowed, the Unknown River has been navigated. Shall I conclude with a triumphant boast, and affirm that although Gaul and

Roman have dwelt upon its shores, and reddened it in sanguinary conflict, its perfect exploration was reserved for the audacity of an Englishman ? Let me rather, more modestly, rejoice in sharing that capacity for taking pleasure in the beauty of natural scenery which belongs to so many in our own time. It is this, much more than any particular satisfaction in the somewhat monotonous business of paddling, which constitutes the principal charm of all canoe voyages ; and it is this, more peculiarly and especially, which made privations light to me, and labor pleasant, and time swift, during the weeks I spent in, 'An Etcher's Voyage of Discovery.'

RESULTS.

A FEW words concerning the especial purpose of this voyage — etching from Nature — may possibly be of use to a few readers who may undertake etching tours.

No art is more agreeable for direct work from Nature than etching is. The rapidity of it, and its freedom, are greatly in its favor, and so is its remarkable independence of damp and wet. Many of the plates in this series were immersed in the river, after being etched, when the artist was upset; others were executed in bad weather, with the rain literally pouring over the copper in a manner which would have rendered any other kind of drawing quite impossible. In the course of the excursion I did sixty plates, from which these are selected. It is better, I think, to be rather prolific in production, and select afterwards the plates which seem most successful, than to spend much time in correcting bad plates in the studio. My advice to etchers would be to spend time rather in doing many plates than in polishing and mending a few. This may be contrary to the feeling of some painters, who rightly, in their art, obey the maxims of Boileau; but whatever value an etching may have depends mainly on the inspiration of the moment. If it were only possible to possess that inspiration always, the

22

art would be easier than it is. The only consolation I have to suggest for the many failures and the disappointing uncertainty which ever attend it, is that it leads us to work from Nature, and look at Nature, in the most essentially artistic spirit.

THE END.

www.ingramcontent.com/pod-product-compliance
Lightning Source LLC
Chambersburg PA
CBHW020320140726
47905CB00013B/1670